T0406053

Falling Like Leaves

Falling Like Leaves

MISTY WILSON

Margaret K. McElderry Books
New York Amsterdam/Antwerp London
Toronto Sydney/Melbourne New Delhi

MARGARET K. McELDERRY BOOKS
An imprint of Simon & Schuster Children's Publishing Division
1230 Avenue of the Americas, New York, New York 10020

Cover design by Debra Sfetsios-Conover

Interior design by Irene Metaxatos
The text for this book was set in Loretta.
Manufactured in China
First Edition
10 9 8 7 6 5 4 3 2 1
CIP data for this book is available from the Library of Congress.
ISBN 9781665975209 (hardcover)
ISBN 9781665975193 (paperback)
ISBN 9781665975216 (ebook)

To all my PSL-drinking, sweater-wearing, apple-picking,
***Gilmore Girls*-watching, pumpkin patch-going,**
candy corn-eating, fall-loving readers.
This one's for you.

May we all find our Coopers.

Falling Like Leaves

Chapter One

Caviar is disgusting, and anyone who says otherwise is a liar.

Still, I roll the eggs around in my mouth as if they're a fine wine, just like Dad told me to do before he abandoned me in the corner to go talk to one of the many white-haired men at this event. If I weren't at the Street Media Corporation annual gala, I would spit it out in a heartbeat. But I can't embarrass Dad by being the Girl Next to the Fake Plant Spitting Expensive Food into Her Napkin. So I let them sit in my mouth, hoping they'll just dissolve so I don't have to force them down.

A small band plays in the front of the sparkling room full of expensive dresses and tuxedos. Four couples make use of the hotel ballroom's dance floor while the rest of the attendees either stand around mingling or sit at the tables adorned in white luxury linens and orchid centerpieces. Tonight's gala is both a celebration of the company's profitable past year and a networking event with potential investors. Everyone who's anyone in New York City is here, dancing and laughing and meeting wealthy new faces.

And I am simply an intern lucky enough to have an important dad.

"Ah, you've found the rare delicacy," Mr. Street says, startling me as he appears at my side. He nods at the caviar spoon in my hand. There's no way I'm insulting the host of the party—not to mention the CEO and founder of the news conglomerate—so I swallow the melting eggs and shoot him a grin. Or what I *hope* looks like a grin.

"I have. They're delicious," I lie, holding back a gag.

"I hear you should press them against your soft palate to truly experience the buttery flavor and unique texture." Mr. Street shakes his head. "Personally, I've never understood the appeal, but to each their own."

You've got to be kidding.

I could have been standing here exchanging quippy lines about how repulsive these eggs are, and how everyone in the room is surely faking their enjoyment of them, but instead I'm one of the fakers.

I deflate at the missed networking opportunity.

"How has your internship been so far, Ms. Mitchell?" Mr. Street asks, the light from the crystal chandeliers reflecting off his kind brown eyes and balding head.

"It's been great," I tell him. "I'm learning so much."

This is only half true. It's hard to learn from lower-level journalists and content creators when I've grown up the daughter of Brad Mitchell, president of Street Media. I was five years old when Dad first taught me all about journalistic integrity and source anonymity. And although this is my first summer at the company in an official capacity, I've shadowed him the last two summers, learning the company ropes, interviewing techniques, how to write a compelling article, and how to recognize and filter bias. Dad says journalism is in my blood and that one day, when he retires, I'll take his place. All I need is solid experience and the right contacts.

In other words, the Streets.

"That's fantastic." Mr. Street takes a sip from his champagne flute. "Have you worked on any assignments you've particularly loved?"

The highlight of my whole summer has been tagging along with a reporter covering the Model Icon Fashion Show, but I know better than to say that.

"I've really enjoyed dipping my toes into foreign affairs. Covering the European Parliament election and the situation in Ukraine has been really eye-opening."

"Oh yes, your dad did mention your interest in overseas matters. Did you know I started out as a foreign-affairs reporter?"

I did know that, of course, because a good journalist does her homework.

"Oh wow. I had no idea," I say, leaning in and feigning interest. "Do you have any good stories from those days? Or any wisdom to impart?"

"Now, Ellis," I hear from behind me as my dad joins us, placing his hand on my shoulder, "you cannot monopolize Edward's time tonight. As the host, he has too much schmoozing to do."

Mr. Street chuckles. "Unfortunately, I'm afraid that is true, but perhaps we can all get lunch together next week."

"I would love that," I say.

"Check my calendar with Anita and get it set up, Brad. I have a feeling your daughter is going to do big things. Her passion simply emanates from her." Mr. Street beams at me. "Go get yourself more caviar before it's all gone, Ms. Mitchell."

He heads toward a group of bigwigs in a heated debate, and Dad turns to me, his Work Smile shifting to his Dad Smile, a difference that is probably imperceptible to anyone else. His eyes linger on my shirt and his smile slips away.

"Is that one of your . . . creations?" he asks, disappointment dripping from each word.

I tug self-consciously at the fitted halter top that I made out of a thrifted oxford. The addition of one of Mom's decorative cameo brooches and the floor-length silk Carolina Herrera skirt push it comfortably into black-tie territory, but Dad seems to think otherwise.

"It is . . . ," I confirm, now regretting not wearing something simpler.

"Well, it seems you made a good impression, regardless."

I shrug. "I didn't really say much of anything."

"Did you bring up foreign affairs like we talked about?"

I nod. "I did."

Dad winks at me. "Good going, kid. I'll get lunch set up on Monday." He points subtly to a curvy blond woman in her mid-thirties wearing a gorgeous gold dress. "Why don't you go introduce yourself to Catherine Howe? She's an executive producer at WorldNet Studios."

Dad flashes his Work Smile at a group of old men across the room before leaving me standing alone in the corner again.

My phone buzzes in my clutch purse, and even though I shouldn't, I take it out to check the message.

Foodie Fernie: **hurry and finish up at that snooze fest. Party at my place! Jordan's here ;)**

I put my phone back into my purse and sigh. I'd love to ditch this stuffy gala and hang out with friends for a change. I'd love to show off my outfit to people who would actually care how cute I look tonight. But if I'm going to get into Columbia and then get a job at Street Media, I have to put in the work. I don't have time for parties or boys or, lately, even my best friend.

So, I push my shoulders back, ignore my screaming feet, and head over to introduce myself to Catherine Howe.

Soft sunlight filters through my bedroom window as I lie on my stomach in bed, staring at the daunting Columbia application on my laptop. Outside, the soundtrack of the city plays on repeat—horns honking, a construction crew shouting, sirens blaring, pigeons cooing. Anxiety balloons in the space between my ribs as I enter my contact information—which is further than I got last time I opened the application.

Maybe I'm more nervous about college than I thought.

I click on the next section of the application and immediately bury my face in my plush white comforter. I don't know why this is so stressful. I *want* this.

I lift my head back up, and my gaze falls on the other tab I have open: the FIT home page. Last year I took fashion merchandising as one of my electives at school, and my teacher suggested

I look into the Fashion Institute of Technology, claiming I have a real aptitude for fashion. Of course, that's not part of my life plan. Dad and I agree that journalism is a much more practical career path, and I've been working toward Columbia my whole life. But it won't hurt to check out the FIT application—just to see what it entails.

I'm definitely not procrastinating on the Columbia application.

The website loads, and I click on the admissions page, a sense of calm washing over me, probably because it doesn't represent my entire future or the pressure that comes with it.

I'm reading through the essay prompt—*Tell us why you're interested in fashion, including your experience and inspiration*—when there's a knock at my door.

"Come in!" I click on the portfolio requirements as Dad opens the door, his eyes tired and his posture slumped—a completely different person than he was last night at the gala. He trudges over to the bed and sits.

"What's up?" I ask him. "Are you okay?"

"Your mom—" He stops as his gaze catches on my computer screen, and he narrows his eyes. My stomach plummets. "What are you looking at there? I thought we discussed this."

"We did." I close my laptop. "It's nothing."

"You're very talented at designing clothes, Ellis, but we agreed that's just a way to show Columbia that you have diversified interests."

"I know. I was just looking. I figured it couldn't hurt to apply to FIT as a backup school, though. Everyone applies to safety schools."

"Uh-huh . . ." Dad nods slowly. Skeptically. "Well, keep your eye on the ball. Don't let your hobbies distract you from what's important. You have to be tenacious and focused if you're going to be successful."

"I know, Dad. I already started filling out the Columbia application. Don't worry."

Even if it was just my name and address.

"Good. Anyway, I came in here to tell you that your mom and I need to talk to you." He stands and rubs the back of his neck. "She's waiting for us in the living room."

I draw my eyebrows together. Something is *off*. "Okay . . ."

I leave my computer on my bed and follow Dad to the living room, where Mom is sitting stiffly on the gray leather couch, wringing her hands and staring at the floor, her strawberry-blond hair pulled back in a messy bun. The dark circles under her eyes match Dad's. Warning bells go off in my head.

She looks up when I sit on the sofa next to her. "Good morning, honey."

"Morning . . ." I glance at Dad, who's staring at the wall behind me. "What's going on?"

"Well," Mom begins, "we wanted to talk to you about something. I'm sure you've noticed that things between your dad and me have been . . ."

"Rough?" I supply.

"Exactly. Things have been *rough* lately. There's no easy way to say this, but . . . we've decided to take some time apart."

Panic seeps into my chest. "Are you getting a divorce?"

"No," Dad says quickly.

Mom shoots him a glare, then settles her eyes on me. "Let's not get ahead of ourselves."

I shake my head. "Okay, well, I know you two have been fighting a lot, but can't you work it out?"

"No, we can't. Not this time," Mom says. "But your aunt Naomi has some extra space at her house, and I think some time apart will be best for all of us."

I look at Dad, hoping he'll object. Hoping he'll have some other solution. He *always* has a solution to everything.

But he only continues to stare at the wall, his jaw twitching.

"Dad? Say something. *Do* something."

"There's nothing to do, Ellis. The decision's been made," he says, finally meeting my eyes. Stubble shadows his face, and his hair looks as though he's run his hand through it a hundred times. He looks *defeated*.

"It'll be tough for the family not to be together, but we'll get through it," Mom says, offering a weak smile.

"How long will you be gone?" I ask.

Mom's eyes widen a bit, some realization dawning on her. "Oh. Well, you're coming with me to Bramble Falls."

"What?" I stop breathing. "No, I'm not. School starts this week," I remind her.

"You'll go to school in Bramble Falls for a little while," she says. "We'll be back by Thanksgiving."

"Absolutely not. I'm *not* starting at a new school. Dad, tell her."

Dad pinches the bridge of his nose. "Like I said, the decision's been made, Ellis. You heard your mother."

I stand, now hovering over Mom, who sits with her lips

pressed tightly together, avoiding looking at me. "I'm not going to freaking Connecticut. You can't make me leave my home and my friends and my school during my *senior year*! What about my commitments? I mean, I'm volunteering at the nursing home, and I'm still doing my internship at Street Media after school three days a week. And I'm finally the editor of the school newspaper this year! I'm sorry, but no. I can't leave. Being here is imperative to my getting into Columbia. Why can't I just stay with Dad?"

Mom finally looks at me, her face hard and unreadable. "This isn't up for debate." She stands. "We're leaving first thing tomorrow morning, so you better go pack."

"*What?* I don't even get to say goodbye to Fern or give my jobs any notice? I'm supposed to have lunch with Mr. Street this week. Please, Mom, don't do this."

My heart thuds wildly and unshed tears blur my vision. I can't believe this is happening.

"Staying isn't an option," she says, her eyes glassing over. "I'm sorry."

I turn my back to her. "Dad, please," I beg, walking over to him, blinking rapidly in my refusal to cry.

Dad pulls me into a hug and kisses the top of my head. "It's only temporary, Ellis. Your internship will be waiting for you, okay? I'm sure Mr. Street would love to have lunch when you get back."

I pull out of his arms, shaking my head in disbelief. How can he just let this happen?

I clench my teeth as my eyes dart between my parents. "I hate you both for doing this."

"Ellis—"

My bare feet pound against the hardwood floor with each step toward my bedroom, cutting off whatever empty argument my mom was about to offer. I slam my door behind me and walk over to my window, where, finally, I let my tears zigzag freely down my cheeks.

Outside, the sun washes over the city. People go about their Saturday morning as if the whole world didn't just flip upside down and catch fire. As if my whole life weren't just upended. As if my whole future weren't just crushed.

Until I started high school, my parents and I used to visit my aunt Naomi and my cousin Sloane every summer. So I already know what I'm walking into.

I already know there's nothing for me in Bramble Falls, Connecticut.

Chapter Two

Mom and I arrive in Bramble Falls early on Sunday. The newly risen sun reflects off the morning dew and paints the town in a golden hue. Sugar maples line the quiet streets, their green leaves clinging to the dregs of summer the same way I'm clinging to home, relentlessly resisting the inevitable change.

The passenger-side window is cold against my forehead as I take in the small town, which looks exactly the same as it did when I was a kid. Small houses sit atop small, perfectly landscaped yards. A few people walk their small dogs down the sidewalk.

Everything here is small.

I already miss New York City. I miss its vastness and its sounds and its bustle. I miss its food and its buskers and its bookstores. Hell, I even miss the trash and the awful smells and the subway.

I do not belong here.

Mom stops at the only traffic light in town and turns to me, grinning, as if everything is fine and normal. Her lips move, and

Gracie Abrams's voice fades as I pull out my AirPods.

"What?" I ask.

"I said it's beautiful here, isn't it? Do you remember all of this?" She gestures at Bramble Falls's town square in front of us.

The white gazebo where my cousin Sloane and I used to eat picnics and meet up with her friends sits surrounded by the same freshly cut grass that always felt like silk beneath my bare feet. The green lawn is dappled with trees, their branches casting shadows over beds of orange and maroon mums.

"Of course. I wasn't in the womb the last time we were here," I say dryly.

Mom frowns and accelerates when the light changes. We follow the road around the square, passing the old hardware store with the same sun-bleached TOOLS & MORE! sign that's always been in the window, the diner where Sloane and I used to get thick malts and chili dogs on unbearably hot summer days, the tiny post office where I used to mail postcards to my friends back in New York, and the market where I (accidentally) stole something for the first time.

Yeah, the quaint town is pretty, and I have a lot of fond childhood memories here. But warm memories aren't enough to extinguish my bad mood. This place isn't *home*, and I'm not going to pretend to be excited about moving just to make my mom happy—especially when it's her fault I'm stuck here. I get that she's going through a lot, but I still don't understand why I had to come with her. It can't be to stave off her loneliness, since she'll be living with Aunt Naomi and Sloane. It can't be to help her avoid homesickness, since home is evidently the last place she wants to be. Every avenue of thought leads me to the same conclusion: that she's doing it out of spite, trying to get under Dad's skin, and I'm collateral damage.

As we drive past a tiny greeting-card store, a woman with curly brown hair and deep wrinkles smiles and waves at us. Mom waves back.

"Do we know her?" I ask.

"No," Mom laughs. "People here just wave to each other. She was being *friendly*."

"Right."

Mom sighs. "This is going to be good, Ellis," she says, staring at the road ahead of her. "For both of us."

I turn off my music and put my earbuds away because Aunt Naomi only lives a couple blocks from downtown. "Sure."

Silence stretches between us as we turn onto Saffron Lane, and the small, white colonial house with its bright blue door and shutters comes into view. We haven't even pulled into the driveway when my aunt comes running out of the house with a face-splitting grin, her arms held out, ready to wrap us in hugs.

Great.

Mom swings our BMW into the driveway and barely throws it into park before she's out of the car, hugging her sister. A second later, Sloane saunters out with a smile that matches her mom's. While I look more like my dad, Sloane is her mom's replica, sharing the same shoulder-length, pale blond hair, thick bangs, sky-blue eyes, and matching flannel shirt.

"Hey, Ellis," Sloane says, wrapping her arms around me the moment I step out of the car.

"Hey," I mutter, patting her on the back. I hate that the excitement over seeing my cousin again is tainted by my circumstances.

Yet another thing my mom ruined.

She pulls away and sets her hands on my shoulders. "Are you doing okay?"

I get that she's trying to be nice because she knows about my parents, but I can't stand the pity in her eyes. I do *not* need pity. I just need to go home.

"I'm fine," I answer, forcing a close-lipped smile. "How are you? It's been forever."

"I'm great!" She takes a step back, plastering on a grin so wide I'm surprised it doesn't hurt her face. "We're so excited to have you stay here, especially this time of year!"

"Oh, yes, Ellis," Mom says, stepping beside me. "You're in for a treat. Nowhere else does autumn quite like Bramble Falls."

"I'll take your word for it," I say. I could not possibly care less about autumn in Bramble Falls. Or anything in Bramble Falls, for that matter.

Aunt Naomi pulls me into a tight hug, and the warmth of her embrace and the long-forgotten scent of her coconut shampoo dull my sharp edges just a bit. "Gosh, I've missed you." She lets me go and tucks my long, dark brown hair behind my ears, her eyes traveling over me, taking in my Khaite jeans and cropped sleeveless sweatshirt. "Wow. You have really grown up since I last saw you."

"Hasn't she?" Mom says, beaming at me.

Aunt Naomi frowns at her. "I can't believe you stayed gone for so long. I feel like I've missed so much."

Mom's shoulders droop. "Life happened."

"It sure did, didn't it?" Aunt Naomi shakes her head and gives Mom a look only a sister could decode. Then she turns back to me and smiles. "Well, you're here now. Let's get you squared away."

Mom pops the trunk, and I grab one of the only two suitcases of clothes she let me bring after reminding me that Aunt Naomi's house isn't big enough for my expansive wardrobe.

But, apparently, it's big enough for my sewing supplies, which she insisted on packing, despite the fact that I've barely touched any of them in over a year.

I don't spare the sewing stuff a glance before lugging my suitcase up the porch steps behind Aunt Naomi and Sloane. Mom follows with her bags, and we stop inside the entryway and set our luggage on the floor.

The house is small—go figure—but well-loved. To our left, a beige slip-covered couch sits beside a blue gingham lounge chair in front of a small flat-screen television in the carpeted living room. Unevenly hung photographs and art projects in mismatched frames cover the walls, and every shelf is jam-packed with knickknacks and books. Straight ahead, I catch a glimpse of the tiny L-shaped kitchen, where potted plants bring life to the place, and the counter is filled with corny coffee mugs that read things like YOU ARE BEAUTIFALL, SPICE, SPICE, BABY, and YOU'RE THE APPLE OF MY PIE.

It's a far cry from our spacious, well-kept NYC apartment, but Aunt Naomi's house has always been oddly charming and cozy.

"Why don't we show you your rooms, and I can give you a tour later," Aunt Naomi says. "It's been so long since you were last here, some things might have changed."

I scoff. This is the type of place where nothing ever changes.

Mom shoots me a glare, then nods at Aunt Naomi. "Sounds good."

The four of us head upstairs to the guest bedroom.

"Annie," Aunt Naomi says to my mom, "this will be your room."

The light blue bedroom is simple, with a queen-sized bed against the wall, a desk in the corner, and a single mahogany dresser.

Mom sets her suitcase on the floor. "This is perfect, Naomi. Thank you."

Aunt Naomi smiles and motions for me to follow her. "Ellis, I was going to set you up in Sloane's room," she says, "but your mom said you'd probably prefer to have a space of your own."

Oh, thank god.

Aunt Naomi leads us down the hall and stops at a door I've never opened before. In fact, I have no recollection of this door at all.

"Unfortunately," she continues, twisting the door's wobbly knob, "we're out of bedrooms." She pulls the door open and begins climbing a creaky set of steps.

I reluctantly follow her. The temperature rises as we reach the landing, where rays of sunlight shine through the window, turning floating dust particles to glitter.

"Sorry, it's kind of stuffy up here," Aunt Naomi says, pushing open the heavy wood-framed window.

I glance around at the giant room spanning the length of the house.

It's filled with boxes, most of them overflowing with what

appears to be the entire autumn section of a party store—plastic pumpkins, fall leaf garlands and red, yellow, and orange artificial plants, wooden fall ornaments, autumn wreaths, and knitted coasters in the shape of pumpkins and apples.

I love a hot pumpkin spice latte and a warm sweater as much as the next person, but this seems a bit overboard.

I follow Aunt Naomi through the narrow path between the boxes, brushing away spiderwebs—both real and fake—until we reach a cleared-out space under one of the gables, where, presumably, I'm supposed to sleep.

There's a standard bed with what looks like a vintage Laura Ashley bedspread and an antique-looking wrought-iron bed frame, a single whitewashed dresser, and a few rugs Aunt Naomi has layered across this section to cover the floor.

But none of them cover the fact that this is an *attic*. I can't help feeling like Sara from *A Little Princess*. I sigh. At least there's a window.

"I know it's not perfect," my aunt says quickly, no doubt noticing my hesitation. "But I hope you'll be comfortable. . . ."

I glance at my mom, who nods at me, prompting me to thank my aunt for her hospitality.

"Thanks," I mumble. "It's great."

I'm beyond angry at my mother for putting me in this situation, but it isn't Aunt Naomi's fault. I *am* grateful she made space for us, even if this is the last place I want to be.

We'll be back home soon enough. *This is only temporary,* I remind myself. Sloane comes panting up the steps, carrying the box with my sewing machine and materials.

"Sloane!" my mom chirps. "You didn't need to bring that up. Ellis and I would have taken care of it!"

I let out an annoyed huff. Bringing it was her idea. There was no way I was hauling that thing up two flights of stairs.

"It's no problem, Aunt Annie. Happy to help! Where would you like it?"

Before I can tell her it doesn't matter because I don't really sew anymore, Aunt Naomi chimes in. "Oh yes, that's right! Annie said you design clothes, Ellis, so I brought up a table for your machine." She points to our left at a dusty antique sewing table with a small stool. Sloane waddles over to it and drops the box with a grunt. "Now, I know you probably use all kinds of special city fabrics for your outfits, but we do have stacks of boxes up here with donations from last month's clothing drive. We had so many come in, the donation center said I'd have to bring the rest back in December. So you're welcome to whatever you find."

I decide not to tell her that almost all my creations have been made from thrifted oxfords and instead opt for "Um, thanks. Sounds good."

My aunt claps and beams at us. "Great! Well, I was thinking I'd make everyone breakfast. What do you think?"

"I'm starving," Mom says. "Ellis?"

"I just want some coffee, honestly. I don't suppose this place has entered the twenty-first century and gotten a Dunkin'? Or any coffee shop, for that matter?" I ask.

Mom sighs, exasperated, but Sloane laughs and says, "Still no Dunkin'. *But* we do now have the Caffeinated Cat." I cock an eyebrow at her. "It's a cat café. The coffee is to die for, and the cutest adoptable cats wander around inside. Trust me, you'll love it. I'll walk there with you."

"Oh. You don't have—"

"Don't be silly. I'm not letting you walk around town by yourself on your very first day," she says. "Come on."

We all leave my dusty bedroom and file down the stairs.

"You two have fun," Mom says, mouthing the words *be nice* at me as Sloane and I head out into the crisp morning air, a welcome reprieve from the hot attic and Mom's suffocating presence.

For two blocks, Sloane talks incessantly about her best friend, Asher, her mom's job, the theater camp she attended this summer, and how excited she is for school to start the day after tomorrow—a fact I'm choosing to ignore because it's nausea-inducing.

Along the way, we walk by several houses where people are sitting on their porch, sipping coffee, and reading the newspaper. All of them seem to know Sloane. Closer to town, we pass the local bookstore and the Bramble Falls florist, where a handwritten sign is already advertising fall flowers.

Finally, we arrive at a teal-colored building located on the corner of Peach Street and Oak Avenue, almost directly across the road from the town square. I don't remember what was here the last time I was in Bramble Falls, but now a wooden sign with the words THE CAFFEINATED CAT hangs above its door.

Sloane holds the door open for me, and I step into the coffee shop, careful not to let any of the roaming felines out. The blended scent of coffee and sugar rides the air, making my mouth water and perking me up before caffeine has even hit my tongue. The line is six people deep, so I study the chalkboard menu behind the counter while we wait.

Not a pumpkin spice latte in sight.

"What are you getting?" Sloane asks as we step closer to the front of the line, a fat calico cat nuzzling her calf and making circles between her legs.

I sigh. "I have no idea. I don't—" I'm about to turn to her when my eyes snag on the guy behind the counter. I squint as if it'll make me believe what I'm seeing. "Sloane, is that . . ."

There's no way.

Sloane follows my gaze and smirks. "Cooper Barnett? Yeah. You remember him?"

Of course I remember him.

I remember Sloane introducing us the last time I was here. He declared us best friends the second she left to spend the summer traveling with her dad before he passed away.

For those two short months, I remember us being inseparable.

I remember drinking Capri-Suns and eating Cool Ranch Doritos together at the lake on the outskirts of town, his noodly limbs stretched out on the dock while he rambled on excitedly about the history of confectioners' sugar or the science behind using salt in bread dough.

I remember racing our bikes down Willow Creek Lane, our shoulders pink and our freckles popping, before he wiped out trying to dodge the only pothole in town.

I remember sneaking into the Bramble Falls drive-in theater on classic-movie night. He couldn't stop crying at the end of *Free Willy*.

I remember eating entire boxes of Popsicles just to get to the jokes on the sticks while we swung in the hammock together in Aunt Naomi's backyard.

And a girl always remembers her first kiss.

But . . .

"I don't remember him looking like *that*," I say, unable to reconcile the cute, lanky boy I used to know with the specimen standing three people in front of me. "When did he get so . . ."

"Hot?" she asks with a giggle.

I shrug. "I mean, yeah."

His once-short brown hair has now grown out in thick waves that curl at the tips of his ears and flop over his forehead, and a cream-colored apron is tied around a tall, fit body. We inch closer, and I notice the smattering of light freckles across his nose that I never appreciated when we were younger. He still has his full cheeks, punctuated by a single dimple, but now they're accompanied by an angular jawline that adds a hotness to his boyish charm.

In the words of what I imagine might be on one of Aunt Naomi's coffee mugs: *Un-freaking-be-leaf-able.*

"He hit a growth spurt sophomore year," Sloane whispers, pulling me from my trance. "Then he ditched those nerdy round glasses he was always pushing up the bridge of his nose and, if I had to guess, probably started using the school's weight room."

The lady in front of us picks up a fluffy white kitten from the floor and moves to the end of the counter. We step forward, and my stomach does a weird little swoop.

Cooper Barnett is wildly beautiful.

"Hey, Sloane," he says, grinning at her. He glances at me for a split second before opening his mouth to ask Sloane what she wants. But then he does a double take, his smile falling and his amber eyes widening as they fix on me.

How did I forget how stunning his eyes are?

"Hey, Coop," I say, my lips curling upward into a grin I can't contain. His jaw flexes, but he says nothing. It occurs to me that maybe he doesn't remember *me*. "Ellis Mitchell . . . Sloane's cousin."

I glance at Sloane standing beside me, watching Cooper with a furrowed brow.

"I know who you are, Ellis," he says, a sharp edge to his voice.

"Oh." My smile wavers. "Good. It's been a long time. How have you been?"

"Busy." He turns back to Sloane. "What can I get for you?"

Um, okay, then.

"I'll just have a green tea, please," she says. Then she turns to me, shifting her weight uncomfortably. "What about you, Ellis?"

"Do you happen to have a secret pumpkin spice latte that's not on the menu?" I offer him my warmest smile, trying to thaw his inexplicably frosty attitude toward me.

"No." He looks at the line behind us and sighs, obviously wanting us to move along. "I'd recommend the harvest spice latte. It has pumpkin spice, hazelnut, and gingerbread. It's the closest you're going to get in Bramble Falls, and it's a million times better."

"I doubt that," I tell him. "But okay, you've sold me. I'll have the biggest harvest spice latte you've got."

He nods, taps on the screen in front of him, and gives me the total, avoiding looking at me the whole time. I swipe my card, and Sloane and I move to the other end of the counter to wait for our drinks.

"What the hell was that about?" Sloane hisses.

"I was going to ask you the same thing. When did he become such an asshole?"

"He didn't! Cooper's basically the nicest person I know. What'd you do to him?"

"Nothing! I haven't been here in *years*. We were really good friends before I left." I don't mention the kiss. She'd wonder why I never told her about it back then. I doubt she'd believe the truth—that it wasn't a big deal. Plus, it's irrelevant because it didn't change things between Cooper and me. "We even texted after I went back home."

"You did?"

"For a little while, before we both got too busy with school. But nothing explains his attitude toward me. We didn't get into a fight or anything."

"I don't know, girl. Cooper doesn't dislike anyone. Whatever you did must have been pretty bad."

"I didn't do anything!" I yell, sending a cat skittering behind a trash can and capturing the attention of two women waiting for their drinks—and, of course, Cooper. My cheeks flare, and I look down at the square toes of my black leather Stuart Weitzman boots.

When our drinks are finally called, we grab them, but just before we leave, Sloane leans over the counter.

"Hey, Cooper," she calls. "You still coming over later?"

He nods. "I'll be there at six."

She gives him a thumbs-up, and I follow her toward the door.

"What's happening later?" I ask her, stepping over a tabby cat in a green sweater.

She flashes me a giant grin over her shoulder. "It's September, which means it's officially Falling Leaves Festival season."

"Okay? And what's that mean?"

Sloane stops walking, and I nearly spill my latte as I bump into her. She pivots to face me.

"It means we have a lot of work ahead of us," she says. "Bramble Falls is known for going *all out* in the fall. There are fall-themed activities every weekend throughout September and October. You know, apple picking, hayrides, corn mazes, pumpkin carving, a fall scavenger hunt, a double-feature horror-movie night at the drive-in, the Autumn Spice Sprint, the Boots and Blankets Bonfire, and the Pumpkin Prom."

"The . . . Pumpkin Prom?"

"It's a costume party with lots of dancing," she says, practically shaking with excitement. "All of it leads up to the big festival the first weekend of November to conclude the season. It's pretty much a huge all-day party. In New York you have the Macy's Thanksgiving Day Parade. Here we have the Bramble Falls Parade around the square!"

I stare at her, dumbfounded by how giddy she is about these events.

"People come from all over for the Bramble Falls experience," she continues. "It's a ton of fun, but it also generates lots of money for the town. And since my mom is the mayor and the head of the tourism board, it's our job to plan, set up, and participate in the events. And since Cooper's mom is on the board too, he helps out a lot. He's coming over later to carry the heavier boxes down from the attic because it's finally time to turn this town into an autumn oasis!"

"Got it. . . ." I clear my throat, my curiosity getting the best of me. "So, are you and Cooper, like, together?"

"Definitely not," she says. "Don't get me wrong, he's hot, and he's super sweet. But I'm not interested. Why do you ask?"

She gives me a knowing smile, and I roll my eyes.

"I was just wondering," I say. "Now walk. Let's get out of here."

Sloane obeys, sipping her tea and turning around. The bells above the door jingle as she steps outside.

Before leaving, I glance back at Cooper and find him watching us. Our eyes lock for what feels like both only a moment and a thousand years before he looks away.

I don't want to care about the fact that Cooper seems to hate me—the same way I don't care about anything else in this town. I wish I could forget about him the same way I've forgotten about him the last three years.

But now that I'm back here and I've seen him again, I can't shake the nostalgia. Memories of the best summer I ever had with the sweet boy from Bramble Falls wrap around me like a blanket. And as I catch up with Sloane outside, the promise of a new season filling the air, I can't help but wonder who Cooper Barnett is now—and what spending a fall with him would be like.

Chapter Three

Ringlets of sweat-soaked baby hairs stick to the back of my neck as I stand on an old wooden chair, forcing a plastic spring-tension curtain rod between the center support beam and the attic wall. If I'm going to be forced to stay here, I need some semblance of privacy should someone need to come to the attic.

Once I have rods hanging on either side of the support beam, I climb down from the chair and stand back to look at my new bedroom walls—gauzy white curtains that I made from some vintage tablecloths in the stack of clothing-donation boxes. The lacy edges felt like the right kind of shabby-chic vibe, and, as much as I would never admit this to my mom, using my sewing machine helped quell some of my anxiety about being stuck here.

"Oh, that's a great idea," Mom says, startling me. "Sorry. I didn't mean to sneak up on you. Those fans are loud."

I pull open a curtain, exposing three fans, all oscillating on their highest settings. "Loud but necessary."

"No kidding. It's like a sauna up here." She steps past the

curtain and surveys my tiny living quarters. "I really am sorry about the attic."

I shrug a shoulder. "Better than sleeping in Sloane's room."

Mom turns and sits on the bed, getting a better look at the curtains. "So you made those, huh?"

"Don't get too excited," I tell her. "I was sewing out of necessity, not desire."

"Well, either way, they look great."

"Thanks."

There's an uncomfortable pause before she continues. "I appreciate you making the best of this. You're a good kid." I nod and cross my arms over my chest as I stare at the floor.

Mom bites her lip and places her hands on her knees as the fans combat the awkward silence between us.

"Look," she finally says, "I know you're mad at me, but maybe try to think of this as an opportunity for you to be a normal teenager for a bit." My eyes dart to her. "Things don't have to be so grueling right now. You have the rest of your life to work."

"I don't *want* to be a 'normal teenager.' I want to get into Columbia."

"And you will. I'm just saying, try to have some fun while you're here. Hang out with Sloane, enjoy the town's charm, work on your fashion stuff. . . ." She pauses, hesitating; then: "Maybe do the things you like instead of worrying about making your dad happy."

My eyebrows shoot up. "You say that like everything I do is for Dad's sake." She says nothing. "You're wrong. I *am* doing the things I like."

I haven't been working on my clothing designs lately because

I haven't had time to go thrifting, let alone spend hours constructing new pieces.

It has nothing to do with my dad.

She nods once. "Okay."

Her tone doesn't say *okay*, though. Her tone says she doesn't believe me. It says she's simply being agreeable. Like always.

"And I don't want to enjoy the town's charm," I continue, searing irritation sweeping through me like wildfire. "I want to be in the city, attending my prestigious high school and finishing my internship, which other people would kill to have, so that I can carry out the plans I've been working toward for the last three years. We're talking about my *whole future*, Mom. Just because *you* don't have a job doesn't mean other people aren't worried about getting one!"

Mom's face crumples, her calm expression turning hurt, and my stomach knots. It's not untrue—after all, Mom gave up her career at an art gallery in the city to stay home and raise me—but I didn't mean to make it sound like being a stay-at-home mom is a walk in the park.

I swallow and look at the floor. "I'm just saying I want to do big things, okay? So what if what I want aligns with what Dad wants for me? He's helping me reach my goals. Being here is a step backward, so stop trying to make this a good thing."

Mom pushes off the floral comforter and stands. Her lips part like she's going to say something, but then she presses them together instead, pivots away from me, and walks across the attic and down the steps.

I groan and flop onto the bed.

My phone has sat silently on the worn dresser next to me all day. I grab it, glancing at the time—5:46 p.m. I find Dad in my contacts and press the green call icon.

Despite Mom being the one who was home with me all the time, I've always been closer with my dad. Mom helped me with homework, but Dad kept me motivated. He pushed me to get perfect grades, to get involved, to work hard, to try new things, to think about the future.

He's brilliant and selfless and *adored* at Street Media. Even when I was little, following him around his office carrying his stapler and the brass paperweight from his desk, I knew I wanted to be him.

He travels a lot for work, so I've gone weeks without seeing him. But the distance between us now feels different. I hate him for letting this happen, but I also *miss* him.

The phone rings. And rings. And rings. When his voice finally carries across the line, my eyes sting. *You've reached Brad Mitchell. Leave a voicemail and I'll get back to you as soon as possible.*

I hang up and swipe my thumb, scrolling until I get to Fern's name.

She answers on the first ring.

"Ellis! Tell me everything!"

My heart lurches at the sound of her voice.

"It's awful," I tell her.

"You haven't even been there twelve hours yet."

"I know, so that says something."

She huffs. "What's so bad about it? Other than the fact that you aren't here with me, obviously."

On the other end of the line, something scrapes across the floor. I picture my best friend pulling a chair out from her small white kitchen table and folding herself into it like a pretzel, the way she always does when she talks on the phone. It makes me homesick.

"They don't have PSLs here for starters." Fern gasps. She might be a foodie, but we both lean into our most basic instincts when it comes to fall. "Exactly. And I'm pretty sure the guy who works at the coffee shop hates me."

"You've already made an enemy? I'm impressed."

"My mom got me registered for school, but they don't have a large enough student body to offer AP classes here. And they don't have a school newspaper."

"This is, like, your worst nightmare."

"It gets worse," I tell her. "I'm staying in the attic."

"Ellis, no. Hop on a bus out of there right now. You can live with me," Fern says. And I know she means it.

"If only. At least then I wouldn't keep fighting with my mom."

"It's that bad?"

"Worse than bad." I sigh. "Tell me something about home. How was your housewarming? I can't believe I missed it."

As real estate investors, Fern's wealthy parents got her an apartment for her eighteenth birthday. We have plans to live together while I attend Columbia.

"Oh my god, I wish you would have come. It was wild."

Fern proceeds to tell me about her night of boys and drinking and karaoke and her encounter with the NYPD and her old, grumpy neighbor. She lists every New York City influencer who attended and all the plans they made to collaborate.

I met Fern when we were both on the school newspaper two years ago. At the time, she dreamed of having her own advice column, but ultimately—and accidentally—she made a name for herself as a restaurant reviewer on social media. With untamable red curls, fair skin, and bright green eyes, she's undeniably gorgeous. She's also inarguably hilarious. And in the last year, she's risen to fame, traveling the country and finishing school online while making tons of money in endorsements as a teen food critic—both because her videos are entertaining and because she's always right about the food. We've barely been able to keep up our weekly Thursday night dinners at Nom Wah, our favorite dim sum place in Chinatown, thanks to her heightened profile.

Her name and career are taking off, and opportunities are presenting themselves left and right. Meanwhile, I'm stuck here in a stalemate.

"Jordan kept asking about you," she says before I hear her take a sip of what I'd guess is her green smoothie. I roll my eyes. "Stop rolling your eyes."

"How do you know I rolled my eyes?" I laugh—a sound foreign to me at this point. Between working constantly and listening to my parents' endless fighting these last few months, it's been hard to muster a sincere smile, much less an actual laugh.

"I know you. Look, I know you say boys are a distraction—"

"Because they are," I shoot back.

"But they don't have to be. He knows you're busy, and he's okay with it. Give him a chance."

"I'm not looking for a relationship right now."

Relationships are time-sucking obstacles on the way to a destination.

"Okay, but it doesn't have to be something serious," Fern says. "Once you're back, you could just have some fun. Be casual."

Casual is all Fern knows—she's commitment-averse.

Unfortunately, I made time to go to Fern's rooftop party four months ago and found myself staring into Jordan's dark eyes, lined with thick black lashes, his impeccable black hair blowing in the breeze, and I kissed him. I *tried* fun and casual, but then he got attached.

And even if I knew him well enough to like him, I'm too busy for a relationship. So, lesson learned.

"I don't do fun and casual. I'm not interested, Fernie. I'm sorry." Maybe I'll have time for boys after I get into Columbia, but until then, I'm laser-focused.

Fern's sigh nearly blows me over all the way from New York. "Just think about it, Ellis. Listen, I gotta go. I'm meeting up with Franky for dinner at the Nervous Donkey."

My stomach grumbles. "Ugh, I've been dying to eat there since they opened."

"I know, babes. We'll go when you're back."

"Let me know how it is," I say.

"You can watch my video," Fern says. There's some shuffling on her end. "Let me know how school goes Tuesday."

I smother my groan. "Yeah, sure."

"Love you, Ell. Bye!"

The line goes dead. I toss my phone on the mattress next to me and lie like a starfish, closing my eyes and letting the air from the fans wash over me. Maybe this is where I wake up and find out this has all been a nightmare.

I'll open my eyes and be in my bedroom in NYC, sunlight pouring through my giant window, photos of Fern and me tacked up on the pale pink walls, my toes sinking into my soft white rug on my way to sit in my armchair and sketch some designs.

A soft knock pulls me from my daydream.

"Ellis, we're coming up," my mom calls from downstairs. She hasn't once announced herself today. I sit up and listen closely.

"Of course I remember you," my mom says as two pairs of footsteps grow closer. "Ellis talked about you for *months* after we last left here. I think it was the best summer she ever had."

"Oh yeah?" a deep voice full of doubt says.

Oh no.

No, no, no.

I completely forgot Cooper Barnett was coming over.

Chapter Four

"Ellis, come out here and help us," Mom says, her voice just outside the curtains now.

I look at my plain gray shorts and sweaty yellow tank top, covered in dirt and dust from trying to clean my small section of the attic all day. I don't have a mirror, but I can picture my high ponytail, loose and messy, and what's left of my makeup smudged under my eyes.

There's no way I'm going out there looking like this.

Mom rips the curtain open.

"Are you ignoring me?" she asks, barely looking at me.

"I was sleeping," I lie. My eyes flit to Cooper, who turns quickly toward the boxes full of decorations, pretending he wasn't watching us.

"No, you weren't," Mom says. "Now get up. It's all hands on deck."

"Whatever," I mutter.

I trudge out of my makeshift bedroom and into the cluttered

attic, folding my arms over my shirt to hide how filthy I am.

"Ellis, you remember Cooper, right?" Mom asks, gesturing at him. "You spent the summer after eighth grade with him."

I chance a look at Cooper. He glances at me quickly before picking up a box. Judging by the way his biceps and back muscles strain against his white T-shirt, I'd guess it's a heavy box.

"Yeah," I reply. "We actually talked earlier today."

Sort of.

"Oh, excellent!" Mom says, her smile growing. Aunt Naomi and Sloane climb the steps behind Cooper.

"Hey, Naomi," Cooper says. "Should I put this in the living room?"

"That'd be perfect," Aunt Naomi says.

He carries the heavy box down the steps, and Sloane hands me a light one, offering a nervous smile.

"Are things going any better with him than they did earlier?" she asks quietly while Mom and Aunt Naomi sort through boxes, picking out the heavy ones for Cooper.

"He hasn't tried to kill me, but he also hasn't spoken to me."

"Are you going to ask him what his problem is?" Sloane asks. "Because I'm dying to know."

I'm dying to know too. But I'd rather not have an audience of nosy relatives when I ask him.

I shrug. "Maybe eventually." I step around her with the box. "But right now I just want to get this job done and take a shower."

We spend the next hour carrying boxes from the attic to the living room, Cooper acting as if I'm not there and me wishing I weren't.

By the time we finish, the five of us are dripping sweat, and I'm forcing myself not to stare at Cooper's flushed cheeks or the toned stretch of abs beneath his shirt when he lifts it to wipe his forehead.

He is the definition of a distraction. I might actually be lucky he wants nothing to do with me.

"I ordered pizza," Aunt Naomi announces, continuing to pull decorations from the boxes in the living room. She sorts them into piles only she and Sloane can make sense of. "It should be here any minute."

"Oh. I actually have to go," Cooper says. "I told my mom I'd be home by seven. I'm already late."

"You didn't think I'd let you come over to help and not feed you, did you?" Aunt Naomi asks. "Don't worry—I already texted your mom to let her know."

Cooper forces a smile. "Oh. Okay. Awesome."

"Cooper, I've never heard you be so quiet," Sloane says before chugging a bottle of water.

His eyes connect with mine for such a brief second, I question whether I imagined it. Then he shrugs. "I'm just tired. The shop was busy today."

"Cooper works at the Caffeinated Cat," Sloane tells my mom.

"Oh, how neat. I'll have to check it out this week," Mom says. "I'm thinking of applying for a job at the art-and-crafts store next door."

I raise my eyebrows. *This is news to me.* "You are? Why?"

Mom grins. "I miss working, and I'd like to pay some form of rent."

"Oh, stop that," Aunt Naomi says, waving off Mom. "I don't want your money."

Cooper's brow furrows in confusion. "Rent? How long are you visiting?"

"Ellis didn't tell you when you talked earlier? We've moved here," Mom says. "Temporarily!" she adds, seeing my horrified face. "We're around long enough for me to get a job, though."

Sloane throws her arm over my shoulder. "And long enough for Ellis to go to school with us. Isn't that exciting, Coop?"

What an instigator.

I can't read his expression—shock mixed with a pinch of dread, maybe?

He doesn't reply before my mom says, "Maybe you two will have some classes together."

His eyes lock on mine. "Yeah. Maybe."

Sloane turns to me. "I'll give you a tour Tuesday morning and show you where the office is."

"Thanks."

Sloane is only a junior, so I'll be on my own this week if Bramble Falls High is anything like my old school, where the grades are in different halls and rarely interact.

The doorbell rings.

"Come in!" Aunt Naomi shouts.

My head whips to her. People just invite people into their homes here without checking who's at the door first?

A short, plus-sized Black kid with fun blue hair, a nose ring, and a THEY/THEM button pinned to their red Cheesylicious uniform walks in carrying two pizzas.

Their eyes wander over the boxes and decorations until they find Aunt Naomi hidden among the mess. They grin. "You want this in the kitchen, Naomi?"

"I'll take them," Cooper offers, grabbing the pizzas. "What's up, Sterling?"

"Just living the dream," they reply with a wide grin.

Sloane steps forward and hands them money. "You want a piece for the road?"

"Thanks, but naw, I'm pizza'd out," they say with a wave of their hand.

"There's no such thing," Sloane insists. "But okay." Sterling tries to hand her change, but Sloane pushes it back toward them. "Keep it."

"Thanks," they say.

"Sterling, this is my cousin Ellis. She'll be going to school with us," Sloane tells them. "Ellis, this is Sterling. They're a junior."

I offer them a smile. "Nice to meet you, Sterling."

"You too." Sterling sticks their hands in their pockets and turns to the group. "Well, I gotta get going on the next delivery. Good luck with the decorations, everyone. See you next weekend, Naomi."

"Thanks, Sterling," Aunt Naomi says.

"So, what event is happening next weekend?" I ask after Sterling leaves and everyone is making their way to the kitchen for pizza.

"Saturday is apple picking at the Vanderbilt Orchard," Aunt Naomi says with excitement.

I nod as I place two pieces of cheese pizza on my plate. "Cool."

"Are you going to come?" Sloane asks. "We can always use more volunteers to work the registers, give tours, help people pick apples, load cars, or show attendees where the bathrooms are. . . ."

I stop with my pizza halfway to my mouth. "Oh, um, I don't know. I mean, starting at a new school is a lot. I might need to see how this week goes first."

Mom's face oozes with disappointment.

"Makes sense," Sloane says. She takes a bite of her pizza.

"We totally understand," Aunt Naomi adds with an empathetic smile. "This is a big change for you."

Cooper stays quiet but looks deep in thought. With his mom being on the tourism board and him being here tonight, I can only assume he volunteers at the events. So he's probably relieved by my answer.

A half hour later, Cooper heads home without so much as a goodbye in my direction, and I head to the shower. But just before I hop in, someone knocks on the bathroom door. I swing it open and find my mom standing there.

"You will help next weekend," she says, her voice low and stern. The sternest I've ever heard from her, actually.

"Mom—"

"Your aunt is letting us stay here for free. She filled her fridge and went out of her way to set up rooms for us, and she asked for nothing in return. The least you can do is volunteer at weekend events."

"So, I'm being punished for your decision to move us here?" I ask, fury building in the pit of my stomach. This isn't fair. Isn't it punishment enough that I'm here at all?

"It's not a punishment, Ellis," she says, annoyed with me. "Volunteering your time is a kindness, and it's the right thing to do. They're family, and they're helping us. You can hate me and treat me like I'm the worst person in the world, but I didn't raise you to act spoiled and entitled. Frankly, I can't believe I have to have this conversation." She turns, but as she walks away, she adds, "You'll be there next weekend. It's not up for discussion. But if it makes you feel better, think of it this way: helping the local government will be a great activity to add to that high school résumé you've been so concerned about."

She disappears down the steps, shaking her head, and I close the bathroom door.

For the next twenty minutes, my tears are washed away while the sound of the shower drowns out my sobs.

Nothing is how it's supposed to be. I'm surrounded by family in a town where everyone knows everyone. Yet I've never felt so alone in my life.

Chapter Five

Sloane drives us the two miles to Bramble Falls High, where the original brick structure with two large white pillars sits on a lawn dotted with trees both big and small. Sprawling acres of infinite woods sit behind the building, the early morning sun captured in a thick mist overhead, giving the picturesque illusion that the trees are glowing.

Sloane parks in the student lot, and we climb out of her junky brown hatchback. After spending the final day of summer break holed up in my room yesterday, working on my Columbia application while everyone else celebrated Labor Day with a cookout and friends in the backyard, I tossed and turned all night, my brain a never-ending carousel of thoughts—about my fight with Mom, about my dad still not calling me back, about my first day of school. When my alarm went off this morning, I'd just fallen asleep.

I looked at my single rack of clothing, full of the basic fall essentials I thought I might need for the next three months, and sighed, trying not to think about what fun, quirky outfit I might be curating if I were back in New York. Instead I pulled out a sleeveless white button-down dress I made from an oversized men's oxford and paired it with red tube socks and some soft brown Gucci loafers. To finish it off, I tied a green-and-red Gucci ribbon underneath my collar and secured it with mom's cameo brooch. I curled my hair into loose waves and tried to hide my tired eyes with concealer and mascara. Now I'm running on adrenaline and the harvest spice latte Sloane and I stopped for because I would have died without it. Luckily, I didn't have to endure Cooper's death stare at the crack of dawn, since Sloane said he doesn't work mornings on school days.

As we walk up the short flight of concrete steps toward the front door of the school, a few girls run over to us and throw their arms around Sloane, squealing about how much they missed her despite seeing her around all summer. My heart twitches with what I think might be . . . jealousy?

I have plenty of acquaintances in New York—ones who are in the same extracurricular clubs, ones I compete against for better grades, ones I commiserate with about upcoming tests, ones I walk into school with. But Fern is the only close friend who's ever lasted. Everyone else got tired of me saying I was too busy to hang out. After I blew off enough parties, they stopped inviting me. I go to a competitive high school, so everyone is focused on their academics. But in their free time, my old friends do what other teenagers do—movies, parties, sleepovers, shopping, dates. My "free time" is allocated to anything and everything that will help me get into my dream college or eventually get me a job at

Dad's company. In high school, friends quickly became a thing of the past.

Fern and I work only because we don't require too much of each other.

Sloane introduces me to everyone, including her friends Hannah, a curvy white girl with wavy brunette hair and cute denim overalls, and Preeti, a stunning Indian girl with eyelashes to die for, both of whom I met many summers ago but barely remember. They all disperse, some going to find their lockers and others going to find more of their friends, and Sloane grins at me.

"You're going to love it here," she says.

I give her the best smile I can muster given the circumstances. *Sure.*

Sloane pulls me through the propped-open double doors into the school. A blue Bramble Falls High banner hangs from the ceiling of the commons, where students loiter, catching up with friends or sitting at tables staring at their phones. Ahead, freshly painted white walls are lined with blue metal lockers.

"The freshmen and sophomores are down that hall," Sloane explains, pointing to a hall to our right. "I'll be with the juniors in that middle hall, and you'll be down there." She points to the hall to our left. "It's super easy to navigate. Each grade level is set up in a U shape with both ends leading here. It's impossible to get lost."

"Good, because I have the worst sense of direction," I say.

"I remember," Sloane says with a chuckle, probably recalling when I managed to get lost at the mall during one of my summer visits here.

Sloane shows me the gymnasium and the auditorium, the art

room, and a music room that also serves as the band's practice space throughout the winter. Once our short tour of the school is over, she leads me to the heavy mahogany door of the main office.

"Welp, I probably won't see you today, so good luck, have fun, and I'll meet you at the flagpole out front at the end of the day," Sloane says, her eyes catching on somebody behind me. "Ash, wait up!" She gives me one last look. "And let me know if you need me to punch Cooper."

I laugh. "I never knew you were so violent."

"Just sayin'"—she throws an arm over my shoulder—"I've got your back."

"Noted," I tell her. Sloane drops her arm to her side and grins at me before practically jogging over to a cute Asian guy wearing basketball shorts and a hoodie, an orange backpack slung over one shoulder. He smiles as she approaches, and she says something that makes him laugh before she ruffles his black hair. They disappear down the junior hall, and I turn toward the office, take a deep breath, and pull open the door.

After having me pick my classes and showing me where my locker is, the administrative assistant leaves me to navigate the senior hall alone.

Luckily, Sloane was right. It's easy enough to find my first class, where I sit at a desk in the back of the room. A few people glance at me. Some whisper to their friends, asking who I am, saying they hadn't heard anyone new moved to Bramble Falls. Someone says they heard from somebody named Forrest who heard from someone named Betty Lynn that I'm from New York, reminding me that I'm in a small town with a robust gossip mill.

Mr. Beck, the physics teacher, has me introduce myself to the class because, despite this being the first day for everyone, I'm the only stranger. He begins going over the syllabus, launching into a speech about his grading scale, the makeup policy, and the importance of science to the human race.

When he starts his slide presentation—telling us it'll be posted online but that note-taking is good for information retention—the guy next to me leans over.

"Hey, new girl, can I borrow a pen?" he whispers.

I fight the urge to roll my eyes. Who doesn't bring something to write with on the first day of class?

I reach into my backpack and grab my purple pen with the light purple pom-pom on top and hand it to him, not missing his iceberg-blue eyes set against tan skin. His blond hair is long and styled on top but fades to short on the sides.

It seems Bramble Falls is the secret hub for hot guys.

He looks at the fluffy pen and grins. "Thanks," he whispers. Then he bites his bottom lip. "Um, can I also have a piece of paper?"

I look at him, deadpan. "Seriously?"

He shrugs, and I tear a piece of paper from my notebook—my notebook filled with purple-lined paper because there's no reason notes can't be cute.

"Thank you. Again," he whispers with a flirty smile. He eyes the paper, then lifts it to his nose. "Is this scented?"

It is. "Shhh."

"Where'd you get this paper? I need to get some."

"Yeah, you really do," I whisper.

He laughs. "I'm Jake, by the way."

Mr. Beck's gaze snaps to us. I ignore Jake, and in my periphery he faces the front of the room and leans back in his chair, giving our physics teacher his attention. Or at least pretending to.

I'm pretty sure he's writing a note on that piece of paper.

The remainder of class passes quickly, and after two more uneventful classes, I walk into calc with my shoulders back, trying to exude a confidence I don't actually have—one of Dad's secrets to success.

"Never let people see your weaknesses," he always says. "Success is all about perception. Put on a smile and fake it till you make it."

I'm so busy trying to decide if I should sit in the back again or if I should stop hiding and grab a seat up front that I almost don't notice Cooper sitting in the second row of desks. He's wearing a pair of cuffed jeans over brown suede boots and a plain gray T-shirt. The kids filing in behind me begin filling the seats, so I move forward, my feet finding their way to the empty desk next to him.

His eyes dart to mine, then travel over my outfit before he averts them. "Ellis."

"Cooper." I unzip my backpack and dig a new notebook and pencil out. "I didn't know you were in this class."

"Yeah, well, we don't talk, so why would you?"

I draw my eyebrows together. "And whose fault is that?"

His head whips to me but he says nothing as he stares at me, the muscles in his jaw ticking.

"What's your problem?" I finally ask.

"The fact that you don't know says a whole lot," he replies. He grabs the stuff from his desk, stands, and throws his backpack over his shoulder. I watch as he asks someone to trade seats with him, and a second later he's sitting next to a blond girl, and a freckly redheaded guy has moved to the seat next to me.

What the hell?

I spend the rest of class distracted, racking my brain for hints of what went wrong. The last time I saw Cooper before we left that summer, we sat in the meadow at Starglow Summit talking about everything and nothing. He braided my hair—having apparently learned by braiding breads—and we made plans for all the things we were going to do in the future, as if we weren't closing the book on summer. As if I weren't leaving Bramble Falls.

Before we parted ways, I wanted to hug him, but I wasn't sure if that would be weird, so instead I just told him I'd see him next summer. He'd pushed his glasses up his nose and nodded. He looked like he was going to cry—by then I'd learned that Cooper was a crier—so I thought it'd be best if I didn't drag out the goodbye.

When I returned home, we texted nonstop for a while, often late into the night, but then school started, and the texts became less frequent. I don't remember the last message between us, but I'm certain no one was upset.

I have to be missing something. But I don't want to ask him because is it more messed up that I potentially did something to upset him years ago or that I don't remember doing it?

Cooper is out of the room before the bell to switch classes is even done ringing. I sigh, pack up my stuff, and head to lunch.

Back in New York, I go to the library and do homework during my lunch period. The librarian lets me eat in there with the agreement that I leave without evidence that I've ever been there. I doubt that'll fly here as the new girl. So I leave my stuff in my locker and follow the rest of the seniors to the commons.

After grabbing a lunch tray, I walk between tables with the excruciating task of trying to figure out where I'm going to sit among hundreds of people I don't know.

"New girl," someone says. I turn my head in the direction of the familiar voice and find Jake grinning at me. He scoots over to make space. "You can come sit with us."

Jake is surrounded by boys who either nod or simply stare at me. Two of them are muscly and wearing white tees with a Bramble Falls football logo on the chest. A couple of girls smile at me before going back to chatting.

And Cooper is sitting across from him. Because *of course they're friends.*

I look around the room for any other familiar faces, but I didn't talk to anyone else in my morning classes. So I nod and squeeze in next to Jake.

"Thanks," I say.

"Everyone, this is Ella," Jake says.

"Ellis," I say.

"Right. Sorry. This is Ellis," he says.

"I heard you're the mayor's niece," one of the guys says, licking orange Cheeto residue off his thick fingers. He flicks his head like he's twitching as he tries to get his ash-brown hair out of his eyes.

"Yep," I confirm.

"No shit," Jake says. "You're Sloane's cousin?" He takes a bite of his turkey and lettuce sandwich.

"I am."

He studies me, chewing, then finally says, "You two do have the same eyes."

"We do," I say, unsure how to respond to his observation of the only feature I got from my mom.

"She talks a lot more than you," he says. "Not in a bad way. Sloane rules. I mean, not that *not* talking is a bad thing either. . . ." I stare at him. "I'll shut up now."

The guys at the table laugh, and when Jake blushes, I can't help but join them.

I push around a cherry tomato on my tray and try not to look at Cooper, even though I swear I feel his gaze on us.

Cheeto Fingers points to my tray. "You gonna eat that or . . . ?"

"Are you saying you want it?" I ask him.

"If you're not—"

"Don't take her food, Slug," Cooper says to Cheeto Fingers. "Give her time to eat."

I'm torn between thinking it's sweet that he's telling his friends to back off my lunch and annoyed that he won't talk to me but he'll defend my food.

In any case, my appetite disappears when I don't sleep, so I grab my apple, then hand my tray to the guy. "It's all yours."

"Thanks." He picks up the grilled cheese sandwich and shoots Cooper a smirk.

"This is Slug, by the way," Jake says.

". . . Slug?" I cock an eyebrow at the nickname. At least I hope for his sake it's a nickname.

"Slowest guy on the football team," Jake says. "But he's a lineman, so it's fine."

"I have no idea what that means, but okay," I say.

"I think we met a long time ago, actually," Slug says. "During one of your summer visits. Probably went by Brent then, though."

"Oh?" I rack my brain. "I don't remember you."

"Shocking," Cooper mutters under his breath.

Jake looks at him, confused. "And this is Cooper."

"We've already met," Cooper tells Jake.

"Oh," Jake says, peeling an orange. He turns to me. "Didn't realize you already knew people here."

"I don't really," I say. "At least not anymore."

Cooper's amber eyes meet mine as Slug says with a mouthful of bread and cheese, "So, you're probably stuck helping out with all the fall events, huh? Living with Mayor Sullivan, I mean."

"It's seeming that way," I answer, tearing my eyes from the boy sitting across from me.

Jake pops a slice of his orange in his mouth. "Well, I'm working the register at the orchard this weekend. Coach makes every player volunteer for one fall event, so I figured I'd get it over with. We can be volunteer buddies," he says, softly bumping me with his shoulder.

"Yeah, okay," I say, earning me another one of his pearly-white grins.

Jake seems like the popular guy who can talk his way out of

bad grades using his charm and good looks—the type of guy I can't stand—but he does seem nice. And if I'm stuck volunteering anyway, at least I'll be hanging out with someone who could potentially be a friend.

And Mom does have a point about adding it to my college applications—maybe I can get Aunt Naomi to write a recommendation letter. Then it'll be worth it, especially because I don't have a bunch of AP classes and extracurriculars to pad my résumé with here.

I take a bite out of my apple, a sense of calm settling in now that I have a plan.

Bramble Falls might not have a whole lot to help my chances of getting into Columbia, but it does have the Falling Leaves Festival. And I'm going to use that to my advantage.

Chapter Six

Sloane talks nonstop on the way home from school. About Asher (he finally got his license), about her classes (she has a notoriously hard Spanish teacher), about the newest book in her favorite series (it releases next week), and about my new friend.

"Is Jake not ridiculously hot?" she asks.

"He is," I agree. "Not really my type, though." Not that I have a type, but if I did, he wouldn't be it.

"Please. He's everyone's type. Well, everyone who's into guys, anyway. Athletic, funny, nice." Taking her eyes off the road, she turns to me. "You can't judge him for not bringing supplies to class."

"It's a major red flag," I half joke.

Sloane rolls her eyes playfully as we pull into the driveway. We grab our backpacks and head inside, where Aunt Naomi is sitting in the living room, still sorting the autumn decorations.

"Hey, girls! How was your first day?" she asks, grabbing a pile of orange candlesticks of various lengths from a box.

"Good for me. But don't ask Ellis. She had to share her school supplies," Sloane says with a twinkle in her eye.

I slap her shoulder. "Shut up. Who doesn't bring supplies to class on the first day!"

Aunt Naomi holds up a finger. "I'm with Ellis on this one."

Sloane shakes her head. "Of course. You two type-A organizational freaks would agree that not bringing supplies is blasphemy. But it's Jake, and if you're going to be friends with him, you might as well get used to it."

"Jake Keller?" Aunt Naomi asks. "In that case, I take it back. He's sweet and helpless, like a lost puppy. You might as well keep a notebook and pencil just for him in your backpack."

I slip off my shoes. "I think maybe I need new friends."

Sloane laughs, and I follow her into the living room.

"So, can I ask a favor, Aunt Naomi?"

She sets down the coasters she's holding and looks at me. "Anything."

"Would you be willing to write me a recommendation letter for me to add to my college applications if I volunteer for the town's fall events?" I ask.

"Oh, that's a fantastic idea," she says. "I can't believe we didn't think of that earlier. The Bramble Falls tourism board would be a great addition to your résumé. Of course I'll write a letter. Does that mean you've reconsidered then?"

"Yeah, I think it'll be good experience." Or at least look like good experience to colleges.

"Excellent! I'll get you assigned to something for Saturday," she says.

"Actually, could I work with Jake?" I ask.

Aunt Naomi looks at me, then at Sloane, who presses her lips together trying not to smile.

"It's not like that," I tell them. *The guy doesn't even bring a pencil to class,* I want to scream for the umpteenth time.

"Mm-hmm," Sloane hums.

"I believe you, sweetie," Aunt Naomi says unconvincingly. "And, yes, I'll see if I can make sure you're with him."

"Thank you. Do you know where my mom is?"

"I think up in her room," she says.

"Okay, thanks."

I'm climbing the steps, calling Dad for the hundredth time, when Sloane shouts, "I have Jake's number if you want it!"

"No thank you!" I yell down behind me as Dad's voicemail pours through the phone speaker. Again. I end the call with a sigh.

Upstairs, Mom's door is cracked.

I knock lightly. "Mom? You in there?"

Classical music plays quietly from inside. I've never heard my mom listen to classical music in my life, but she's humming along. She knows this piece.

I push the door slowly open, revealing my mom in a chair at the window, a large canvas on an easel in front of her. A palette sits on the nightstand beside her. She brushes a bright red across the canvas, completely lost to the world. The same way I get when I'm creating clothing designs.

Or *used to get*, I should say, seeing as I haven't been doing much creating lately.

The music crescendoes, growing bigger. Louder. Intense.

And Mom's strokes become wider. Longer. Bolder.

I stand out of her line of vision as I watch her blend colors and create shapes and strategically leave negative space until a painting of a river flowing through a small town with a cityscape in the distant background is rendered on the canvas in front of her.

"Wow," I breathe. Mom's an *artist*. She's basically Bob Ross, and I had no idea.

Mom jumps, spinning around with her hand over her chest. "Ellis. You almost gave me a heart attack!"

"Sorry. I knocked. . . ."

She blows out a deep breath. "It's okay."

"Why didn't I know you could do that?" I ask, motioning at the colorful painted landscape.

She gives me an almost *sad* smile. "I didn't know for sure if I still could. I haven't painted in almost two decades. But I filled out an application at the arts-and-crafts store today, and just being in there made me want to pick up a brush again."

"You're so good at it," I say, stepping closer. I inch toward the canvas until I'm close enough to lean in and take in the intricate details. The way she used white highlights in the water to make it appear to shimmer. The way some strokes of the tree branches are heavier than others, adding dimension and demanding attention. The subtle yellow lines that blend seamlessly into the background while still looking like rays of sunlight.

"Thanks, honey. How was your first day?"

I turn away from the canvas. "It was okay. But I was wondering if you've talked to Dad. He hasn't answered any of my calls."

Something unreadable passes over Mom's face before she

shakes her head. "No, I haven't. I'm sure he's just busy with work. He'll call you back."

"Yeah. I guess so," I say, trying to shake off the feeling that something is wrong—something other than the fact that I should be in New York with him right now. "Well, I better go study."

"Studying on the first day?" Mom asks, her eyebrows near her hairline.

I laugh at how appalled she is by the notion. "If I'm going to be here, without AP classes and a boatload of extracurriculars, I'm going to need straight As."

"You've always gotten straight As."

"Because I've always studied. Even on the first day," I remind her.

She sighs. "Fine. But I support you getting a B once in a while, you know?"

"Over my dead body, Mother."

She laughs but says, "I'm serious."

"So am I." I head for the door, stopping just before exiting. "Hey, what are you going to do with that painting when you're done?"

"Oh, I don't know. Probably throw it away so it doesn't clutter up Aunt Naomi's house."

"Can I have it?" I ask.

"Um, sure, but why? It's not anything spectacular," she says, frowning at the canvas.

I want to tell her *I* think it's spectacular. I want to tell her I love that the cityscape reminds me of home. I want to tell her that it makes me feel sad because the small town is in the forefront, and

I want to tell her I love that she was able to create something that makes me feel *anything* because art has never done that before.

But instead I tell her, "It will liven up my attic bedroom."

She nods with a hopeful smile. "Yeah, okay. I'll bring it up after I'm done and it dries."

"Awesome."

Heading to the hallway, I glance back at the painting one last time, where the fading city feels like a depiction of a distant memory.

I want to tell her that I'm afraid of that becoming a reality.

Chapter Seven

The Vanderbilt Orchard is a twenty-acre plot of land on the edge of town, with evenly spaced trees in long rows and wood-burned signs labeling the types of apples people can expect to pick in various sections of the expansive field.

Sloane is popping popcorn and handing it out to kids. Mom is dispensing cute brown baskets to visitors picking apples, while Aunt Naomi is walking around making sure everything is running smoothly.

Cooper's been helping wherever he's needed, and although he's passed by several times, he hasn't acknowledged me. But after stressing about it all week, I've decided I don't care. Between Sloane, Jake, and even Slug, I'm slowly making friends.

Cooper Barnett can kick rocks.

Inside a log cabin at the edge of a small gravel parking lot, I'm bagging apples, pies, caramel dip, and knickknacks after Jake rings them up. We've been inside working since I got here two hours ago, and honestly, it hasn't been half bad.

"Thirty dollars and ninety-five cents," Jake says to me as a middle-aged lady approaches with a basket full of items.

I eye the items in the basket, assessing. "Higher. Thirty-four twenty-five."

Jake shakes his head at me and greets the lady. He rings up her items while I lean over him, watching the total go up, up, up—until it stops at thirty-three dollars even.

Jake shoots me a smirk. "I win. Again."

"But I'm closer!" I whine.

"But you went over. Sorry, loser."

I give him a shove and he laughs.

"That's no way to talk to a girl, Jake," the lady scolds him with a tsk.

I lift my chin and try not to laugh. "Yeah, Jake, you're hurting my feelings."

He turns to face me, his expression faux serious. "I'm sorry, Ellis. I didn't mean to offend you." The corner of his mouth slides up. "But the runner-up in a two-person competition *is* in fact a loser. I didn't write the dictionary."

The lady grabs her bag and walks away, shaking her head.

"Have a good day, Mrs. Miller!" Jake calls after her.

"She hates you," I laugh.

"Meh, Mrs. Miller has hated me since I was eight and she caught me eating the huckleberries she planted in her backyard."

"Wow, such a menace," I say as a new customer steps up to the counter.

"Eight fifty," Jake mutters under his breath.

"Six seventy-five."

Jake rings up the items, but a commotion behind me steals my attention. I turn around to find a short, elderly woman, probably in her eighties, blushing as she tries to keep a small but wild child from opening a package of caramel apples. She has short, bouncy curls that make her head look like a cotton ball, and her lips are painted a bright pink.

"I'll be back," I tell Jake. Then I approach the woman. "Can I help you with anything?"

She seems to hesitate before taking her eyes off the boy. "Oh no, dear. I'm just waiting for one of the volunteers to finish in the orchard. I'm not as nimble as I once was, especially on uneven ground or ladders." She points to the living tornado. "Harley struggles with patience, so I thought if I let him walk around in here while we waited . . ." She trails off. "Well, you can see how that's going."

Behind me, Harley is tossing peaches into the air. "Look, Grandma! I can juggle!"

A peach lands with a dull thud on the ground, undoubtedly now bruised. The woman sighs.

"Why don't I take you guys so you're not stuck waiting in here?" I offer.

"You don't have to do that. I know you have another job to do," she says. "I'll just take him back outside so he stops destroying the place."

"I really don't mind," I assure her. "Harley," I call, motioning him over, "put those peaches back and come on. We're going to pick some apples." The boy jogs over, his tiny feet nearly tripping over themselves.

We're about to exit the shop when Aunt Naomi stops us.

"You're taking them through the orchard?" she asks, her eyebrows raised.

"Yeah, is that okay?"

"Sure, yeah. It's just that you don't know your way around. . . ."

"That's all right. It's just rows of trees," I say. "Plus, I'm sure there are plenty of people out there who can help me find my way around."

"It's twenty acres, though," the woman next to her says. She's vaguely familiar, and at first, I can't place her. But then I notice her eyes—the same striking amber as Cooper's. Her gaze homes in on something behind me. "Coop, can you go with Naomi's niece? She's taking these two apple-picking. I don't want her to end up getting lost like the Turners did last year."

I don't glance back at Cooper, and I don't give him a chance to reply. "What about Jake?" I hitch my thumb in the direction of the register. "He can help me."

"Jake has a long line right now," Aunt Naomi says. "I'd rather not switch out the person dealing with the money without balancing the drawer first, and I don't really have time for that."

"Don't worry, Cooper knows his way around," his mom adds with a friendly smile.

Too bad getting lost is the least of my concerns right now.

I haven't talked to Cooper since the first day of school and didn't plan on talking to him again before going back to New York. With the exception of a few glares I catch him shooting my way, he mostly avoids me, even at our shared lunch table. I can't believe I'm being forced to hang out with him today.

Accepting my fate, I huff and turn to find Cooper already scooping Harley up and setting him on his broad shoulders. Harley giggles as he fists Cooper's hair, tugging on it as if holding on to reins.

"Giddy up!" he calls.

"Oh, dear . . . ," Harley's grandma mumbles. But Cooper takes it in stride, telling Harley to be sure to hold on tight.

"Let's head out," he says, giving the old woman a smile. A stupidly beautiful smile.

"Hey, new girl!" Jake shouts from across the store. "It was eight seventy-five. Loser." He winks at me before turning back to his line. I smile and shake my head, catching Cooper watching us before he makes his way out the door toward the fields.

I sidle up next to the woman and link my arm through hers. "I'm Ellis."

"Lovely to meet you, Ellis. I'm Dorothy."

She places her soft hand on my forearm and lets me lead her outside.

It's a cool September day following a heavy morning rain, and the grass is still wet, leaving my boots soaked as we saunter through the field of trees. In just the past week, leaves have begun to change, the lush green now giving way to hints of the yellows and reds to come. Families roam the area, picking various types of apples and placing them in their baskets, some climbing the wooden ladders placed throughout the orchard for whoever might need them.

Before long, Dorothy and I fall into an easy conversation

about Street Media and my college plans. She's eager to tell me about her daily walks with the friends she affectionately calls her "girls," their Sunday games of bridge, her favorite characters in *Law & Order: SVU*, and her old job as a travel agent.

We're strolling beneath the overcast sky, goose bumps covering my arms and the sweet scent of apples tickling my nose, when Harley tugs hard on Cooper's hair and shouts, "Stop here!" Cooper winces as he stops at a tree filled with bright red apples. Harley wiggles off Cooper's back and stares up at the apples dangling from every branch. "I want that one."

We all crane our necks, searching for the specific apple he's talking about.

"This one?" Cooper asks, tapping one of the high-hanging fruits.

"No. The one all the way up there." Harley's chubby finger points beyond where Cooper can reach.

"Harley, no one can reach the ones up there. Choose one of these," Dorothy says, gesturing to the apples on the lower branches.

Harley stomps his foot, his face puckering into a defiant pout. "No."

"It's no problem, Dorothy. I'll grab a ladder," I say. I let go of her arm. "You wait here."

After weaving through two rows of trees and ducking beneath low branches, I get to the closest ladder I can find. It's folded and leaning against an apple tree. I heave it upright and begin walking it into a horizontal position when Cooper's hand reaches around me.

"I got it," he says, grabbing the ladder.

"I can get it," I tell him, not bothering to mask the annoyance in my voice as I let go.

"I know you can." He lifts the ladder with ease. "But you don't have to. And I can probably get it over there faster, which is vital because there's no telling what sort of trouble that kid will get into if we leave him alone for longer than thirty seconds."

I smile because he's right. "Or even longer than three seconds, really."

"You're right. His energy is unparalleled," Cooper says, exposing the first crack in his icy demeanor by smiling back.

"Harley, get down from there!" Dorothy calls as he swings from a branch like it's a gymnastics bar. "You're going to get hurt!"

As we arrive with the ladder, the apple tree shakes, higher and higher, until Harley pops out with his arms and legs wrapped around a skinny branch as he maneuvers toward the apple he picked out.

Cooper and I stop in our tracks and stare up at him.

"I couldn't stop him," Dorothy says, worried.

The apple trees aren't especially tall, but this one is high enough that if he falls, he'll definitely get hurt. He reaches out to pluck an apple from its branch, and my stomach drops, panic seizing me when his hand slips. The apple falls to the ground, and he screams, wrapping his arms and legs tightly around the branch as he begins to cry.

"It's okay, Harley," I call up as Cooper sets up the ladder. "Hold on. I'm coming up to get you."

"Okay," he whimpers.

Cooper looks at me. "I should climb up and get him."

I shake my head, stepping onto the first rung. "You're stronger, so you should hold the ladder for us." Plus, the sheer look of horror on his face reminds me that he's afraid of heights, a detail I won't rub in right now. Not when he's finally talking to me again.

He nods and grips the ladder rails, clearly relieved. "Yeah, okay."

I climb the rungs until I've reached the top. Harley is still a foot above me, but I can't get any closer. "All right, buddy, I'm going to need you to crawl this way." I hold my arms out, ready for him.

He looks at me, unsure, then blows out a puff of air before nodding. His movements are slow and deliberate as he inches toward me.

"Okay, let your feet drop but keep holding on, and I'll grab you," I tell him once he's above me, the weight of him making the branch droop in our favor.

He unwraps his ankles from around the branch and lets them fall into my left arm while I use my right to hold on to the ladder and balance.

"I have you, don't worry. Now let go."

With tears in his eyes, Harley lets go of the branch, and his full weight falls into my arms. I slowly lower him in front of me until his feet are on a ladder rung.

"You climb down first," I tell him, but I'm not sure he even hears me. Because the second his feet hit the ladder, he takes off.

"Thank you both so much!" Dorothy says, clutching her chest.

Harley's eyes scan the ground. "Where's my apple?"

Cooper walks over to where Harley's apple rolled and picks it up. "It's right here. It didn't make it far."

"Oooh, thank you!" Harley darts underneath the ladder, bumping the unstable base with his shoulder, causing it to tilt too far to the right.

Everything after happens quickly.

The ladder shifts and begins falling over. My scream gets caught in my throat.

I try to leap off, but my shoe catches on the side rail, twisting my ankle and my free-falling body.

The ladder hits the ground just as I fall into Cooper's outstretched arms. He's breathing fast and hard, pure panic on his face.

His horrified eyes lock on mine as he seems to process that he caught me.

"Are you okay?" he asks.

"I . . . think so?"

He lets out a huge breath and closes his eyes for a second. I can almost feel the relief rushing through him. Then he says, "You were right about the three seconds."

It takes me a second to realize he's talking about how long Harley can be unattended, but once I do, a laugh bubbles out of me. Cooper's lips slide into a lopsided grin.

"You said a potty word!" Harley shouts at me.

"No, I didn't." I pause. "Did I?"

"You definitely did," Cooper says, amused.

"You said 'shit,'" Harley tells me.

Dorothy gasps. "Harley Andrew Dempsey! You do not use grown-up words!"

"She's not a grown-up and she said it," Harley points out. "And you didn't yell at her."

"She isn't six years old, and she isn't mine to yell at," Dorothy tells him.

"No, I shouldn't have said it either," I tell him. "When I get home, I'm putting myself in time-out for using a potty word."

Harley looks at me like I'm bananas. "Who puts themselves in time-out? You're weird."

Cooper laughs as Harley runs off, leaving his apple on the ground beside us.

"I'm going to put you down, okay?" Cooper says, pulling my attention back to him.

A blush spreads across my chest when I realize my arms are wrapped around his neck, as if holding on for dear life. I nod and let go, and Cooper sets me on the ground. But a sharp pain shoots through my left ankle, and I fall back on my butt.

"What's wrong?" Cooper asks, squatting next to me. "Did you hurt your foot?"

"My ankle, but I'll be fine," I say, pushing back up but bearing my weight on my right foot.

"I'm so sorry, Ellis," Dorothy says to me.

"Nothing to be sorry for," I say, trying to smile through the pain.

"Harley, get over here," Dorothy calls.

Harley comes barreling over, and Dorothy makes him apologize, even though he clearly has no idea what he did wrong.

"I think we ought to head back and get some ice on that ankle," Dorothy says.

Without warning, Harley jumps on Cooper's back, climbing him like he climbed the apple tree.

"Nope," Cooper says, unwrapping Harley's arms from around him. Harley's feet drop to the ground. "It's Ellis's turn. Can you lead the way, though? I don't think I know how to get back."

"What are you talking about? I'm not getting on your shoulders," I say.

"You can't walk all the way back on that ankle," he says. "I'll carry you on my back."

"Isn't there, like, a golf cart we can use or something?"

Cooper stares at me.

"Fine," I grumble. "But that's a long way for you to carry me."

"I'll be just fine," he says, kneeling down.

I limp over and set my hands on his shoulders as he reaches back and scoops his hands under my thighs and stands effortlessly.

"Are you going to be okay, Dorothy?" I ask.

"I'm not as spry as I once was, but I'm not bedridden yet, honey. Didn't I tell you about my daily walks with my girls?"

"Okay, point taken," I laugh. "But the ground is uneven, like you said, so please be careful."

Cooper walks slowly in the direction of the orchard shop, trying not to outpace Dorothy, while Harley runs figure eights around trees.

"Doesn't he ever get tired?" I ask Dorothy.

"Oh no. He's like the Energizer Bunny," she says. "In fact, it seems the more he does, the more energy he has, like the activity charges his internal battery."

Harley runs by with his arms spread wide, pretending to be an airplane, and I try not to think about Cooper's muscles beneath my palms. Or how he smells like sugar and citrus and laundry detergent. Or the heat radiating from him, warming me from the inside out.

Instead I try to focus on my throbbing ankle. Because I can't be attracted to a guy who wants nothing to do with me. A guy I'll likely never see again after I leave Bramble Falls.

"You know," I say to Cooper, "the last time I was here, I was the one giving you a piggyback ride."

Cooper laughs. "Don't remind me."

"Oh, but I'm going to. You'd just jumped off the floating dock at the lake . . ."

"Ellis, come on," he whines, but I can hear his smile.

"And you burst out of the water crying."

"I had a rusty fish hook in my toe!" he exclaims.

"Yeah, but I didn't have to carry you because of the injury. You ended up on my back because you were sobbing so hard about the possibility of getting tetanus."

"A legitimate concern," he says in his own defense.

"The hook barely broke your skin. You didn't even bleed," I laugh. "There was no reason you couldn't have walked."

"Did you go to the doctor?" Dorothy asks, reminding me that we're not alone.

"Don't, Ellis," Cooper says quickly.

"Three times!" I say, cracking up. "He went three times that week because he said the doctor was wrong. He was convinced he was dying."

Dorothy laughs with me, and Cooper squeezes my thighs,

making my insides crackle and hiss like a blazing fire.

"Yeah, yeah," he chuckles. He shakes his head. "I hate you."

The sentiment snaps me right back to reality. He can't see me, but I nod, my smile faltering and my voice becoming quiet. "Yeah, I know." And I can't stand it, despite trying to convince myself I don't care.

Once we're out of the field, Dorothy and I wait in the parking lot with Harley while Cooper goes inside to get a bag of apples for them to take home since apple-picking didn't go as planned.

"Dorothy, it was so nice meeting you," I say as Cooper gives her the free apples.

"It was lovely meeting you, too," she tells me.

Dorothy wrangles her grandson into the car, and they drive off. Cooper carries me inside, toward a hallway at the back, and sets me down in a small employee break room.

"Sit." He nods at a chair. "I'll be right back."

"O-kay . . ."

Cooper returns five minutes later carrying a first aid kit and an ice pack wrapped in a thin towel. He sits in a chair across from me, scoots close, and pats his leg, nodding at my foot.

I reluctantly lift it, and he takes it in his hands, slipping off my boot and dropping it onto the floor. He pushes up my pant leg, and I shiver when his soft fingertips graze my leg.

"I can do this myself," I tell him.

He looks up through his thick lashes, giving me a look that says, *Shut up.*

I look away because those hypnotizing eyes might kill me otherwise.

"Where does it hurt?" he asks.

I touch the outside of my ankle. He nods and places the ice pack on it, holding it as he clears his throat.

"I'm sorry," he says.

"For what?"

"I shouldn't have walked away from the ladder, especially with Harley running around. I wasn't thinking."

"Oh." For some reason I thought he was going to apologize for how he's been toward me since I arrived. I thought maybe we could be friends again. I *hoped* we could be friends again. "It's okay. I'm sure my ankle will be better by tomorrow."

He nods, but he still looks torn up about it.

"Besides, you *did* save my life," I tell him.

"I doubt you would have died," he says, his lips inching into a grin.

I shrug. "Could have. But now we'll never know."

He sets the ice pack on the table and unravels an ACE bandage, circling it around my foot then up and around my ankle.

He hands me the ice pack. "You'll want to hold this on there. Twenty minutes on, twenty minutes off."

"Okay. Thank you."

Cooper stands and holds his hands out for me to take. I scan them, finding the scar on his left thumb from when he burned it on a baking sheet the last time I was here. It's faded now—white instead of bright pink—but it's there. Yet another reminder of how different things used to be between us.

I place my hands in his and try to ignore the soft buzz his touch elicits inside me. And as he pulls me up, something comes over me and, without really thinking, I find myself saying, "So, um, would you maybe want to go get tacos when we're done here?"

When he doesn't immediately answer, instead seeming to study me, my cheeks flood with heat, and I silently berate myself. His friendliness today doesn't negate the fact that he's acted completely disinterested in connecting with me since I've gotten to town, and I feel stupid for getting caught up in the moment.

"Tacos?" he finally says, his expression unreadable.

I train my gaze on Cooper's shirt instead of those captivating eyes and bite my lip, wondering if I should tell him to forget I said anything. Wondering if I could get away with telling him I was just kidding. "Uh, yeah. We could go to that cute stand we used to stop by every day after swimming?"

"That place closed," he tells me, his tone flat as he drops my hands. "It's an ice cream stand now." He takes a step backward, not meeting my eyes, and I can tell he's shutting down again. "I'm going to get back out there."

I nod, trying to hide my embarrassment. "Oh. Yeah, okay. Thanks for your help."

"No problem." He runs his hand through his hair as he looks at the floor. "Sorry again about your ankle. I'll see you around, Ellis."

I wilt as he disappears through the doorway, leaving my extended olive branch snapped in half on the break-room floor.

Chapter Eight

When Sloane and I walk into school on Monday, homecoming posters line the walls of Bramble Falls High. The excitement is palpable. Whispers of dates and dancing fill every classroom. In classes, homecoming dinner plans are already being made, and girls are scrolling online shops, searching for the perfect dress.

By Wednesday, however, the buzz has mostly died down as everyone begins the wait to see which brave soul will be the first to initiate an invite.

Meanwhile, I'm just trying to get from point A to point B on a bum ankle without being late.

Jake sets my lunch tray on the table and lets me slide into my seat before sitting down beside me.

"Wow, how chivalrous of you to carry the lady's lunch," Slug quips. Jake gives him the middle finger. He's been carrying my backpack and my books for me all week, following me around while I limp from class to class. The swelling in my ankle has gone down, but it still hurts. I could probably carry my own stuff, but Jake insisted. I don't know how much chivalry has to do with it, though. Helping me has been getting him out of the first few minutes of his classes.

Cooper shows up to lunch late, but when he does, he joins farther down the table with the cute blond girl he sits next to in calculus. In class earlier, he stayed on the opposite side of the room. When I passed him in the hall, he didn't so much as glance my way.

I try to forget the fact that I caught a glimpse of the boy I used to know on Saturday because, apparently, we're back to pretending we don't have a history. He's not being snarky toward me anymore, but he's still aloof. Detached. *Avoidant.*

Which I guess is good, because the more I think about this past weekend, the more embarrassed I become to have put myself out there only to be rejected.

"I'm having a party on Friday," Jake says. "My mom's going on a business trip."

"Cool." I take a bite of my food.

"You going to come?" he asks.

"No."

He chuckles. "Not even going to think about it, huh? Just no?"

"There's nothing to think about," I tell him with a shrug. "I have to study for physics."

He furrows his brow. "But it's on Friday night."

"Yeah, I heard that part. Still, I'll be studying."

Slug laughs and shakes his head.

Jake's face contorts. "Freak."

I laugh. "Listen, we can't both be slackers. How will you pass physics if I don't study?"

Jake looks away guiltily, probably figuring out that I caught him copying my pop quiz today. "I don't know what you're talking about. But even if I did, I'd say I'd rather you come to my party and we fail physics together."

"Not going to happen." I put my hand on his shoulder as the bell rings. "Sorry, Jakey."

"Aw, you have a little pet name now," Slug says.

"It sounds like a toddler name," Jake grumbles.

"Well, if the shoe fits . . . ," I say.

Slug laughs and Jake stands, frowning at me.

"I'm so nice to you, and yet this is how you treat me," Jake says.

I laugh. "You're nice to me so that I'll let you copy my quizzes."

"No, that's just a perk." He sighs and grabs my tray. "Maybe you can study extra hard tonight and tomorrow, then you won't need to study Friday."

"Maybe. But probably not."

"Just tell him you'll think about it," Slug tells me. "I can't listen to him bitching and moaning about it all week."

I laugh. "Fine. I'll think about it."

Jake's whole face lights up. "Hell yeah."

I wait while he dumps our trays, and when he comes back, he holds out his hand. I take it—even though I don't need it—and he pulls me up.

"You sure you don't just want me to carry you to class?" he says.

"I'm sure. I'm fine." I don't need any more boys carrying me anywhere.

He loops his arm through mine. "Okay, then let's get you to art."

I nod and let him lead me through the throng of seniors in the commons.

But feeling eyes on me, I glance over to find Cooper watching us.

I offer him a small smile, but with a twitching jaw he turns away and pushes through the set of double doors leading outside.

"Hey, Ellis," Dad says when he answers his phone on Friday night.

We've exchanged a few texts since my move to Bramble Falls, but they've been brief and half-hearted, a quick **Hope you had a good day at school** or **I forwarded your mail to your aunt's** or **Do you know where Mom keeps the iron?** I miss having actual conversations with him, but he's always so busy, it's been impossible to get him on the phone. Until now.

"Hey, I can't believe you answered," I say, grinning as I curl up in my bed.

"Yeah." Something clinks in the background, and he sounds distracted when he says, "Just got home from work."

"Oh wow. Another late night at the office. Have any fun plans tonight?" I ask, knowing he never does anything fun—except work, because that's his idea of a good time.

"Not really. But, hey, did you need something?" he asks. "I'm about to go grab some takeout. . . ."

"Oh," I say, my smile falling. "Yeah, no, I don't need anything. Just wanted to talk. I miss you."

He sighs. "I miss you, too, Ellie Belly. But you and Mom will be home soon. It'll be like you never left."

But we did leave. Mom dragged me away from my life there, and I won't ever forgive her for it. "Yeah. You're right. I just wish 'soon' wasn't so far away."

"I know, but it'll fly by." Dad's keys jingle. "All right, well, give me a call tomorrow. Have a good night, Ell."

"Okay," I say, even though I know he likely won't answer when I call tomorrow. "Love you."

"Yep. Love you. Talk soon."

Dad ends the call, and I toss the phone on the bed beside me as Sloane flings open my curtain and drops a large pile of fabrics in various colors and materials onto my bed, offering the perfect distraction from my disappointing phone call.

"Good grief, how are dresses so heavy?" she says.

"Um, why are you bringing me a pile of fifty dresses?" I ask, eyeing them.

"Because the apple cider tea party is tomorrow. I already got my dress months ago, but we have to pick one of these for you to wear." She sits on the edge of my bed. "All of them have fancy matching hats and gloves, but I would have needed another two arms to carry those up too."

"And why do you have so many dresses?"

"Mom takes tea party dress donations whenever someone is done with one they've worn in the past. So these are all pre-owned but also very cute, in a very specific sort of way," she says. "I'll hold them up so you can pick one."

"Can't I just wear one of my own dresses?" I ask, even though I know I didn't bring anything remotely suitable in the pared-down basic wardrobe I squeezed into my two measly suitcases.

She shakes her head. "Nope. These are tea party appropriate—big and fancy and outlandish. You have to embrace the absurdity, though. As long as you don't mind wearing secondhand stuff? I know you're big into fashion in the city. . . ."

"No, it's fine. I go thrifting all the time. Or at least I used to." I maneuver my way to the other end of the bed.

"Okay, cool. I'm sure at least some of them will work." Sloane stands and holds up the first option—a puffy dandelion-yellow dress with squared shoulders and a V neckline. "This one looks like it'll fit." I scrunch my face, and Sloane laughs. "Okay, so that one's a no," she says, tossing it to a new spot on the bed.

"A big no," I confirm. "Even if I'm embracing absurdity."

We continue through the pile, laughing and cringing at some of the options. I ultimately select an off-the-shoulder A-line dress in pistachio green. It's satin and tea-length and, honestly, show-stoppingly adorable.

Sloane picks up the pile of dresses. "Okay, so I was waiting until we were done to say anything, but . . ."

"But . . . ?"

"I'm supposed to make sure I get you to Jake's party."

"Oh yeah? Says who?" I ask.

"Jake, obviously. He's texted me six times in the last twenty-four hours to remind me. And since you're not actually studying tonight . . ."

"I don't know. I just don't really feel like going." Spending the night at a party where I know almost no one doesn't sound that great. "Are you going?"

"I *will* if you want me to take you. But I wasn't planning on going otherwise."

"Then my vote is no, we don't go."

"Okay, do you want to watch a movie?" she asks.

I glance at the old TV and even older DVD player my aunt dragged up here a couple days ago. It sits on a small stand, not hooked up or plugged in.

"What movie?" I ask, trying to remember the last time I sat down and actually watched a movie. I honestly don't know.

Sloane shrugs. "*Practical Magic*? 'Tis the season, after all."

"I've never seen it," I tell her.

Sloane gasps and drops the pile of dresses on the floor. "Ellis, how are we related?" She grabs the unruly cords and plugs the TV in, then tosses the remotes on the bed. "I'll get the DVD and popcorn. You turn everything on."

"Okay."

"Be prepared to fall in love with these two sisters and their aunts," Sloane calls as she hops down the stairs.

Twenty minutes later, my cousin and I are lying on our bellies on my bed, getting crumbs and kernels in my sheets, and watching Sally take measures not to fall in love.

It's the most fun I've had in a really long time.

Chapter Nine

When Sloane and I arrive at the town square the next day, Aunt Naomi is already there directing volunteers to their assigned places. I watch her, in awe of how she can be in charge of so many people, have so much to keep organized and running smoothly, and still manage to be warm toward people and not at all frazzled.

In the gazebo, a violinist in a gaudy pink dress sets up her music stand. Round white tables, ranging from two-tops to six-tops, are placed across the lawn. Ceramic teacups with delicate fall patterns sit on matching saucers atop cream cotton tablecloths. Golden-orange wildflower centerpieces donated from a local flower farm top off the look.

“Oh my goodness! You two look gorgeous,” Aunt Naomi says as Sloane and I approach.

“We look ridiculous,” I correct her.

“You don’t feel like you’re dressed for the Kentucky Derby?” Aunt Naomi asks, gesturing at her very large hat.

"I think we'd look a little extra even at the Kentucky Derby," I laugh.

"Extra is good. You remember that," she says with a wink.

"Do you need anything before we go to the raffle-ticket table?" Sloane asks, her eyes scanning the square for something—or someone.

"Oh no. You're good to head over whenever you're ready. You girls have fun!" Aunt Naomi waves at someone behind us, and she's gone in a blink.

We take a short walk around the square, and Sloane points out what will be happening in the various locations throughout the day. I'm so busy getting the tea party rundown that I don't notice Cooper sitting at the raffle table until we're standing right in front of it. He's staring at his phone and doesn't seem to notice us, either, which is good because I can barely look away.

He has on a dark green tie and gray suspenders over a white dress shirt that fits him snugly in all the right places, and his sleeves are rolled up to just below his elbows. Although I can't see his full outfit behind the red BRAMBLE FALLS APPLE CIDER TEA PARTY RAFFLE banner hanging from the front of the table, his top half is enough to stop me mid-sentence.

He finally looks up, catching me staring. "What's up?"

"Um, what are you doing?" I ask him.

"What do you mean?" he asks, confused.

"Sloane and I are working this table. You should ask Aunt Naomi where you're supposed to—"

"Actually," Sloane interjects, "my mom made me a greeter."

I look at her. "What? When?"

"She just told me this morning."

Sloane has always been the worst liar. We could never get away with anything when we were younger if it meant her having to tell our parents a fib. And this lie is written all over her pretty face.

"But you *just* asked her—"

"Anyway, you two have fun! Bye!" She turns and nearly sprints away.

I sigh and sit in the chair next to Cooper.

"Sloane's an awful liar," Cooper says, scrolling on his phone.

"Yep."

"So . . . why'd she tell Naomi to trade our jobs?" he asks, setting his phone right next to mine on the table between us.

"I have no idea, but if I had to guess, I'd say it's because she can't stand when people don't get along and she thinks if we're stuck next to each other all day, we'll become friends again."

Cooper nods but says nothing as he looks out at all the dressed-up people arriving. An awkward silence fills the space between us, the shared memory of his rejection last weekend hanging in the air.

Finally he says, "I ran into Dorothy last night."

"Oh?"

"She brought Harley to Cheesylicious for dinner. Stopped by my table just to rave about you."

I grin. "Aw. I really liked her, too."

"Well, as a Bramble Falls native, I feel like it's my responsibility to make sure you're informed about the people here," he says. "Especially if you might become friends with them."

I narrow my eyes at him. "What's that supposed to mean?"

"You know how Dorothy kept mentioning her walks with 'her girls'?"

"Yeah . . ."

"Well, she and her friends are well-known around town as the Gossip Girls."

"Like the show?" I ask.

"More like they're the heart of the Bramble Falls gossip mill."

My jaw drops. "Shut up. Cute elderly Dorothy? Not possible."

"It is possible. They're the eyes and ears of this place. They walk in circles around the town square every day, getting their steps in and sharing rumors."

"Cooper, stop it right now," I laugh. "I don't know if I should believe you or not."

"I'm not lying!" He laughs, gracing me with his dimple.

"Dorothy?" I shake my head. "This is so scandalous."

"Just thought you should know, in case you end up talking to her more," he says.

"Thanks. I'll be careful not to share my deepest, darkest secrets."

He grins at me, his eyes lingering on mine before a shadow is cast over us.

"Can I get two tickets?" someone to my right says. Cooper's gaze is still fixed on me when I look away, giving a tall white woman with light brown hair my attention.

I pull two tickets off the roll, and she hands me two dollars, which I hand to Cooper to put in the cash box. Once the woman leaves with her tickets, I put their matches in the large raffle-ticket spinners in front of the two baskets she is hoping to win—one with free passes to various upcoming Bramble Falls events, including the homecoming game in a couple of weeks, the double feature horror night at the drive-in movies in October, the community theater's presentation of *Wicked* in November, and the Snow Ball in December, and one basket filled with treats from the Caffeinated Cat. I haven't tried the pastries there yet, but my mouth waters just looking at them.

"I need a harvest spice latte," I say, realizing my stomach is empty. "Do you mind manning the table alone for a few minutes?"

"Um, yeah," Cooper says, standing. My eyes wander to his dark gray dress pants, which fit him *perfectly*. If staring at him were an Olympic sport, I'd win gold. I swipe at my mouth just in case I'm drooling in public. "I'm not going to let you walk all the way there on a bad ankle. You watch the table. I'll be right back."

"It's been a week. My ankle is fine," I argue, pulling my eyes back to his (impossibly handsome) face. "Even if it wasn't, it's literally across the street." But he's already on his way. "Cooper, stop! I can—"

"I can't hear you!" he calls without looking back.

"At least take my credit card!"

He ignores me and keeps walking.

In the time that he's gone, I sell twenty raffle tickets between four people, and all four put their tickets in the Caffeinated Cat basket. So when Cooper shows up with my latte and a dark red cookie, I'm ready to see what all the fuss is about.

I break it in two. Inside, swirls of something white mix with the buttery soft dough. I offer him the smaller half, which he declines.

I shrug. "Fine. More for me. What kind of cookie am I about to eat?"

"Red velvet marshmallow," Cooper answers as I take my first bite.

It's possible I moan.

Cooper laughs. "You like it?"

Okay, yeah, I definitely moaned.

"'Like' doesn't cover it," I say after I swallow. "This is the sexiest thing I've ever eaten."

Cooper's eyebrows draw together, but he wears an amused smile. "Did you just call food sexy?"

"I called this red velvet cookie sexy, yes. Try to tell me I'm wrong."

He laughs. "I wouldn't dare."

"Good. You should be fired from your job, by the way."

"And why's that?"

I gesture at what's left of the cookie in front of me. "Because I've been here two full weeks. I've gone to that café every single day for coffee. And *not once* did you insist I get one of these. Worst employee ever." I shake my head, take another bite, and fill my cheek with the gooey goodness. "And depriving me of these this whole time? If you didn't already hate me, I'd fire you from our friendship. Worst ex-friend ever."

Cooper shifts in his seat. "I don't hate you."

"Please." I lick the marshmallow off my finger. Cooper's eyes track it, and a strange warmth floods my cheeks. I put my hands in my lap. "You've made your feelings clear."

"'Hate' is a strong word."

"Oh, okay. Would it be more accurate to say you 'strongly dislike' me?" I ask. "Because that would be disappointing. At least 'hate' implies something matters enough to be able to elicit such a strong feeling."

"You mattering isn't really the issue," he grumbles.

"Okay, then tell me, what is the issue, exactly?"

A phone vibrates loudly on the table between us. We each look down to check where it came from. My phone is lit up.

Pen Thief Jake: **Hey, you. Missed you last night ☹ What are you up to today? Working the ACTP?**

He arches an eyebrow. "Pen Thief Jake? Is that Keller?"

"Yeah, he asked to borrow a pen on the first day of school and never gave it back."

"Do all of your contacts have nickname reminders of who they are?" Cooper asks.

"Pretty much." I take the final bite of cookie, closing my eyes as I savor the taste.

"Am I still in your phone?" His question is hesitant. Nervous.

I open my eyes. "Yes."

He picks up his phone, hits a few buttons, and sets it back down just as my phone vibrates again.

Summer Cooper: **What's my reminder nickname?**

"Interesting. I thought it'd be something like Crying Cooper or Pooper Cooper or Self-Tanner Cooper," he says.

I snort-laugh. "Any of those would have worked. I guess I was being generous."

Cooper's bright eyes crinkle in the corners as he laughs, and I have to avert my eyes.

He is actually Too Much to look at.

Our laughter dies as the pretty girl from calculus and lunch approaches Cooper's end of the table. She has sun-kissed highlights in her straight, long blond hair, a button nose with full lips, and a daisy-yellow dress. Her bright eyes are fixed on Cooper.

Which, understandable.

"Hey, Coop," she says. "How's it going over here? I thought you were a greeter today."

"Hey," Cooper replies, angling himself toward her. "Yeah, I was. Got swapped with Sloane, though."

"I just saw the greeters sitting at a table drinking apple cider," she says. "Sucks you don't get to enjoy the party."

Cooper shrugs, unaffected. "We're having our own party over here."

I laugh. "If this is your idea of a party, you need to get out more."

He turns to me, a smirk playing on his face. "*You* skipped out on Jake's last night so that you could study, but *I'm* the one who needs to get out more?"

"Hey, I ended up watching *Practical Magic* with Sloane," I say defensively. Plus, who needs a social life when I'm not going to be here long enough to make any real friends, anyway?

"Love that movie," Cooper says.

"Really?" I ask, skeptical.

"Really," he says. "The idea of being able to cast a spell so you don't fall in love? If only."

I tilt my head, trying to make sense of his comment, when the blonde clears her throat.

"I'm Chloe," she says, cutting in and offering a small wave. "You're Ellis, right? We sort of eat lunch together but haven't actually met."

"Yeah, nice to officially meet you."

"Cooper said you two used to be friends," she says.

"Yeah." I glance at him. "Used to be."

"I'm glad my old dress came in handy," she says, her eyes trailing over me. "Looks way better on you than it did on me."

"Thanks," I force out. I try not to compare myself to other girls, but the idea of a who-wore-it-best moment between me and Chloe threatens even my sense of self-confidence.

She turns back to Cooper, whose eyes are on me. "Speaking of dresses," she says, and he gives her his attention. "My mom and I went shopping this morning, and I got my homecoming dress. I'll send you a picture so you can match the color."

Oh.

Cooper and Chloe are a thing.

I don't know why that never occurred to me. I've seen them together a thousand times over the last two weeks.

I also don't know why I hate the idea so much.

Get a grip, Ellis.

"Sounds good," Cooper says to her.

Chloe smiles. "Okay, well"—her eyes bounce between me and Cooper—"I'll leave you two to your private party. Nice to meet you, Ellis. See you later, Coop."

I stare ahead, out at the couples and families sitting at the tables drinking their apple cider and having a good time.

"The dress does look good on you," he says quietly to my left.

I close my eyes and press my lips together. I know he's trying to be nice and make me feel better, knowing I'm probably comparing myself to his gorgeous girlfriend since she wore it last year, but *do we have to talk about the dress?*

"Thanks." I turn to him. "So, you and Chloe, huh?"

"What about us?" he asks, even though we both know what I'm asking.

"She seems nice. You two are cute together."

"Oh yeah?" He chews the inside of his cheek and says nothing else as an announcement is made, reminding people about the raffle. People swarm the table, and Cooper and I are busy for the next twenty minutes, falling into an easy flow, working seamlessly together.

Once the rush clears, Cooper says, "Chloe and I aren't together."

"Really? Are you sure?" I ask.

"I think I'd know," he says.

"Does Chloe?"

He draws his eyebrows together, in either confusion or annoyance—hard to say. "Yes, she's aware. Why are you asking?"

I shrug. "Was thinking I might become one of the Gossip Girls."

But my joke doesn't land. Cooper only continues staring at me, waiting for a real answer.

"You're going to homecoming together, and she definitely seems into you. I was just curious," I say. "I'm only here a couple of months, but I'd still like to know what's going on around me. That's all."

"Right," he says. But he's looking at me like I just admitted to being into him. Like I just asked him out. A combination of panic and embarrassment sends me into fight-or-flight mode.

"What about Jake?" I blurt, as if I care in the slightest whether Jake is single. And I think it's safe to assume I'd know by now if he weren't.

Cooper looks away. "Jake's single." He taps his thumb on the table a few times before adding, "And so is Slug, in case you were wondering."

We both know I wasn't.

"Okay, and what about Sloane and Asher?" Now, *that* is something I actually am curious about.

Cooper cracks a smile and turns my way again. "I mean, they say they're only friends, but . . ."

"I know, right?"

He laughs and all the tension between us seems to dissipate.

A few minutes later, Aunt Naomi tells us we don't need to sit at the table anymore. So Cooper heads over to where Chloe is hanging out, and I join Sloane, Preeti, and Asher at their table.

But no matter how hard I try, I can't stop glancing at him.

And even if they're not together, I can't stop being jealous of whatever it is between him and Chloe.

Chapter Ten

"Ellis, I'm so sorry," Sloane says breathlessly as she jogs to the flagpole after school on Tuesday. "I forgot drama club starts today." She hands her keys to me. "You can take the car—shit, no you can't. Girl, we have to get you your license."

"I don't need a license in the city. It's okay. I'll just do my homework while I wait."

"Are you sure? I feel bad that you're stuck at school," she says.

"I'd be doing the same thing at home. It's fine." I really don't mind, but I was looking forward to kicking off my boots and lying in bed with my work.

"Okay. I'll meet you in the commons in an hour and a half, then," she says. She dashes away, and I head back inside.

Inside, a few stragglers stand around talking. Jake, Cooper, and Slug are hanging with some friends at a table, so I head over there.

"Hey, new girl. What are you still doing here?" Jake asks.

I set my backpack on the table. "Do you still call me new girl because you can't remember my name?"

"Of course not, Ella," he says. I punch him in the arm, and he laughs. "I'm kidding! Jeez. It's Ellis from here on out. But seriously, what are you still doing here?"

I sigh. "Sloane has drama club, so I'm stuck here." Then an idea occurs to me: "Unless you can give me a ride home?"

Jake frowns. "I have football practice in five minutes. But I could skip."

"Won't you be benched for your next game if you skip?" Cooper says.

Jake shoots him a glare that clearly says, *Shut the hell up, man,* then turns to me. "It'll be fine. I'll take you."

"No, I'll just wait. It's not a big deal," I tell him. I appreciate that he's willing to miss practice to give me a ride, but it's really not that important.

"Coop could probably take you," he says with a shrug. He turns to Cooper. "You're heading out, right?"

"No," I say quickly. "I'll just wait for Sloane." Things with Cooper are still confusing. It's like we've left something unresolved and are dancing around it whenever we talk—even though I don't know what *it* is. I never know where we stand, and, honestly, I really don't feel like getting emotional whiplash today.

"Nope, let's go, Mitchell," Cooper says, slinging my backpack over his shoulder with his own. "I'll drop you off."

"You really don't have to."

"I know." He makes his way toward the door. I hesitate for a minute before I sigh and head after him, grateful that my ankle is completely healed as I jog to keep up with his long strides.

"Bye, *Ellis*!" Jake calls from behind me. I wave and follow Cooper through the double doors outside.

In the parking lot, I hop into his rusty burgundy truck, and he puts our backpacks in the small space between us. He pulls out, and we drive the next few minutes in silence.

Until I can't take it anymore.

"Can I ask you a question?"

He glances at me. "Okay."

"Why do you act like you don't know me at school?"

"I don't know what you're talking about," he says.

"Cooper."

"What?"

"Come on. It's just the two of us. No excuses, no distractions. Tell me why, after we had a good time at the apple cider tea party, you went back to keeping your distance. Tell me what I did wrong. Why you have a problem with me," I say, exasperated. "I get that I should know, okay? I feel bad that I don't. But I can't fix it if you don't tell me."

Cooper's knuckles turn white for a second, then his grip on the steering wheel relaxes. "Okay." He sighs. "When you left, I thought we were friends. I was mad when you ghosted me."

"Ghosted you? What do you mean?" I ask. "If I recall correctly, we just got busy."

"No, Ellis. *You* got busy. *You* stopped calling me back and would text one-word answers. Then *one time* I didn't want you to feel bad for completely ignoring me for a week, so I said it was okay because I had been busy that week too. And then I never heard from you again. As if me saying I was busy that one time meant it was okay for you to just stop talking to me altogether. I was . . ." He takes a breath and shakes his head. "I was *hurt*, okay? I felt like you'd been waiting for permission to forget about me. You coming back just surprised me and brought up a lot of old feelings."

My heart sinks. "Cooper . . ."

He shrugs nonchalantly, but we both know it's an act. "We were just kids."

"We were . . . but I'm still sorry." I swallow. "And even sorrier that I got too busy to realize what I was doing. I didn't mean to ghost you."

He glances at me then back at the road ahead. "It's fine. Really."

But it doesn't feel fine. It feels like I severely messed up something special.

And the worst part is that I didn't even miss him until I saw him again.

I *had* forgotten about him.

Cooper pulls up to Aunt Naomi's house and turns to me. "Look, we share mutual friends, and it seems we're going to be running into each other a lot on the weekends. So it's not like avoiding you is really an option." I frown, and he adds, "But, honestly, you kind of make it impossible to stay mad, anyway." His lips slant into a seemingly sincere smile. "We're good, Ellis. Really. Don't worry about it."

I nod, but I can't look at him. I can't offer him a smile. I hurt him enough to make him hold a grudge for the last three years. And I don't blame him.

"I'll see you tomorrow," I mumble as I climb out. "Thanks for the ride."

"No problem."

I watch his truck pull away, leaving me standing there, full of regret, wishing I could change the past.

I climb the steps to my room on Friday afternoon and find Mom's painting hanging on the wall. I collapse onto my bed and study the highlights and shadows she's added. It's remarkable how she brought a made-up landscape to life, like fictional characters in a book, only she managed to do it in a single still image.

She started her job at the art store last week and has been painting in all her spare time. I've never seen her so happy. So *alive.* Maybe Bramble Falls *is* good for her. Maybe this is exactly the break she needs in order to be happy at home again.

I still don't see why *I* have to be here, though.

I roll onto my back and call Dad's phone, sighing when he doesn't answer, even though I figured he wouldn't. Aside from a few texts—mostly him explaining that he's busy and promising to call me later—I've barely talked to him this past week, despite my *many* calls.

I'm very well acquainted with his voicemail.

But this time I'm not giving up that easily. I dial his extension at Street Media.

"Brad Mitchell's office," his assistant answers.

"Hey, Kara. It's Ellis."

"Oh! Hi, Ellis! How's your vacation going?"

What.

Dad seriously told everyone I'm on *vacation*? So they'll think I'm the type of person who just blows off a job to take an extended trip?

"It's . . . okay," I reply through clenched teeth. "Is my dad around? I couldn't reach him on his cell."

"He's not, unfortunately. Is this an emergency? I might be able to reach him. . . ."

"Oh no. No need to do that. Do you know when he'll be back?"

She clicks around on her computer. "He has his schedule blocked off until four o'clock, but he's at the club with Mr. Gableman, who, as you know, loves to hear himself talk. Plus, he's showing his new intern the ropes, so I imagine he might be gone a bit longer."

The wind is knocked out of me. "His . . . new intern?"

"Talia, yes. Has he not told you about her?" Kara says. "She's only been here a week and a half, but she's fantastic. She's a sophomore in college. Very driven girl. And a fast learner."

"I see," I say, although I barely hear myself through the whooshing in my ears.

"Of course, you'll always be our favorite, though," Kara adds.

I squeeze my stinging eyes closed.

"Right. Okay, well, thank you, Kara."

"Any time. I'll let him know you called," she says.

I nod even though she can't see me, and I hang up.

Dad didn't waste any time replacing me. After telling me my internship would be waiting for me when I get back. He found time to hire someone else—someone with more availability because she's in college, someone *fantastic* and *driven*—but he hasn't found time to call me back. He hasn't found time to even ask how I'm doing here.

Which, at the moment, isn't great.

But I refuse to lie here and cry.

I crawl out of bed and head downstairs. Sloane and Asher are in the living room eating Pop-Tarts with notes scattered in front of them.

I should be doing homework, too. But I *need* a distraction, and there's no way I can focus on school right now.

"Hey," Sloane says, her head tilted. "What's wrong?"

"Nothing. You guys want to go get dinner?" I ask.

Asher taps his phone, and the screen lights up. "At three fifty p.m.?"

I bite my lip. "An early dinner."

"I can only eat dinner today if someone is spoon-feeding me while I highlight," Sloane says, gesturing at her notes. "I copied these from Asher. I haven't actually paid attention in class since school started, and we have our first quiz Monday."

"But it's Friday," I say.

"Oh, that's rich coming from you," she says with a laugh. "We won't have enough time to study this weekend with the fall events on both days, so we're cramming now instead."

"Sorry," Asher says. "Mr. Winston is notoriously hard. I don't want to start off in a hole I have to dig myself out of."

"It's okay." I head over to the door and slip on my black leather boots.

"You're going alone?" Sloane asks, her eyebrows skyrocketing up her forehead.

I shrug. "Yeah." I get how shocking it must be for Sloane, a girl with a plethora of friends, but I'm used to being alone. I don't mind it.

Usually, anyway.

"You don't have to do that," she says, clearly rattled by the idea. "I can order takeout. You can hang out with us and do homework."

I offer her a smile, hoping she doesn't feel bad, and open the front door. "Thanks, but I'll be fine. Good luck studying."

As soon as I'm outside, I unlock my phone and begin scrolling through my contacts, suddenly wishing I had more friends in Bramble Falls. I scroll until I reach SUMMER COOPER. Even his name in my phone is a reminder of what I threw away.

I sigh. I can't text him, especially now that I know he has pent-up resentment toward me, despite him saying we're good. Plus, the last time I asked him to get food with me, he shot me down.

A girl can only take so much rejection.

I scroll back up to Jake's contact. He might not cause the same heat in my stomach that a glance from Cooper does, but he's been a great friend since I moved here.

Me: **I'm hungry.**

Pen Thief Jake: **lol try eating?**

Me: **Eat with me.**

Pen Thief Jake: **yeah? name the time and place**

Me: **How's five minutes? The diner?**

Pen Thief Jake: **oh shit ok might be closer to 15 but ill be there**

Chapter Eleven

"Why are you so gross?" I ask, popping a waffle fry into my mouth. Jake and I are sitting in a corner booth at the diner, having arrived just before the dinner rush, both of us with smash burgers on our plates. Jake's is half gone even though it only arrived ten seconds ago.

The jukebox is playing some country song as the booths along the walls begin to fill. The shiny black-and-white checkered floor glints from the low-hanging lights above. The walls are covered in photos of celebrities who have eaten here over the years.

"Just got done with football practice," Jake says after swallowing. His hair is wet with sweat, and his cheeks are flushed. "Was about to shower when you texted." I dip a fry into my ketchup, nodding. "It was a good surprise, though."

"Wish I could say the same about your smell," I say.

Jake laughs. "Sorry. *Someone* gave me an unrealistic amount of time to get here." He picks up a fry. "So, why *did* you text me?"

"What do you mean? Am I not allowed to eat with friends?"

"Are we friends?" he asks. His expression says he's serious.

I stop with a fry halfway to my mouth, a blush painting my cheeks. "Oh. Are we not?"

"I don't know. You blew off my party. And you never text me back."

"It was just a party," I say with a shrug. "And you've only texted me, like, once."

"Three times, and you haven't responded to any of them," he says. "I was convinced you gave me a fake number."

"Probably should have," I joke, trying to push away the prickle of shame that crawls up my neck at the realization that I really have been an asshole. But Jake doesn't laugh. "Okay, I'm sorry about the party. And about not texting you back. I've just been busy. Usually, I'll see a text and plan on responding once I'm done doing whatever, but then I forget about it entirely. Still, it was messed up to ignore you but then text you when I wanted something. I'll try to do better."

And I mean it. Jake's the only person who's gone out of their way from day one to befriend me in Bramble Falls. He deserves better than me using him as an ice pack for my bruised ego since Dad apparently finds me so easily replaceable.

Jake nods. "Okay."

A grin creeps across my face. "But I texted you today because Sloane couldn't come."

Jake barks out a laugh. "Ah, I see. I'm your second-choice friend. Sounds about right."

"More like my only friend. I love Sloane, but she's got a whole life here, with her own friends and her own stuff going on."

"You'll make more. You just got here."

We both take bites of our burgers and chew while we people-watch. I don't bother telling him I'm not great at making friends. Or at least not at keeping them.

"It'd probably help if you got out and did things with people, though," he says, leaning back in the red vinyl seat and wiping his hands on a napkin.

I shrug. "Maybe. But I'm not here long enough to really worry about it."

"When do you leave?"

"Sometime before Thanksgiving."

"That's plenty of time to make friends and have some fun. You don't have to stay holed up in your room studying all the time," he says.

"I leave the house. I've been helping with the fall events," I remind him.

"Yeah, that's a start. But it's still *work*."

"Okay, and what would you suggest I get out and do here in Bramble Falls?"

Jake ponders the question. "For starters, I'd say come to my parties."

I roll my eyes. "I think we've established that already."

"Football games."

I scrunch my face. "That does not sound like fun. I don't know the first thing about football."

"I'll teach you, and then you can come cheer me on." I continue grimacing at him, and he laughs. "Listen, Taylor learned a thing or two about the sport, and now she loves it. So, don't knock it till you try it."

I arch an eyebrow. "Taylor . . . ?"

"Swift. Obviously."

"Right, obviously. I guess I just didn't realize you two were on a first-name basis," I laugh. "I'll think about it, okay?"

"That's all I ask."

"All right. What else?"

"Homecoming's around the corner. That's a great place to have fun and hang out with friends."

"I've never gone to homecoming. It's not really a thing in New York."

"Tell me you're joking," Jake says.

"Nope. Kids usually just party in the penthouse of whoever's parents are away on business that week."

"Ellis. You have to go, then. It's your last high school homecoming." He bites his lip and casually shrugs a shoulder. "I could take you."

My eyebrows lift. "Take me . . . to homecoming?"

He lets out a nervous chuckle and looks at the table. "Yeah, why not?"

"I, um . . ."

I try to imagine that night. Everyone else will be there. I'm sure Sloane will go with Asher. Cooper will go with Chloe. Jake and Slug will be there.

And I'll be sitting at home. Alone.

My brain does a quick catalog of my grades, my upcoming tests, my schedule. I have nothing going on that weekend, and teachers have purposefully not put a test near the big dance. I have no reason *not* to go. . . .

"All right, yeah. Let's do it," I tell him.

Jake beams and says, "Really? You'll be my date?"

"Yeah, why not?" I say, grinning at how his face has lit up. Then I pause, considering the possibility that Jake might think we're heading in a direction I have no interest in going with him. Just in case, I add, "Why do you seem so surprised? We're just going as friends. People do that all the time, right?"

"Sure. They do." Jake reaches over and takes one of my fries. "I guess I sort of figured someone would have already asked you."

"Because I'm so popular here in Bramble Falls?"

He shrugs. "Because you're hot."

I laugh. "Well, I'll let you know if I decide to trade you for some other, more appealing suitor who might ask me in the coming weeks."

"More appealing than me? Yeah, right," he scoffs, and I toss a fry at him, which he catches in his mouth.

Attending my first high school homecoming my senior year is not something I had on my bingo card. Especially not in Bramble Falls. And especially not with Jake Keller.

But I have to admit, even if making friends here is pointless, I'm sort of excited.

Jake and I walk around town, sipping harvest spice lattes while he shows me places I'm already familiar with.

Places that hold memories with Cooper.

But I don't say anything because Jake's excited to share his small town with me.

We stop by the bookstore, where Cooper and I used to sit in the kids' fantasy section while he'd read to me—until an employee would tell us to either buy the book or leave.

We visit the candy store, where Cooper once choked on a jawbreaker. It was the one and only time I've ever had to save someone's life, and the one and only time he ever hugged me.

We check out the record store, where Cooper and I bought stacks of ninety-nine-cent used CDs by artists we'd never heard of, then listened to them on his mom's old stereo, sorting them as either "cool finds" or "trash."

I push the memories aside and try to be present. Because that summer is long over, and so is whatever Cooper and I had.

I made sure of that.

When the sun begins to set behind the Bramble Falls Public Library and an evening chill sets in, Jake and I part ways.

When I get back, Aunt Naomi's house is dark from the outside, but as soon as I open the door, three women come running at me.

"Ellis!" Sloane screams, grabbing my arms and jumping up and down.

"Uh, yeah . . . ? What's happening right now?"

"You have a homecoming date!" Mom squeals like a teenager.

"Oh my god, is that what all this is about?" I ask. "How'd you even find out? I just left him ten minutes ago."

"It's a small town, honey. Everyone knows everything within five," Mom says. "So, tell me all about this boy."

"He's eye candy," Sloane tells her. "And he's on the football team."

"Okay, this is a good start," Mom says, bobbing her head.

"You've actually met him," I tell her. "He's the guy who was working the register at the apple orchard."

"Oh yeah! He was a sweet kid," Mom says. "Very cute."

"Jake is great," Aunt Naomi adds. "He's goofy and a bit irresponsible, but he's a good egg."

"He's fine." I shrug.

"You said you'd go to a dance with him," Mom says. "You've *never* gone to a dance. You must think he's more than just 'fine.'"

"Okay, you're all being weird about this," I say, taking a step backward. "It's just a dance, and we're going as friends."

Mom nods. "Well, I'm just glad you're making friends and *doing* things." She reaches up and softly runs her thumb over my cheek. "I just want to see you happy."

"I know." I bite my tongue. I don't have it in me to fight right now, but I'm dying to tell her that if she really wanted to see me happy, she wouldn't have made me leave New York. She would have let me stay with Dad. I'd be taking more challenging classes at a more impressive school, some other girl wouldn't have my internship, and Dad wouldn't have forgotten I exist.

"I really don't think you two will just be friends for long," Sloane says, giddy.

"Even if I liked him—which I don't—I'm not here long enough to start anything with someone. Plus, my focus is still on getting into Columbia. Not on boys."

Aunt Naomi turns and heads toward the kitchen, calling over

her shoulder, "I got Chinese. Come eat and tell us all about how he asked you."

Mom follows her, and just as I'm about to head to the kitchen, even though I'm stuffed from dinner with Jake, Sloane steps in front of me.

"Did you run into him there or did you text him to meet you?" she asks.

"Why does that matter?" She raises her eyebrows, looking at me expectantly. I sigh. "I texted him."

She squeals and runs toward the kitchen. "I knew it!"

"You three are exhausting," I mutter, laughing as I follow behind her.

I sit in the empty spot at the table with my second dinner in front of me, and I rehash my entire afternoon with Jake as if I'm talking with girlfriends. As if *we're* the town Gossip Girls.

And it feels . . . nice—even if they are excited for no reason.

Chapter Twelve

Mom turns down a narrow dirt road and drives nearly a mile before she reaches an archway that reads PEARSON PUMPKIN FARM. Clusters of maple and oak trees reflect off a small pond to the right of the entrance, and a field of tall cornstalks sits to the left. Soon the road opens up to a large asphalt parking lot, where Mom pulls into a spot.

It's a balmy autumn day, and the sun sits high in a bright blue sky. The puffy white clouds look straight out of one of Mom's paintings. As she leads me to a stand-alone brick building, we pass a concession stand selling coffee, apple cider, and caramel apples. The sweet smells mix deliciously with the earthy scent of the changing leaves. I wish I could somehow roll it into a fall-scented candle.

We walk into the small building and find Aunt Naomi talking with a couple of volunteers I recognize from around town. She lights up when she notices us. Once she sends them on their way, she greets us with hugs.

"Ellis, I assigned you to work with Cooper today. Is that okay?" Aunt Naomi asks.

Working with Cooper all day is going to make it really hard to ignore the awkward tension between us, but I don't want to complicate things for Aunt Naomi, so I shrug and say, "Sure."

"Great!" She looks at her phone. "He should be about to take the first group to the pumpkin patch if you want to head out to the trailers."

She points me in the right direction, and I make my way over. I find Cooper leaning against a tree, wearing a simple black T-shirt and dark khaki pants with black Chucks, talking to Sterling, the pizza delivery kid. He laughs at something Sterling says, and I stop in my tracks.

Why do I love that sound so much? And why do I wish I were the one causing it?

"Hey, Ellis," Sterling says, noticing me standing there watching the two of them.

I wave and finish making my way over. Nearby, a line of people are standing at a trailer filled with bales of hay. A trailer being pulled by . . . horses?

"Um, why are there horses?" I ask.

"Tried to pull the trailer full of people myself, but couldn't get it to budge, so . . . ," Sterling says with a grin.

"Ha-ha," I deadpan. "I just mean, aren't these things usually pulled by tractors?"

Cooper pushes off the tree. "Maybe at other places, but in Bramble Falls, the horses are part of the pumpkin patch experience."

"You two have fun with that," Sterling says, saluting. "I gotta get back to the concession stand. A customer just showed up."

"I don't love horses," I tell Cooper. I look nervously over my shoulder back toward the food. "Maybe I can switch jobs with Sterling."

"Have you ever even been around a horse?"

"Irrelevant. Their teeth are big," I tell him.

"They don't bite," he says, smiling. "Usually."

I frown. "Comforting."

"You'll be okay. I promise."

"But they're huge. Especially *those ones*," I say, gesturing at the giant monsters attached to the trailer.

"It's not like you have to get on them. We're going to sit on that built-in bench at the front of the trailer. I'll have the reins. You just have to ride next to me and help people when we get to the pumpkin patch."

I gnaw at my lip, then finally nod. "Yeah, okay."

I follow Cooper over to the trailer, and he tugs the collapsible steps down so people can climb onto the platform filled with hay bales. As he gets people situated, I slowly inch toward the front to look at the horses. They're massive, but I have to admit they're also breathtaking.

When I was younger, I always begged my parents to take me on the horse-drawn carriages in the winter in the city. Dad would scoff and say those things were for tourists, and Mom would give me a weak smile and agree.

"They're Clydesdales," Cooper says, coming up behind me. The black one in front of us nods his head. "This is Ink."

"And the other one?"

"Coffee."

I look at the brown horse, the color of coffee beans. "Those are great names." I inch closer to Ink, and his eye watches me. "I always wanted to be an equestrian when I was little."

"Yeah? And now you're afraid of horses?" Cooper asks.

I shrug. "Well, I liked the *idea* of riding them as a kid, but I'd never been around them. Then I got older and realized just how big they are."

"They're gentle giants." He takes a step to his left and pets Ink on the nose. Then he reaches out and wraps his fingers gently around my forearm and pulls me toward him. "Come pet him. He won't bite you. Or kick you. Or stomp on you. Or whatever else you're afraid of."

Cooper is just behind me, his body close enough that I feel *safe*. Slowly, reluctantly, I reach up toward Ink's nose, right where Cooper was petting him.

But then Ink shakes his head, abrupt and quick, and I rear back with a scream.

"Fuck!" I hear as my head rams into something—or someone.

When I whip around, Cooper is bent over, holding his face.

"Oh my—I'm so sorry!" I tell him. He doesn't respond as his back rises and falls with deep breaths. "Are you okay?"

He holds up a finger, telling me to give him a minute.

"Coop, I'm sorry." I put my hand on his shoulder.

"I'm fine. I just need a second."

I press my lips together and nod, even though he's not looking at me.

A great start to making things right between us.

When he finally stands upright, his eyes are watering.

And his nose is bleeding.

"Shit," I mutter. "Okay, you wait here. I'm going to go get tissues. Or something."

The entire sprint back to the small building where Aunt Naomi has set up base, I'm grateful I was smart enough to wear my thrifted Frye boots, the kind that can handle a little hay and dirt. Once I'm there, I grab a whole box of tissues and sprint back.

When I get to the trailer, Cooper is finishing apologizing to everyone for the delay. He's plugging his nose as he makes his way over to me.

He points to my mud-covered feet. "Your boots are ruined."

"I'm not worried about them. Your nose, on the other hand . . ." I pull three tissues from the box and hand them to him.

Cooper takes the tissues from me. "My nose will be fine."

I shake my head. "I'm really sorry."

"Please stop apologizing." Cooper shoves a tissue up each nostril until they're stretched wide and white is hanging out. A laugh bursts out of me, and Cooper smiles. "First you bust my nose; then you laugh at me for bleeding. Damn, Mitchell, you're brutal."

"Sor—"

He slaps his hand over my mouth. "Don't say it."

I nod and he moves his hand. "Good thing I wore a black shirt today, I guess."

We both look down at the darker spot from where he used his shirt as a tissue before I got back.

"If you hadn't, we could have just told everyone this was a haunted hayride."

He grins. "True. Okay, you ready?"

"Maybe I should stay back."

"Nope." He grabs my hand and pulls me toward the front of the trailer. "We're going to turn this day around."

He helps me up onto the bench seat behind the horses, then climbs up and sits beside me. He makes an announcement to the people in the trailer behind us, letting them know we're about to go, then takes the reins.

"Are you sure you know what you're doing?" I ask.

"Nope," he says. "This is my first time ever driving this thing, but I'm sure we'll survive."

I look at him. With tissues hanging out of his widened nostrils, he looks completely unserious despite his serious expression. "Don't mess with me, Cooper Barnett."

He laughs. "I know what I'm doing. I've done this every year since I was thirteen. Before that, I rode with my dad. Stop worrying."

I hold on to the railing beside me. "Okay."

Cooper clucks his tongue and gently slaps the reins against Ink's and Coffee's backs, and we're off.

The horses pull us down a dirt path lined with trees. I smile at the gentle clacking of hooves as we ride beneath canopies of red, yellow, and orange. A gentle breeze sweeps through the trees, and colorful leaves fall like rain all around us. I laugh, and when I turn to Cooper, he's watching me with a smile.

"You're like a little kid," he says.

"Shut up. I am not."

"It's cute." He shrugs.

I blush as I stick my tongue out at him, and his smile widens. I have to force myself to look away.

When we get to the pumpkin patch, Cooper lets everyone out of the trailer. They disperse, looking for the perfect pumpkins for the pumpkin carving party tomorrow. When I notice a woman trying to carry two pumpkins by herself, I head over to help her.

"I can carry one of those for you," I tell her, taking one of the pumpkins.

"Thank you so much," the woman says.

I let her know I'll put it in the trailer; then I help a kid pick a pumpkin from her selection of three nearly identical ones she's torn between.

"You picking one for tomorrow?" Cooper asks before we head back.

"I probably should."

Everyone climbs into the trailer, and Cooper and I walk around until I find the perfect pumpkin—one that actually inspires my idea for what I'll carve into it.

Cooper's face contorts when I get it back to the hayride. "Of all the pumpkins here, why are you picking the ugly, warty one?"

"You'll have to wait until tomorrow to find out," I say as I climb onto the bench.

"Ah, intrigue." He grabs the reins. "Guess I have no choice but to hang out with you tomorrow, then."

My eyes whip to him. Is the icy wall between us finally melting for real? Does he *actually* forgive me for blowing him off years ago?

Trying not to read too much into it, I face forward and bite back a smile as he gets the horses moving. "Guess so."

When we get back, Cooper goes to grab an ice pack and throw away the bloody tissues. We spend the rest of the day making trips to the pumpkin patch, and as the hours pass, his swollen nose begins to shrink back to normal.

By the end of our last trip, the sun is low in the sky, and the temperature has dropped. "Do you need help with anything?" I ask as Cooper unhooks the horses from the trailer.

"Yeah, come here." He walks Ink around the trailer until he's standing beside the bench. I keep my distance as I approach. "You have to get closer to get on him."

"Um, what? I'm not getting on that thing. He hates me."

"He doesn't hate you. He just happened to shake off flies when you were going to pet him. This is your chance to live out your equestrian dream. Sort of. I'll hold the reins and walk with you. Your only job is to not fall off."

"No. Nope. Not happening. I've seen enough movies to know that if something spooks this guy, I'm done for."

Cooper laughs. "All right, fine. What if I ride with you? Just a short walk down the trail and back." I gnaw on my cheek, considering. "I'm not going to make you. If you say no, I'll drop it. I just think you'll enjoy it."

Climbing on the horse with Cooper *is* a chance to take a step forward in our friendship and leave behind the mistakes I made with him.

And remembering the heat that fizzed through me when he gave me a piggyback ride at the apple orchard, I can't say I'm not tempted by the thought of being that close to him again. . . .

So, against my better judgment, I say, "Yeah, okay. Let's do it."

Cooper grins, his dimple popping and his eyes bright.

I follow him up to the bench, and he climbs onto the giant horse. He takes the reins and scoots forward on Ink's bare back, leaving space for me to climb on behind him.

"Just swing your leg over and hold on to me," he says. My limbs shake as I slide on and grip the back of his shirt. He lets go of the reins, reaches for my hands, and moves them to his waist. "I'd feel better if you weren't relying on my T-shirt to save you from falling."

"Got it," I say, my body thrumming at the electrifying feeling of being this close to him.

"Ready?" he asks.

"Not really."

"I'm not going until you're ready," he tells me.

"Okay, fine. I'm as ready as I'm ever going to be."

He nods and squeezes his calves, and we're off. I squeal and grasp on to him tighter.

"You good?" he asks.

I'm not falling off. I'm not being kicked. I'm fine. "Yes?" I answer. But it comes out with less conviction than I intend.

We're walking down the dirt path when Cooper veers left and heads into the woods.

"Um, where are we going?" I ask.

"Just for a walk."

The woods are filled with birds chirping and bugs buzzing and trees rustling in a whispering breeze. I close my eyes and listen. It's a calming symphony I've never heard in the city.

It almost doesn't feel real.

I open my eyes to the sound of rushing water. Cooper has brought us to a river lined with trees and brush. Ink walks along it, carrying us back in the direction of the stables.

"How'd you learn to ride?" I ask.

"Dad used to be a farmhand here when he was younger. I spent every summer here with him. Except for *our* summer—I ditched him that year. Anyway, he taught me, but it's not something I really do a lot. Or ever, anymore."

"Why not?"

"I never wanted to be an equestrian," he says, smiling as he looks back at me out of the corner of his eye. He shrugs. "And I got busy with other stuff."

"Like working at the Caffeinated Cat?"

"Yeah, among other things."

Cooper steers us left again, and after a minute we come out of the woods and ride into a large meadow full of wildflowers in the back of the farm.

"Oh my god, it's so pretty," I say.

"Is that why you're squeezing me to death?" he asks with a laugh.

"Oh." I loosen my grip and give him space, the warm autumn air suddenly feeling cold against the areas of my torso no longer pressed against him. "Sorry."

"If you apologize to me one more time, I'm throwing you off this horse."

I laugh. "Okay, sorry!"

"Ellis!"

"It just comes naturally. I can't help it!" My head falls against his back as I laugh harder, and his body shakes with his own laughter.

We get back to the stables, where someone has already taken care of Coffee. Cooper hops off Ink, then helps me down.

"Well, thanks for helping me overcome my irrational fear of horses," I tell him.

"You're welcome."

"And I'm totally not sorry about your nose."

His dimple sinks into his cheek. "Good."

We stand there for a second. There's nothing else to say. The day is over. But I don't want to leave.

"I'll see you tomorrow, Mitchell."

Right. "Okay. Yeah. See ya."

I leave the stables and grab my warty pumpkin from the trailer. Then I head to Aunt Naomi's home-base building, where Mom said she'd wait for me at the end of the day. And the whole time, all I can think about is hanging out with Cooper tomorrow.

Maybe there's still hope for our friendship after all.

I've just finished eating dinner and clearing the dishes when my phone buzzes in my hand. I freeze halfway up the steps when I find Cooper's name lighting up my screen.

Summer Cooper: **How are your thighs? Sore?**

I smile at my phone.

Me: **Are you stalking me or something?**

Summer Cooper: You've never been on a horse, and we rode for a while. Plus, you were so tense, Ink probably has bruised ribs. So, logic says you're probably a little sore.

"Hey," Sloane says as she's passing the steps. I look up to find her watching me, and she waggles her eyebrows. "You talking to Mr. Hot Dog?"

A laugh bubbles out of me. "Mr. Hot Dog? What on earth are you talking about?"

Sloane lets her hair fall into her face, hiding her rosy cheeks. "Dog as in, like, a golden retriever. You know, because my mom referred to Jake as a lost puppy? And he's obviously hot. . . ." She chews her lip for a moment. "Maybe Mr. Sexy Puppy is better."

I snort. "Or maybe let's just call him Jake." My phone buzzes.

Summer Cooper: Leaving me on read. Okay, I see how it is.

"I gotta go, cuz." I sprint up the steps, ignoring the burning in my thighs and Sloane calling behind me, "Tell Jake I say hi!"

Me: Sorry, I was in the middle of CRAWLING up the steps because, yeah, my thighs hate me right now.

I lie back on my bed and bite my nails as I watch three dots appear on the screen.

Summer Cooper: What are you doing now?

I press my lips together, trying to suppress a grin. We're *casually texting* again.

Me: Not sure. Maybe putting on a movie? Aunt Naomi brought up some old DVDs. Unless I want

to watch Practical Magic again, I have to choose between the '90s live action Teenage Mutant Ninja Turtles, Eternal Sunshine of the Spotless Mind, or Spirited Away.

Summer Cooper: All solid choices. My vote is for Eternal Sunshine.

Me: But it's so depressing.

Summer Cooper: It's a perfect movie.

Me: Well, I'm not a masochist, so I'll probably put on TMNT. Donatello's hot.

Summer Cooper: wow lol such high standards

Me: What are you doing?

Summer Cooper: Falling asleep

Me: It's not even 8pm.

Summer Cooper: Well some of us had to get up at 5am to work at the coffee shop only to then be given a concussion while volunteering at the pumpkin patch.

I wince.

Me: **How IS your nose?**

Summer Cooper: **it's fine. I'm just giving you a hard time.**

Summer Cooper: **But I am going to get some sleep. Just wanted to check in on you. I'll see you tomorrow?**

Me: **yeah.**

Summer Cooper: **Enjoy ogling Donnie.**

I laugh out loud.

Me: **Will do.**

Summer Cooper: **Night, Mitchell. Don't let the bedbugs bite.**

Summer Cooper: **But if they do, get a shoe, and beat 'em till they're black and blue.**

I let myself grin at the silly rhyme he used to say to me all those years ago, when he was the last person I'd talk to each night.

Me: **Sweet dreams, Coop.**

Chapter Thirteen

As the town gathers in the square the next day for the pumpkin carving party, gray clouds blanket the sky, hiding the afternoon sun like a secret. Plastic tablecloths, disposable aluminum cooking tins, and paper towels are placed at each station, with carving tools and paint and brushes. Music pours from large speakers inside the gazebo as everyone claims a spot with their friends and family.

"You want to go shopping for a homecoming dress on Wednesday?" Sloane asks as we plop down on the tablecloth where we dropped off our pumpkins last night. "Preeti and I are going to venture to the mall after school."

"Oh. Yeah, sure." I haven't really given any thought to homecoming since I talked with Jake on Friday, but I guess I will need a dress.

"Awesome," she says, stabbing the carving knife into to the top of her pumpkin. She carves a circle, then pulls the stem to take off the top. I copy her and stick the jagged edge of my carving knife into the top of my pumpkin.

"Hey, Coop," she says, looking over my shoulder.

I nearly cut off my finger when she says his name.

"Jumpy today?" Cooper says from behind me.

"Stop sneaking up on people," I mutter without turning around. I don't know why I suddenly feel antsy around him.

After texting with him last night, my mind was an endless carousel of thoughts and confusing feelings that made my insides hum with boundless energy I desperately needed to burn off. So, instead of watching a movie, I pawed through the donated clothes in the attic. I uncovered an entire box of flannel shirts, which aren't exactly the dress shirts I'm used to working with, but the general structure was familiar enough. Before I knew it, I was taking the collar, yoke, and cuffs from a black-and-white buffalo-plaid shirt and splicing it together with the front and back panels of a blue-and-black buffalo-plaid shirt. I ended up wearing it today, since I didn't really bring anything I'd want to expose to pumpkin guts. I like it more than I expected—the softness of the material is different from the stiffer cottons I used to sew with, but it makes for an extra-cozy wearing experience.

And piecing together a shirt is a heck of a lot easier than trying to piece together how exactly I'm feeling about the boy sitting down next to me right now.

I finally turn to him, and I nearly stop breathing. He's wearing glasses. Thick black frames that somehow make him even hotter.

Since when do I have a thing for glasses?

He tosses a green cookie in my lap. I let go of my carving knife and pick it up to examine it, mostly because I need to peel my eyes off him.

"Are those Fruity Pebbles?" I ask of the familiar colorful rice cereal on top.

"Yep." He holds out a cup from the Caffeinated Cat. "And a harvest spice latte."

"For me?" I ask, surprised.

He shrugs. "Unless you don't want it."

"I definitely want it." I take the latte from him. "Did you just get off work or something?"

The tips of Cooper's ears turn pink. "Uh, yeah."

"Well, where's mine?" Sloane asks.

"I had to come see what Ellis is planning to carve into this ugly pumpkin, but I wasn't sure if you'd be over here," he says.

Sloane purses her lips. "Where else would I be?"

"With Asher," Cooper and I say in unison. We look at each other and laugh.

Sloane's cheeks turn pink, and she mumbles, "I'm meeting him in an hour."

"My point exactly," Cooper says. "But do you want me to run back in and get you something?"

Sloane sighs. "No. That's okay." She reaches her hand into her pumpkin and scoops the guts out, then drops them into the tin.

I hold my green cookie out for her to take a bite, since her hands are covered in slime, and she gives me a close-mouthed grin as she chews. Then I take a bite, and my tongue is immediately hit with the sweet taste of sugar and . . . cherries? "Holy crap. Fruity Pebbles and cherries? What is this bizarre but heavenly concoction?"

"Which is better, the red or the green?" Cooper asks.

"How dare you try to make me choose," I say. "That's just cruel."

"Have you tried the lemon one yet?" Sloane asks.

"No! Where's my lemon one?" I ask Cooper.

He chuckles. "I'll see what I can do."

"Where's your pumpkin, by the way?" I ask, chewing the remaining piece of cookie.

He nods to my right, where Chloe is sitting with Slug and Jake. "You should come carve with us. Sloane, you can come too, obviously."

Sloane looks at me, waiting to see what I want to do.

I don't really want to watch Chloe and Cooper being all cutesy together—though I'm refusing not to think too deeply about why—but if I join them, at least I won't be sitting here alone after Sloane leaves.

"Yeah, okay," I say.

Cooper picks up my tray. "You two carry your pumpkins. I'll grab the rest."

Sloane and I head over to the group, with Cooper carrying the tins, tools, and my latte behind us.

"Ellis!" Jake yells when he sees us coming. He pats the spot next to him. "Come sit with me."

I glance at Sloane, and she winks. I roll my eyes just before catching Cooper eyeing us.

I set my pumpkin on the plastic tablecloth and take my latte from Cooper.

"Thanks." I sit next to Jake, and Cooper puts our tins down and sits next to me so that he's between me and Chloe.

"So, you're going to homecoming with Jake, huh?" Chloe asks, leaning forward to talk around Cooper. "Brave girl."

"What's that supposed to mean?" Jake asks.

"It means you're a handful," Chloe says. Her face turns bright red. "And I do *not* mean it the way you're thinking."

Jake smirks. "Nah, then I'd be two handfuls. At least."

Chloe scoffs and Slug laughs.

"Good luck, Ellis," Chloe says, sitting back and dipping her paintbrush into the red paint.

I finish carving the hole on top of my pumpkin, pop off the top, and dig out the guts.

"You look like you're an expert at this," Jake says.

I shrug. "It's not my first rodeo."

He laughs. "No? Were there a lot of pumpkin carving parties in New York?"

"None. But I was always determined to have the best pumpkin on any stoop in the city."

Jake raises his eyebrows. "So, you competed against people who didn't even know there was a competition."

"Yes."

"That tracks," Jake laughs. "Are we competing right now?"

I look at him. "Of course."

To my right, Cooper laughs. "Well, I suck at pumpkin carving, so consider me out of the running."

"I'd shit-talk you right now for bowing out, but you get a pass because you brought me coffee."

"That's obviously why I did it," he says as Chloe leans forward and eyes my harvest spice latte.

For the next forty-five minutes, we all carve our pumpkins and talk about classes and upcoming parties I know nothing about. Eventually, Sloane heads out to meet Asher, and everyone else finishes their pumpkins. Everyone watches me as I put the final touches on my creation. When I turn it around, the group gasps, sending dopamine pulsing through me.

"What the hell? How'd you do that?" Slug asks, staring in awe at the apple tree I carved into the pumpkin.

Jake reaches forward and runs his fingers over it. "You used the freaking pumpkin stem as a tree trunk! That's, like, genius shit."

I laugh. "I don't know about that."

Cooper grins. "You weren't kidding about being good at this." His eyes pause on the pumpkin's bumpy growths. "The wart things are the tops of the trees. They make it appear sort of three-dimensional."

"Exactly," I say.

"Never thought I'd say this, but . . . Jake's right," Chloe says. "This is some genius shit."

Cooper squints at me like he's pondering something. Then he says, "Okay, genius. Do me now."

I raise my eyebrows at him. "What?"

"Wait a second," Jake interjects. He slides his pumpkin over to me and turns it so the uncarved side is facing me. "If you can do people, then do *me*."

I shake my head. "Guys, I've never carved a person. Only

characters. You know, like vampires or Frankenstein. But no one *specific*."

Cooper leans forward and tilts his head. "Huh. Is Ellis Mitchell backing down from a challenge?"

I cross my arms over my chest. I *know* he's taunting me. I *know* this is nothing more than bait.

But, damn it, it's working. I sort of want to try.

"Give me your pumpkin," I say to him. Chloe laughs as a wide grin spreads over Cooper's face.

"But my pumpkin's already in front of you," Jake says gesturing at it.

"Sorry, Jakey. It's first come, first served, and Cooper asked before you." Jake pretends to pout, and I pat him on the leg. "I'll do yours next, don't worry."

"Yeah, yeah," he grumbles.

Cooper grabs Slug's pumpkin and sets it in front of me. "Mine's covered in paint, but here."

A big knobby growth is directly in the center of the uncarved side. *What am I supposed to do with that?*

"Hey!" Slug says, looking at his pumpkin, which has two uneven triangles for eyes and a rectangle for a mouth carved into it. "That's my masterpiece!"

"Don't worry," I say, studying the pumpkin, the gears in my head turning. "I won't mess with that side of it. And you can still display your side. No one wants to see Cooper's face any more than they have to anyway," I tease.

Everyone laughs as I grab my carving tool.

"Wouldn't have to worry about that if you were carving me,"

Jake mutters. I elbow him softly in the ribs, and he throws a playful, arrogant smirk my way.

When I look away, Cooper's watching us. I shoot him a mischievous smile because I know *exactly* what I'm going to do.

An hour later, dark clouds are rolling in. Around us, people are packing up their trays and tablecloths and setting them under the gazebo.

"Are you done yet?" Jake asks with an exaggerated sigh. He's lying next to me with his hands laced behind his head. Chloe and Slug are next to him in a heated debate over recent diss tracks released by two rappers.

And Cooper is sitting directly in front of me.

He's trying to be helpful, making himself available in case I need a reference. Which I don't, because over the last three weeks, I've stolen more glances at him than I care to admit. Instead he's just a distraction. Even when I'm focusing on the pumpkin, I can *feel* his eyes on me, his soft but penetrating gaze burrowing into me, making my blood simmer and adding a splash of pink to my cheeks.

Again, it's a miracle I still have all ten fingers.

"Almost," I tell Jake. "Hand me a paper towel, Coop."

Cooper passes the roll to me. I tear two pieces off, dab them with a bit of red paint, and use them as my final additions before looking at my handiwork. Now, *this* is a masterpiece.

"Okay," I say, pressing my lips together so I don't spoil the reveal with a giggle.

I turn the pumpkin around to show everyone.

Jake, Slug, and Chloe stare at it, confused, but Cooper *erupts* into a full-fledged belly laugh. He's rolling at the joke meant just for the two of us, and god, it feels good to have made that happen.

Chloe looks at us, then back at the pumpkin. She cocks her head to the side. "I feel like I'm missing something."

Slug scratches his chin. "Yeah. It's clearly Cooper, but what's with the paper towel?"

"The ugly knob . . . ," Cooper says between gasps, actual tears in the corners of his eyes as he looks at the red paper towel pieces sticking out of the orifices I created, "is my bloody, swollen nose."

"I don't . . . get it," Jake says.

It's the worst pumpkin I've ever carved. But I managed to get Cooper's hair right, and the dimple carved into the left cheek is a dead giveaway that it's him. I also think I captured his magnetic eyes perfectly.

His laugh is contagious, and soon, the two of us are so busy cracking up, we don't notice the first drops of rain.

But within seconds the sky opens up and dumps on us.

The few remaining townspeople run frantically for the gazebo, but the wind is blowing the rain sideways, and everyone taking cover under it is getting drenched.

Chloe grabs Cooper's hand and pulls him toward the Caffeinated Cat. "Come on! Let's go hide out in the shop!"

Cooper turns around to face me. Our eyes lock, and he's about to say something when Jake takes my hand. "My car's over here. We can wait this out in there."

Cooper's eyes fall on Jake; then he turns and runs, Slug following slowly behind them, his pumpkin in tow.

As Jake tugs me toward his car, I look back one last time. But Cooper's already halfway across the lawn with Chloe, his hand in hers, his back to me.

It shouldn't bother me. It's not like I'm trying to date anyone. And even if I were, it's not like I *like* Cooper.

So why do I care so much that I'm not waiting out the storm with him?

Chapter Fourteen

When Mom gets home from work that evening, I've taken the hottest shower of my life, put on sweatpants and an oversized sweatshirt, and buried myself beneath five heavy blankets in the attic. I'm rewatching *Practical Magic* for the third time while sketching a dress design inspired by the perfection that is the nineties styling in this movie—long and black with a cowl neckline, a low scoop back, and lace straps—when I hear her come up the steps.

"Hey, how was the pumpkin carving party?" she asks when she appears wearing her art-store uniform—black slacks and a yellow polo shirt that reads ART ATTACK in block letters.

I sat in Jake's car for thirty minutes before we checked the radar and decided we were wasting our time. After braving the storm to grab our pumpkins, he asked if I wanted to go to the movies with him, but I was soaked and cold. All I wanted was my bed.

"It was fun before it got rained out."

"I saw your pumpkin downstairs." She sits on the edge of my

bed. "That tree is incredible. I think it might be your best one yet."

"Thanks." Slug took his pumpkin home, but still, my lips tilt upward at the thought of Cooper cry-laughing at our little inside joke. *That* pumpkin will forever go down in history as my best one yet as far as I'm concerned.

Mom peers at my sketchbook, but I snap it closed. I'm not ready to show anyone the stuff I've been coming up with. I'm too afraid that any negativity will burst this bubble of creativity that's been swirling around since we got here.

She smiles at me and says, "I'm really glad to see you sketching again."

Designing and sewing clothes was always my escape from the weight of everyday life, but I stopped having time to escape. And even if I found time, Dad reminded me that fashion was a waste of it. But I shrug like it's trivial and nod at the TV. "I guess I've just had some good inspiration lately."

Mom turns to the screen. "*Practical Magic*? You know, those sisters always reminded me of Naomi and me."

"Yeah? Which one were you?"

She gives me a sad attempt at a smile. "I'll let you figure that out." She stands. "Night, honey."

Her footsteps fade as she goes downstairs. Before she even reaches the bottom, I know exactly which sister she sees herself in: the one who left town and fell in love with the wrong guy.

When I walk into calc on Tuesday, there's a cookie on the desk where I normally sit. Figuring someone else has claimed my seat, I settle into the desk behind it. But as I'm getting my notebook out, I realize the clear cookie wrapper has a sticker on it. *Ellis* is scrawled across it. I scan the room as I slowly move back to my usual desk. Cooper is sitting sideways in his seat, his focus solely on Chloe's animated storytelling.

Ms. Hanby walks in the room, and as she's getting her things prepped for class, I tear off a small piece of the yellow cookie and shove it in my mouth. *Lemon.* I grin to myself.

I glance back at Cooper. He's laughing and saying something to his friends, completely oblivious to me discovering the cookie.

But this has to be from him.

So, what does it mean that he keeps bringing me cookies? Nothing? Do I *want* it to mean something? Does it mean something to *me*? Am I overthinking it? Maybe a cookie is just a cookie.

"Ellis?" Ms. Hanby says.

My attention snaps to her. "Yes?"

She smiles at me. "I asked if you'd want to come up and solve this for us."

Heat rushes to my face. "Oh. Sure."

I shake off my thoughts. And my feelings.

Because, clearly, cookies are a distraction.

Sloane has drama club after school, so I wrap my cardigan around me and head out of the front double doors. The brighter the foliage gets, the more I find myself wanting to be outside. The sun is shining bright today, but the air is cool. I'm sitting against the wide trunk of a tree, sketching, when a shadow falls over me. I cup my hand over my eyes and peer up to find Cooper hovering.

"Scooch over," he says.

I move over until I'm against the giant root extended out from the tree, leaving very little room next to me. Still, Cooper squeezes in between me and a root to his right.

"What are you doing?" He nods at my sketchbook.

"Homework."

"For what class?"

I avert my eyes. "French."

"Chloe said you guys never have homework in there," he says. I look at him, immediately getting sucked into those eyes, and he raises his thick brows. He knows I'm lying. "What are you always drawing in there, Mitchell?"

"Nothing." He's so close, I have to work not to *stare* at the light dusting of freckles on his nose and cheeks. Not to reach up and run my fingers over them.

What the hell is wrong with me?

He reaches over and tentatively grabs the sketchbook, giving me a chance to tell him to back off. But I loosen my grip and let him take it because, for some reason, I trust him with it.

I trust him not to destroy me.

I stare ahead, out at the green lawn peppered with leaves, and the few remaining students lingering in the parking lot, while Cooper flips through my sketchbook and my heart pummels my ribs.

"Ellis, these are . . ." I hold my breath and turn to him. He shakes his head as his eyes wander over the designs. "These are unbelievable." He turns to me. "I didn't know you design clothes."

I shrug. "It's just something I do for fun sometimes."

He's sure to hold my gaze when he says, "You're incredibly talented."

"Thank you," I murmur, ducking my head, flustered by the flattery.

He points to one of the designs—the mixed buffalo-plaid shirt I was wearing at the pumpkin carving party.

"You *make* clothes too?"

"Meh, not often. I taught myself how to sew in middle school, and I got really into making clothes freshman and sophomore year. But then . . ."

"You got busy."

"Yeah."

He looks at my sketchbook and nods, his expression almost *disappointed*. Then he points at the black dress I drew last weekend. "What about this one?"

"I've actually never made a dress before. I usually stick to structured shirts. But I've been watching a lot of *Practical Magic* lately, and I can't get Nicole Kidman's wardrobe out of my head, so I kind of just drew it for fun."

His looks me in the eye, his voice soft and sincere when he says, "It's perfect."

"Thank you," I say, blushing.

"You should make it."

I raise my eyebrows. "You think? I mean, there's no real reason to. Where would I even wear something like that?"

"I don't know. But even if you just wear it around Naomi's house, it'd be worth it. That dress should exist, Ellis."

My cheeks burn at the intensity of his gaze. I look away, suddenly feeling bashful. Exposed. Like he *sees* me. “Yeah?”

“Definitely. Make it.”

I run my fingers over the dress design. Maybe I will.

Chapter Fifteen

My phone rings the following Friday afternoon. After almost two full weeks of spending every spare minute working on my black dress, I've just finished it with the intention of wearing it to homecoming tomorrow night, especially since I blew off going to the mall with Sloane last week so that I could get started on it.

It turned out better than I could have ever anticipated—bold and beautiful, with silky material that hugs every one of my curves and lace that adds a unique flair. It's honestly hot, and I can't wait to show Fern.

I grab my phone off my tiny dresser, expecting to see her name on the screen because no one else calls me.

But it's Dad.

I quickly swipe to answer. "Dad!"

"Hey, Ellis," he says. He sounds upbeat. Happy. Not that I want him to be miserable, but he's not supposed to sound so happy without Mom and me.

"I've been trying to get ahold of you for two weeks," I say.

"I know. I'm sorry. It's just been so busy."

Too busy for your own daughter, I don't say.

"I get it." I sit on the edge of my bed and try to sound natural when I say, "Well, tell me everything. I heard you got a new intern."

"I did," he says. "She's doing well. She caught on to everything quickly. Edward likes her."

"She already met Mr. Street?" It took me *months* to meet him.

"She did, yes." Dad clears his throat. "We had lunch last week."

"Oh. That's . . . nice," I say, my voice catching.

"Now, Ellis, don't get emotional," he says.

"What? I'm not." I totally am. Of course I am. This girl is replacing me. "But what about saving my internship for me?"

"You'll still have a position when you get back, don't worry." There's a rustling sound on the other end of the line. "Anyway, I called you for a reason."

Because apparently just calling to say hi and see how I'm doing isn't reason enough.

Ugh. I try to shake off my negativity. I hate being upset with him.

"I ran into an old friend of mine from college," he says. "His name is Justin Erikson. Turns out, he's on the admissions committee at Columbia. I told him all about you, and he said he'd be happy to talk with you. I told him you're going to school in Connecticut, so it might be hard to come during the week, but he said he'd meet with you this Saturday evening."

"As in tomorrow?"

"Yes, does that work for you?" he asks.

Anxiety blossoms in my belly, the same way it always does when I'm working on my Columbia application, swelling until I can barely hear my dad over my pulse pounding in my ears.

"Are you there?" Dad asks.

"Um, yeah. That sounds great," I tell him. I squeeze my eyes closed and rub circles on my temples. "Do I need to bring anything with me?"

"Couldn't hurt to have a résumé on hand," he says. "Be prepared to talk about everything on it—your grades, accomplishments, jobs, and other commitments. It's not an admissions interview, but it is a first impression, so make it a good one."

No pressure or anything.

"Okay. Sounds good. Does Mom know?"

"I'll call and tell her," he says. "I'll give Justin your email address so you two can arrange a time and place to meet."

"All right. Thanks, Dad. Maybe you and I can get pizza afterward, and you can tell me everything that's been happening at Street Media. I heard you've been meeting a lot with Mr. Gableman."

"Sure," he says noncommittally. "I have to go now."

"Oh, okay."

Not a single question about how life is here. How school is going. If I have friends. Whether I'm on the nonexistent school paper. Nothing.

But he *is* still looking out for me, and we can talk about all that stuff tomorrow night.

"I'll see you this weekend. Love you, Ellie Belly."

"Love you, too."

The line goes silent, and I set my phone back on the dresser and flop onto my bed.

My homecoming dress stares back at me from where it's hanging on the curtain rod, reminding me that now I have to cancel my homecoming plans with Jake.

Chapter Sixteen

A few hours later I'm wearing pigtails wrapped in giant blue bows while Sloane paints my face with black and blue paint. I'm in a pair of her leggings, with knee-high blue socks and a BRAMBLE FALLS HIGH FOOTBALL T-shirt.

"There, all done," she says, stepping back in her matching outfit. She has two buns on either side of her head, and her entire face is painted blue.

I drew the line at painting my whole face.

My reflection stares at me in Sloane's bedroom mirror, walking a fine line between cute and ridiculous. Jake's jersey number is painted on one cheek, and *Go BF!* is painted on the other.

"Are you sure it's normal that we're this decked out for a high school football game?" I ask.

"Girl, we really aren't decked out," Sloane says. "The other superfans are going to put us to shame, believe me."

A horn blares outside, and Sloane grabs her bag and grins at me. "It's time!"

I follow a giddy Sloane down the steps, and at the bottom, Mom throws her hand over her mouth. "I never thought I'd see the day. Ellis going to a football game. Someone pinch me."

"She has to go support *Jakey*," Sloane says, waggling her eyebrows.

I roll my eyes. "Shut up."

Jake begged and pleaded all week for me to come watch the homecoming game. Once Sloane said she was going, I figured why not. I'm not going for Jake, but it did sort of make me happy to see *him* so happy when I told him I'd be there.

Still, people seem to want a spark between us that just isn't there for me.

The horn honks again.

"We gotta go!" Sloane says, pulling my arm. We slide on our shoes and jog out to Cooper's truck. It's too cold for only a T-shirt, but Sloane swears it won't matter once we're there.

"Hop in!" Chloe says from the back of the truck. Her blond hair is in two French braids with black bows, and she's wearing a blue sports bra, short blue spandex shorts, and blue knee socks with white stripes. *Bramble Falls* is painted across her stomach and Slug's number is painted on one cheek and another jersey number I don't recognize is on the other. Somehow she doesn't look ridiculous at all. She looks stunningly sporty.

Once we're in the truck with the other four superfans they've already picked up, Cooper shouts to us to hold on, and he takes off toward the school.

The energy at the game is electric, and within a few minutes of it starting, I'm screaming and cheering even though I have no idea what's going on because it's *infectious*. I take my cues from Sloane, Hannah, and Preeti to my right and try to avoid looking at Cooper to my left.

Because if I do, I might do something stupid. Like touch him.

He had the audacity to show up here *shirtless*, with a football painted on his chest and *Bramble Falls* across his abs, and, to make things more dire, he has on a backward Bramble Falls hat over his floppy hair, black strips of paint across each cheek, and blue basketball shorts.

I'm just saying, it should be criminal to look that hot.

Something happens on the field and the rows of superfans cheer. Cooper grabs my hand and throws our arms up while he shouts at the players. Chloe holds his other hand as she jumps up and down yelling.

He said they're not together, but they are *always* together. And they look *good* together.

There's definitely *something* going on there.

"All right, Mitchell, you ready to start the chant?" Cooper says, leaning into me.

"Uh, no?"

"Come on," he says. "All you have to do is face the crowd and shout, 'Hey, Bramble Falls, let's leave a bruise!' And they'll take it from there."

"Live a little, Ellis!" Sloane shouts over the crowd.

I groan. "Fine . . ." I turn around to face the expansive bleachers full of people.

"Wait." Cooper turns around and kneels down.

"What are you doing?" I'm *not* hopping on his bare back.

"You're too short. You'll blend in with everyone down here, especially with everyone else yelling."

"Then maybe you should do the chant," I say.

He turns his head to look at me. "Ellis, just get on. Stop making everything so difficult." I sigh but put my hands on his shoulders, and he swoops me up. He turns around to face the massive crowd of excited fans. "Be loud!" he shouts to me.

I cup my hands around my mouth, my heart pounding as adrenaline courses through me.

"Hey, Bramble Falls!" I shout as loudly as I can. Everyone in the vicinity turns to me. "Let's leave a bruise!"

"Black and blue," the whole Bramble Falls side of the stadium shouts back, "refuse to lose!"

Everyone stomps their feet against the bleachers, shaking the stands. I yelp and hold on to Cooper as he stomps with them. I'm laughing when I notice Chloe watching us with an expression I can't decipher. Then her gaze meets mine, and she smiles.

"Oh shit!" Sloane yells, pointing to the field.

I know zilch about football, but there's no missing Jake running the ball toward the end zone, faking out defensive players as he zooms by.

My body tenses as I watch him get closer to scoring. "Come on . . . ," I mumble to myself.

Cooper squeezes my thighs like he heard me, and my grip on him tightens. I never knew sports were so stressful.

The crowd erupts when Jake runs into the end zone, putting

us in the lead. Sloane laughs as I scream, "Heck, yes!"

His teammates slap his shoulder pads and shove him and try to hit their helmets on his—a bizarre showing of support and excitement that only exists in football, I think—but he's searching the stands.

And then he finds me. His eyes lock with mine, and he grins and points to me.

Then he holds up his hands in the shape of a heart.

"Oh. My. God," Sloane says as the cheering grows louder.

I laugh, knowing he's referencing Taylor from the first time he asked me to come to a game. *Such a Swiftie.* I let go of Cooper's shoulders and hold my hands in a heart back to him. His grin grows wider before he's running to the sidelines.

Cooper lowers himself. I guess it's time to climb off him.

Once my feet are on the ground, Sloane leans into my ear. "Nothing going on there, huh?"

"There isn't!"

"You guys just put on a whole show for the stadium," she says.

"It was a joke. That's all."

We stay the rest of the game, cheering and laughing and having fun. But Cooper's energy has nosedived.

As we're walking back to the truck afterward, I nudge him with my shoulder. "You good?"

He glances at me. "Yeah, why wouldn't I be?"

I shrug. "I don't know. You seem off."

He furrows his brow at me and smiles, assaulting me with that dimple. "I'm good, Mitchell."

"Okay." I climb into the back of the truck, and Chloe gets in front with Cooper.

And as we pull out of the parking lot and head to the diner, I try to ignore how much I hate it.

Chapter Seventeen

The diner is packed by the time we arrive. Our group of eight is finally seated after waiting twenty minutes. Another ten minutes later, Jake and Slug show up fresh off their win, showered and grinning. Sloane made sure to leave the chair next to me open, so Jake snags it.

As I'm sure she intended.

"Well, how terrible was your first football game?" he asks me.

"You know, I had no idea what was happening, but I had fun."

"I knew you would." He takes a sip of my milkshake. "You picked a good first game. Homecoming is always a blast." I give him a smile, but it dims as I remember that I have to break the news to him about the dance. The idea of telling him now and ruining the buzz from the win seems shitty, but would waiting until the end of the night be any better? At least if I tell him now, he'll be able to shake it off with his friends. There's no good option.

I sigh, pushing down the resentment I feel toward my dad for putting me in this position. "Speaking of homecoming . . ."

"Not sure how I feel about that tone." Then he smiles like he's joking when he says, "Are you backing out on me?"

I stare at him.

"Oh." His smile falls, and he runs his hand through his wet hair. "Um, okay."

"I'm so sorry, Jake. It's just that a really big opportunity came up. My dad called earlier, and he set up a meeting in the city with an admissions guy from Columbia."

"On a Saturday night?" he asks, clearly not believing me.

"I can't meet during the week now that I'm living here, so that's when the guy said he could sit down with me. I swear I didn't pick the time. The scheduling was out of my hands."

Jake looks at the table. "Okay."

Ugh. I am the world's biggest jerk.

"I'm sorry," I say. "Really."

"It's fine." He shrugs. "I get it."

Chloe, oblivious to our conversation, comments on Jake scoring three touchdowns tonight, and he turns to talk to her. Probably so he doesn't have to talk to me. I run my finger down the condensation on my water glass, my mood completely tanked.

I sense someone watching me, and when I raise my eyes, Cooper's staring. And he looks *pissed*.

I arch an eyebrow at him, silently asking why he's looking at me like that. With a tight jaw, he shakes his head and looks away.

What could I have possibly done this time? Did he hear my conversation with Jake? Is he mad at me for not going to homecoming?

A server arrives with our food, and I try to push Cooper's

scowl to the back of my mind as the night turns into laughter and chatter. Over the next hour, Jake makes a show of bouncing back, sucking down three milkshakes and cracking jokes. But I get the sense he's just putting on a front, and it makes my stomach twist with guilt.

The diner grows louder as more post-game groups arrive, and everyone is having a good time. Slug asks out a sophomore he meets at the jukebox. Asher shows up and sits next to Sloane and Preeti, and when "Party in the USA" comes on, he stands on his chair and sings along. Soon *everyone* is laughing and belting the lyrics. Everyone except me. Because I can't get out of my own head. I know how important this interview is, but it doesn't make me feel any better about skipping out on Jake.

I excuse myself and weave through the crowd on the way to the bathroom, desperate for a few minutes alone, somewhere that I don't have to plaster on a smile and pretend I'm not reeling about disappointing my friend.

I lock myself in a stall and let out a deep breath as I lean against the wall, taking a moment to decompress. My phone buzzes, and I dig it out of my pocket to find an Instagram notification—Fern's latest post, showcasing a new dumpling place in Chinatown. I'm suddenly so homesick for our Thursday night dinners at Nom Wah that tears prick at the back of my eyes. I tap the heart on her photo, and I can't help but notice I'm the eight thousandth like. For some reason it makes me feel even more disconnected from her.

I try to shake off my worry that our friendship won't endure the distance between us, and I send her a DM letting her know

I'm coming home this weekend. I slide my phone back into my pocket, unlock the door, and head back out to my friends.

But as I'm leaving the women's restroom, I run into Cooper heading toward the men's.

He stops in the hallway in front of me, and I wait for him to say something. When he doesn't, I give him a close-lipped smile and step around him because, honestly, he hasn't acknowledged me for the last hour, and I already feel shitty enough without having to worry about what his problem is.

But just as I'm passing him, he says, "How could you do that?"

I stop and turn to him. "How could I do what?"

"Cancel on him like that? The night before the dance." He shakes his head. "Don't you see how messed up that is?"

"I didn't have a choice. My meeting—"

"You always have a choice. You say, 'Actually, I have homecoming that night. Can we meet next weekend?'"

"It's not that simple." My dad would have died on the spot if I'd said that. Putting a dance before a Columbia meeting? Ridiculous. And what if rescheduling meant losing the meeting altogether?

"It is. And worse, you don't even seem to feel bad about it."

"Of course I do. It's just . . . this is important, Cooper."

"So is Jake!" he snaps. His cheeks turn pink, and he lowers his voice. "He *likes* you. Don't you get that? He's a good guy, and he was so pumped about you saying you'd go with him. He blew up the group chat for days about it."

"You don't understand." My voice breaks, and I'm afraid if I say any more, I might start crying.

He shakes his head. "It's a shitty thing to do, Ellis."

I stand there, pressing my lips together to keep my chin from trembling, hating the way he's looking at me.

"And yet it's not surprising," he says before carrying on and pushing through the bathroom door.

My stomach clenches. I don't want to be here anymore. I take a few breaths before heading over to Sloane.

"I'm going to walk back," I tell her once I reach the table.

"Why? What's wrong?" she asks.

"Nothing. I'm just tired." I give her my best fake smile, emulating Dad's Work Smile.

Jake ends his conversation with Slug mid-sentence and turns to me. "You're going? I'll walk you home."

"No, stay. Eat. Have fun," I tell him. I feel guilty enough as it is.

"Are you sure?" he asks.

"Yeah. I'm really sorry again about homecoming."

"Don't worry about it. You'll make it up to me later," he says with a wink.

I ruffle his hair, trying to keep things light even though I feel anything but. "I'll see you Monday. Have fun tomorrow."

"Text me so I know you made it okay!" Sloane calls as I head out.

Shrouded in darkness, I walk down Saffron Lane and let myself cry.

If only I could list *messing up friendships* under the skills section of my résumé.

My overnight bag is packed and ready to go by the next afternoon. I've printed out my résumé and steamed the perfect gray

Veronica Beard pantsuit for my meeting—this time I'm leaving the Ellis originals out of it and wearing a crisp Theory button-down. I stayed up late studying potential admissions questions and preparing answers even though I know this isn't an interview.

I'm going to make Dad proud and hopefully secure my place at Columbia.

The bus leaves in an hour, so I lug everything downstairs, ready to go. But instead of Sloane waiting in the living room to drive me to the bus station, Mom is there.

"Can we talk?" she asks.

I set my bag down. "Okay . . ."

"I think you're making a mistake," she says bluntly.

"What are you talking about?" I ask. "How is a college meeting a mistake?"

"It's not. But skipping this dance is."

"God, what is with everyone and this dance?" I groan.

"I don't want you to regret missing it."

"Uh, I'd be far more worried about missing an opportunity to meet with Columbia admissions because I went to a high school dance," I tell her.

"I can call your dad and have him talk to his friend about resched—"

"Don't you dare, Mom. I'm going to this meeting. You already forced me to come here. I refuse to let you take away every shot I have at getting into this school. Just stop it. I'm going."

Mom stands. "Fine. It's your life. But I'm telling you, it's a mistake."

"It's my mistake to make." I grab my bag and head out to the car, where Sloane is already waiting.

"Ready?" she asks.

I get in the car, and we drive to the bus station.

She doesn't say anything about me skipping the dance. She doesn't mention me bailing on Jake. But she doesn't need to. I know my cousin is thinking exactly what everyone else is thinking.

Chapter Eighteen

My whole body is practically vibrating with anticipation as I wait at the bus station.

I finally get to see Dad, and my bedroom with my king-sized bed, and Fern, who I texted on my way here to make sure she was free for breakfast tomorrow before I have to head back to Bramble Falls.

Last night may have sucked, but I'm finally going *home*.

Five minutes before the bus is supposed to arrive, my phone dings.

Pen Thief Jake: hope you have fun in nyc tonight. Gotta tell you tho, you're missing out

A second message comes with a photo of him dressed in his suit, his phone pointed at the mirror and a cute little smirk on his face.

I laugh despite the pang of guilt that snaps me like a rubber band.

Me: The girl sitting next to me agrees. She just asked for your number.

Pen Thief Jake: **Is she cute?**

Me: **Nope, but I gave it to her, anyway.**

Pen Thief Jake: **a true friend**

Me: **I really am sorry.**

Pen Thief Jake: **I know. don't even think abou tit. Just have fun**

Pen Thief Jake: **tit lol where's autocorrect when you need it**

I roll my eyes, laughing to myself as I put my phone in my pocket. But then it dings again.

Dad: **Did you get the email?**

Email?

I open my email app to find one unread message in my inbox—from Mr. Erikson.

Ellis,

I'm so sorry to do this, especially at the last minute, but I have to cancel tonight. Hopefully you get this before you catch your bus. I'd still love to meet with you to discuss your future at Columbia and the admissions process. I'll be in touch soon to set something up for November. Things should slow down for me then.

Best,

Justin Erikson

I don't have time to process the utter relief that creeps into my bones before my phone is ringing.

I swipe up. "Hey, Dad."

"Did you get it?"

"I just saw it, yeah," I say.

"So unprofessional. He always was a flake," Dad says. "I should have known better."

"Sounds like something came up. People get busy."

"Yeah, well," he says. But he doesn't add anything.

"The bus is pulling up, so I'll text you when I'm close, okay?" I say as the bus comes into view.

"What do you mean? Why would you still come?" he asks, truly sounding puzzled.

"Um, because I figured we could still get pizza and hang out?"

"Oh, right. Sorry, Ellie Belly. Tonight's not good for me," he says. "Maybe in a few weeks. I'll have Kara check my schedule and get you penciled in, okay?"

He'll pencil me into his schedule. Like I'm a client.

"We'll be back home in a few weeks," I remind him.

"Well, then, that's perfect." A door closes wherever he is. "I have to go. Sorry again about Justin. Love you."

The line goes dead as the bus comes to a stop.

I look down at my bags, then back at the bus. After how adamant I was that this meeting was too important to miss, heading back to Bramble Falls and telling everyone it was canceled feels too daunting. I could go back to the city and stay with Fern or just lie in my own bed, but being back in New York without seeing Dad somehow feels even worse. I wanted to spend time with him. I wanted him to want to spend time with me, to ask me about how things were going here.

What's the point if he doesn't care enough to make time for me? What could possibly be more important than his daughter, especially on a Saturday night? It's not like he has work.

Although even if he did, the reality is, it would be more important to him.

The bus pulls away, leaving me crying on a bench thirty minutes outside Bramble Falls.

The sky is a marbled canvas of pinks and purples as we head back into town. Mom's quiet in the driver's seat, letting my sleeve absorb my silent tears without commentary. By the time we pull into the driveway, my eyes are puffy, my nose is red, and I'm ready to sleep until Monday. But when we go in, Mom follows me to the attic.

I stop on the steps and turn to face her. "What are you doing?"

"We're going to get you ready for homecoming."

"That's almost funny."

"I'm not joking," she says. "You worked your butt off making that gorgeous dress, you got yourself a date—"

"That date probably hates me now," I say. Even though I know he doesn't. Or, at least, I don't think he does. But another boy—the boy I can't stop thinking about—definitely does.

"Jake doesn't hate you. He will be thrilled when you show up. Don't let your dad ruin this for you," she says.

"My eyes are red and puffy," I whisper, tears springing to them again.

"That will go away while I fix your hair." She gives me a gentle shove. "Get going. You're already going to be late."

When I turn the corner at the top of the stairs, Aunt Naomi is sitting on the bed in front of a mirror that wasn't up here when I left.

"What's going on?" I ask, slowly walking into my makeshift room.

She points to the supplies on the dresser. "Your mom said we were going to have some last-minute homecoming primping to do. I wasn't sure if you would need a straightener, a curling iron, or a crimper, so I plugged in all three. Hoping like hell it doesn't blow a fuse in this old house," she laughs. "But they're all ready to go. So sit."

She stands and gestures at the bed. I sit on the edge, and Mom climbs onto it and kneels behind me.

"Okay, honey, tell me what you're thinking."

I blink away the urge to cry again—grateful tears this time—and explain what I have in my head while Aunt Naomi stands beside us holding clips, bobby pins, and a massive can of hair spray.

When it's time to put my dress on, my mom disappears downstairs for a few minutes before returning with a shoebox. "Don't forget the final accessories!" she says as she lifts the top. Inside are her black patent-leather Louboutin So Kate pumps.

I let out a small squeal and look up at her, grinning. "What happened to packing appropriately for Bramble Falls?"

"You never know when you're going to need a pair of dress shoes." She smiles back. "I brought them just in case."

My body practically slams into hers, and she lets out a grunt as I wrap my arms tightly around her. She squeezes me, and I realize I can't remember the last time we hugged.

How is that possible?

"Thank you," I say into her hair.

"You're welcome." She kisses the side of my head.

An hour and a half later, we pull up to Bramble Falls High. The sun fades on the horizon, leaving behind embers of pink, but as the car comes to a stop, the sky is lit mostly by the giant moon and a million bright stars.

I consider not getting out.

Or maybe getting out and waiting for Mom to pull away, then walking the two miles to the diner.

Because I don't know if I can face everyone. Cooper's mad at me. Slug probably is too. And even if Jake isn't, he probably should be.

"Knock 'em dead, Ellis," Aunt Naomi says with a wink.

"Have fun, honey," Mom says. "Call me if you need me."

With shaking hands, I climb out of the car.

"Thank you both for everything." I close the car door and head up the school's concrete steps, the clicking of my mom's stilettos calming my racing heart.

I pull back my shoulders and lift my chin. Even though I'm upset with him right now, Dad's words are in my head as I open the double doors.

Don't let them see your weaknesses, Ellis. Fake it till you make it.

Chapter Nineteen

The commons is covered in streamers. Helium-filled black and blue balloons flood the ceiling, and colorful disco lights bounce around the room. The heavy bass shakes the dance floor, where kids are packed like sardines, grinding against each other and throwing their hands in the air.

All but three tables have been cleared out to make space for everyone, but plenty of people are hanging out on the outskirts of the crowd. I hug the walls as I make my way around the room, keeping my eyes peeled for any of my friends.

But I hear them before I see them.

"Ellis?" Jake's voice carries over the blasting music.

To my right, Jake, Chloe, Slug, and Cooper are standing with a few other football guys, some of Chloe's friends, and Sterling, whose hair is now dyed pink to match their chic pantsuit. Everyone is sweaty, and the boys have abandoned their jackets. Their sleeves are rolled up, and Jake's dress shirt is unbuttoned, exposing his white undershirt.

Jake's whole face lights up as I approach. "What are you doing here?"

"Ellis!" Slug shouts. Judging by his red-rimmed glassy eyes and the hug he pulls me into, I'd guess he pregamed before the dance.

Even if they're mad at me, I can't contain the smile that tugs at my lips being here with them.

"Hey," I say as Slug lets me go. Chloe smiles sweetly at me, and Sterling gives me a nod. My gaze finally slides to Cooper. I expect to find him glaring or snarling at me, but instead his lips are parted, his eyes traveling over my dress. I blush and turn back to Jake.

"Things didn't go as planned," I tell him, trying to keep all emotion out of my voice.

"Hell yeah!" he shouts. "I mean, I'm sorry, but also, hell yeah!" I laugh, and he looks at my wrist. "I wish I'd known you were coming. I would have brought your corsage."

"I'm not worried about it." I shrug. "I'm just glad I made it."

"Me too."

"I love your dress," Chloe says in her own sparkling green ballgown. "Where'd you get it? I feel like I scoured every store and never found anything like that."

"Oh, I, um . . . I made it," I say, wringing my hands.

"Are you serious?" she asks. "That's incredible."

"Thanks."

"We'd love to stay and chat, Chlo, but we've got places to be." Jake grabs my hand and pulls me onto the dance floor before I even realize what's happening. With the rest of our group close behind, he stops in a small open space and starts dancing, which he's surprisingly decent at.

When I just stand there watching him, he leans into my ear. "Dance with me, Ellis!"

So I do.

My hair has been crimped and teased. It's long and big, just like I imagined. And now it's flying wildly as I move my hips against Jake. As the song goes on, I grow hot, sweaty, and breathless. My thighs burn. I am in no shape for this sort of exercise. I turn to face my date, and he lifts my hands into the air to lyrics about apple-bottom jeans before we all lower our hips to the floor. Which is hard in my mermaid-cut dress. I nearly fall, but Jake catches me, and we both laugh.

As the next song comes on, I catch Cooper dancing with Chloe out of the corner of my eye.

It shouldn't bother me.

His hands on her hips shouldn't matter to me.

Her ass rocking against him shouldn't make me want to burn the building down.

And yet.

I force myself to look away. I'm having fun with Jake. I'm not letting some weird feelings ruin this night.

We dance for another fifteen minutes before my feet feel like they might fall off. Louboutins are gorgeous, but they're not exactly meant for high-exertion activities.

"I gotta go take my shoes off. I'll be back." I shout into Jake's ear. He nods, and I fight my way off the dance floor. I can't leave my mom's shoes anywhere, though—they're too special to risk losing. So instead I head outside and let the crisp night air cool me as I rest my throbbing feet.

I'm sitting at one of the metal picnic tables when footsteps approach.

Then Cooper sits across from me.

"Hey," he says. "Taking a break?"

"Yeah, it's hot in there."

"At least you aren't stuck in long sleeves and pants." His thin black tie is loosened around his neck, his top two buttons undone, and his shirt untucked. His hair is sweaty and disheveled. He looks so good. His eyes dip to the silky black fabric I'm wearing. "I can't believe you made the dress."

"It was harder than I thought. There are plenty of mistakes, things I wish I'd had time to fix. But yeah." I smile, looking at him. "I sort of can't believe I did it either."

"I'm impressed," he says. "It's . . . stunning."

My insides swell with pride, and my cheeks heat. "Thank you."

He takes his phone from his pocket. His thumbs move swiftly over the screen before he looks at me and says, "Text me."

"Um, okay . . ." I grab my phone from my tiny clutch purse and send a text as he sets his phone on the table in front of me.

Dress Designer Ellis: hi?

My heart dances before my brain shuts it down fast, pressure building in my chest. I grab his phone and hit the edit button. *Journalist Ellis.* I pass his phone back to him. He frowns at it but then fixes his face.

"So," he says, changing the subject, "are you having fun? Jake said this is your first school dance."

"It is, and I am, yeah."

He nods, and silence falls between us. I'm dying to ask him

what he's thinking about, but then he takes off his boutonniere and starts pulling it apart, tugging the end of the small black ribbon wrapped around the red rose that matches Chloe's dress.

He reaches over and gently grabs my wrist. He ties the ribbon in a bow around it. "I'm sorry for yelling at you yesterday."

I peel my eyes from his fingers on the soft skin of my inner wrist and look at him, but he's focused on what he's doing. "Thanks for saying that. But you weren't wrong. Even if I didn't feel like I had a choice, it was still messed up."

"It was," he agrees. "But I could have handled it better." He plucks the black berries from his deconstructed pile of flowers and begins weaving the short stems around the ribbon. I'm mesmerized by his delicate movements as he tucks his little white flowers into it. "What happened with New York?"

I sigh. "The meeting was canceled, and my dad had more important things to do than see his daughter."

"I'm sorry."

I shrug. "It is what it is."

His eyes meet mine. "You know you're allowed to be upset. You don't have to pretend it's fine."

I look away. "It is fine."

"Okay."

"It just . . . it feels like things are happening for everyone in New York, like everything outside of this place is moving forward, and I'm . . . stuck. Being here feels like trying to claw my way out of quicksand."

He nods as he sticks one last flower in and lets go of my hand. I stare at his handiwork.

He made me a corsage.

A shiver runs through me, and it's not because of the temperature.

Ed Sheeran's voice spills through the propped open double doors. Cooper pins the red rose back into his pocket, stands, and holds out his hand for me to take. "Dance with me?"

"Um, okay." I swallow and set my hand in his, rising to dance with him.

Barefoot in the cold grass, I wrap my arms around his neck and his arms come around me, his hands resting on my bare lower back. I shudder at his touch, but if he notices, he doesn't say anything.

We sway to the song.

We were just kids when we fell in love,

Not knowing what it was . . .

"Has it really been that terrible?" Cooper asks, his voice low. "Being in Bramble Falls, I mean?"

I look up at him, and he stares back at me with those burnt honey eyes. "No," I whisper. "It hasn't."

His thumb makes slow, soft circles on my lower back, and I melt into him, resting my cheek on his shoulder and closing my eyes. Because it's perfect here. I could live in this moment forever.

We dance like that, beneath the starlit sky, with our hearts beating fast and untamed, and his touch raising the hairs on my neck and arms.

Until someone clears their throat.

I open my eyes to find Chloe watching us. "Cooper, we were

announced as homecoming king and queen. They're waiting for us onstage."

She glances at me again, and I pull out of Cooper's arms. "Well, that's . . . fun. Congrats," I say. "I'll, uh, let you get back to your date." I step over to where my shoes sit on the ground by the table. "Thanks for the dance."

"Yeah," he mumbles.

"Let's go," Chloe says to him.

I slide my shoes on, a thousand frenzied feelings exploding inside of me like fireworks.

Then I watch as Cooper walks back into the dance with his queen, and the denial slips away, giving way to the most heart-stopping and unfortunate realization.

I really, really like Cooper Barnett.

This is *not* good.

Chapter Twenty

I barely slept after I got home last night. After watching Cooper and Chloe be crowned and share a slow dance together (and hating every second of it), I left with Jake. He dropped me off at my door, hugged me goodbye, and, with the most heartfelt smile, thanked me for ultimately showing up. It almost made me grateful that Mr. Erikson canceled.

But after showering, I lay in bed trying to process how this happened. Trying to convince myself it hadn't.

I can't like Cooper. I'm leaving here in a month.

He and Chloe are . . . something.

He's a *distraction*.

Sloane and I spent today lounging on the couch, nursing our sore feet and eating snacks while watching TV. I talked to Fern for a while, and at one point Jake texted just to say he had fun. But it's been otherwise a quiet day.

Until eleven forty-five p.m., when Sloane, Mom, and Aunt Naomi come crashing up the attic steps.

I leap out of bed. “What’s wrong?”

Aunt Naomi pushes the attic window open, and Mom tosses a bundle of blankets out of it. “Nothing,” Mom says. “Come on.”

Sloane shoots me a grin and climbs out onto the roof. She spreads a blanket over the shingles while my aunt and cousin climb out behind her carrying Styrofoam cups and a coffee carafe.

“What’s going on?” I ask, padding over to the window. I stick my head out as they all sit on one blanket and wrap the others around their shoulders. “It’s freezing out there.”

“Oh, suck it up and get out here,” Mom says. I give my warm bed one last longing glance and climb out the window. I sit next to Mom, and she hands me a fleece blanket to cocoon myself in. Aunt Naomi fills the cups and passes them out.

“It’s cider,” she says when I tell her I’m going to pass on the midnight coffee because I’d like to be able to sleep whenever *whatever this is* ends.

I take the cup and let the liquid warm me. “Is someone going to tell me why we’re sitting on the roof in the freezing cold on a school night?”

“Because look at the sky, Ellis,” Aunt Naomi says, full of delight.

I take in the full moon that feels like it belongs to Bramble Falls tonight.

“It’s the harvest moon,” Sloane says. “We come out here with blankets and cider every year on harvest moon night.”

Mom sighs. “I’ve missed this tradition.”

“You used to do this too?” I ask her.

"Oh yeah. Naomi and I used to do this with your grandma," Mom says. "After she died, we continued the tradition. But once I moved to the city with your dad . . ." She trails off, taking a sip of her cider and staring up at the sky.

Aunt Naomi rocks into her. "But you're here now."

Sloane lies back and tucks the blanket under her chin. "I miss Dad. He used to love doing this."

"He really did, didn't he?" Aunt Naomi says. Mom rests her head on Aunt Naomi's shoulder.

Sloane's dad died from unexpected cardiac arrest three years ago. Although I never knew him well, I remember him always being so *present*. He was involved in Sloane's life, always supportive of her acting and often taking her on trips, just the two of them. It's been hard enough being away from my dad for a month. I can't imagine her grief.

"Are you happy with how the Bramble Falls events have been going?" Mom asks.

Aunt Naomi grins. "I really am. Everyone's been having fun. It's truly magical how everybody comes together to make everything perfect in the fall." She sighs. "But I can't find last year's Harvest Hunt list anywhere, so I have to make a new one."

"What's a harvest hunt? Can I do anything to help?" I ask.

"This weekend's fall scavenger hunt," she says. "It's not a huge deal. I just have to make a list of fall items for people to search for."

"I can do that," I volunteer.

Mom turns to me. "Really?"

I shrug. "Sure. I'll have it done by Friday morning so you have time to make sure it's okay and make copies or whatever."

"That'd be great, Ellis," Aunt Naomi says. "Let me know if you have any questions or need help with anything."

The four of us lie shoulder to shoulder for the next half hour, talking about the past and the town and plans for the future. When Aunt Naomi almost rolls off the roof because she's laughing so hard after Mom brings up the time she dated a guy she met at Comic-Con who dressed like a Smurf and ate tater tots for breakfast, we decide it's probably time to go to bed.

I crash the second my head hits my pillow.

Despite yesterday's disappointment with Dad, it's been the longest—but best—weekend.

The Caffeinated Cat is dead on Thursday evening. Cooper is working behind the counter, but aside from taking my order, he hasn't said two words to me.

In fact, he's barely talked to me at all since homecoming.

I don't know why—and I don't have time to analyze it—but it's probably for the best.

Surely crushes die if left deprived of attention, right?

A calico cat hops up on the round table where my papers and laptop are scattered. He bats at my pen until he knocks it to the floor next to a mammoth Maine coon named Marty.

"Jerk," I mutter, affectionately petting the calico's annoying little head.

"We're closing," Cooper says, picking my pen up off the floor and setting it on the table. Marty nudges his head against Cooper's leg, begging for attention.

I tap my phone to look at the time. 7:59 p.m.

"Really?" I drop my head on the table, startling the calico. He leaps down. "Stay open until eleven for me."

"Wish I could. The best I can do is give you cookies and coffee to go."

I perk up, lifting my head. "Yeah?"

"Sure." He peers down at my papers. "What are you working on over here?"

"I volunteered to make the scavenger hunt list for Aunt Naomi, but it's harder than I thought it'd be."

"Don't you just need a list of things for people to find?" he asks.

"Yes, but I wanted to spice it up a bit," I explain. "I've been trying to come up with clues and write riddles people have to solve to know exactly *what* to find. I have an easy, family-friendly list and a list for those who want more of a challenge."

"Leave it to you to go above and beyond."

"Yeah, but I told Aunt Naomi I'd have it to her by tomorrow morning, and I'm nowhere remotely close to done." I sigh. "But I don't want to give up and just hand her a list of items. I volunteered so I could make it more exciting for everyone. This means a lot to Aunt Naomi."

He studies me a second, then says, "Okay. Pack up your stuff. I have to count the drawer real quick, but then we'll go to my house."

"What?"

"I'll help you," he says over his shoulder.

"Seriously?"

"Yeah, why not? With both of us working on it, I'm sure we can knock it out," he says.

Alarm bells go off. *Bad idea, Ellis. Distance yourself, girl.*

"Okay." I internally shake my head disapprovingly at myself as I pack up my computer and Cooper does his closing duties.

This cannot end well for me.

Chapter Twenty-One

The last time I was in Cooper's room, I was kissing him.

But I try not to think about that as we lie on our stomachs next to each other on his bed.

"'I'm orange and roundish and can be found in a patch,'" Cooper says.

I stare at him.

"What?" he says.

"That's way too easy! I'll add it to the family-friendly list, but we're supposed to be starting with the challenging ones so we can get them out of the way before we get too tired to think." I type his riddle into the document. "Try something less obvious, like 'I'm tall when I'm young and short when I'm old. What am I?'"

"Doesn't *everyone* get shorter when they get older?"

I frown. "It's a candle, not a person."

"Ah, yeah, okay. Maybe we can put a hint with it, like something about being in a jack-o'-lantern."

I make a note. "I'll consider it, but then it'll probably have to go on the easy list."

"All right, let's see. 'I'm the color of shit, and I fall from trees. What am I?'" Cooper says, grinning at me.

"A stick?" I guess. "A twig? A branch? An acorn?"

"A brown leaf, Ellis," he says.

"Wow. You actually really suck at this," I tell him with a laugh.

"It's a perfectly good riddle. Not my fault you couldn't solve it." He rests his forehead on his arms and talks into his comforter when he says, "Okay, how about 'I have two legs but can't walk. I have a mouth but can't talk. The sun doesn't bother me, but I wear a hat. I scare birds, but I'm not a cat.'"

I slap his shoulder. "That's a good one!"

He looks up and flashes his dimple at me. "Yeah?"

"Yeah." I force myself to look at the computer and type his scarecrow riddle. "What about 'What asks but never answers?'"

He draws his eyebrows together. "I have no idea."

"An owl."

"That better be going on the challenging list," he says. "Are you actually expecting people to find an owl?"

"They don't have to find a *living* owl. They can get creative. I know for a fact there's a taxidermy owl in the hardware store and a painting of one in the arts-and-crafts store."

"Oh, you're right." He grins. "Okay, cool. We definitely have to people-watch on Saturday. Everyone's frustration will be entertaining."

"You're heartless," I joke. But really, my stomach is doing somersaults because we're making plans to hang out on Saturday.

An hour and a half later, my eyelids are heavy, but there's still so much to do.

"I'm going to go grab some snacks to keep us awake," Cooper says.

"Yeah, okay," I say. "That's probably a good idea."

He slides off the bed and leaves the room, and I lay my head on the blanket and rest my eyes.

Just for a second. Just until he gets back.

An unfamiliar alarm stirs me from my heavy sleep. I groan as I pat the area around me, looking for the source of the wretched sound so I can throw it against the wall.

But my hand lands on something soft. A shirt. A back. A person. My eyes shoot open.

Outside, pale morning sunlight tints the sky a muted orangish-pink, and *I'm still in Cooper's bed.*

My mom is going to kill me. Like, actually murder me.

Where the hell is my phone?

"What are you doing?" Cooper rasps.

"I need my phone. I can't believe I slept here," I say. "I have to text my mom."

"Relax, Mitchell," Cooper says, setting his hand on my arm. I pause to look at him. His eyes are bleary, and he has pillow creases etched into his cheek. And still he steals my breath. "I texted Naomi last night to tell her you'd fallen asleep while working on the scavenger hunt. She said she'd tell your mom. Everything's good."

I shake my head as he turns off his alarm. "There's no way

my mom was okay with me sleeping at a boy's house."

"I'm not just any boy, you know," he says with a sleepy crooked grin.

It's true—Cooper is beloved and trusted by everyone in this little town. Plus, Aunt Naomi is friends with his parents, who—

"Oh my god, where are your parents?"

"Probably downstairs," he says.

My face heats. "I'm going to have to climb out your window."

Cooper laughs. "They know you stayed." I groan, and he gestures at the doorway. "It's okay. I left the door open. That's the rule."

"Oh? Do you have a lot of girls spend the night?" I ask, as if I want to know if the answer is yes.

Cooper blushes. "Well, no. You're the only one."

I hold back a smile, caused partly by his cute bashfulness and partly by the fact that it makes me strangely happy that I'm the only girl who's slept in his bed overnight.

"Okay, well, I'd still rather not face them," I tell him as I reach for my laptop, which is open but asleep. "I have to get going. Maybe I can finish this if I skip first period. I'll probably miss a pop quiz, and if I'm not there, Jake will definitely fail, but—"

The laptop wakes as I pick it up, preparing to close it and pack it into my bag.

What. The. Hell.

There are twenty more riddles and clues written in the doc. Both lists are complete.

My head whips to Cooper, who's sitting there watching me. "You stayed up and finished this?" I ask him.

"It didn't take that long," he says.

A lie. We weren't even close to finished. It took us two hours to come up with the ten we had.

"I can't believe you did this."

He sits up with his back to me and lifts his arms over his head, stretching and yawning. "It isn't a big deal."

But it's a big deal to me. And even though I shouldn't, I throw my arms around him, wrapping him in a hug from behind. His body stiffens. "Thank you," I say. He slowly lowers his arms and pats my hands, which are splayed across his stomach.

"No problem," he says. "Let's go make bacon."

"On a school day?" I ask, letting go of him. "There isn't time for bacon."

He stands, and I pack up my stuff. "There's always time for bacon. You can email that list to Naomi while I cook. Then I'll drive you by your house so you can change." When I don't budge, he sighs. "Ellis, I set the alarm early enough that we would have time to eat. But if you don't get moving, we *won't* have time."

I don't ask any more questions. Instead I do what he says because I'm honestly astounded right now. He finished my project *and* considered breakfast.

Downstairs, Cooper's parents are sitting together at the kitchen table eating cereal and toast. I can't even remember the last time my parents sat together for a meal. Or, really, for anything—other than to tell me they were taking time apart.

"Ellis! So good to see you again," Cooper's mom says.

My cheeks flush. "You too, Mrs. Barnett."

"Coop said you were working on the Harvest Hunt?"

"I was." I glance at Cooper who's setting a frying pan on the stovetop. "But Cooper finished it for me."

"I hardly did anything," he says.

"Come sit," his mom says. "And please, call me Amanda."

I sit next to her and take my computer back out of my bag. "Okay." I open it and try to relax, but my leg won't stop bouncing. I hate making bad impressions on people, and sleeping in Cooper's room does not look good. "Sorry about accidentally spending the night."

Cooper's dad waves me off with a small laugh. "It's okay. I can't tell you how many nights Amanda has fallen asleep in the middle of working on things for the Falling Leaves Festival."

I look at her. "Really?"

"Oh yeah. It's an exhausting time of year. There's always so much to do. We really do appreciate you taking on the scavenger hunt, though."

"No problem." I attach the document and send it to Aunt Naomi. Then I put my computer away.

While the bacon sizzles behind me, Cooper's parents tell me all about next week's Autumn Spice Sprint—which sounds way too athletic for me—and the Boots and Blankets Bonfire that night. And I tell them all about Cooper's awful attempts at fall riddles, some of which have them cracking up.

"So, what are your college plans? It's just about application time," Cooper's dad says.

"I'm going to Columbia," I tell him with confidence. "I've already started filling out the application."

"Oh!" Amanda exclaims. "So you and Coop—"

"Time to go, Mitchell," Cooper says, swooping in behind me and practically tossing a plate at me. "Bacon for the car."

"Okay." I toss my backpack over my shoulder as I stand, then I grab my plate. "It was nice talking to you guys. Sorry again for crashing here."

"We hope to see you again soon, Ellis," Amanda says. "Tell Naomi I said hi."

Cooper and I hop into his truck and scarf down our bacon on the short drive to Aunt Naomi's. He waits in the car while I change my clothes and brush my teeth. My reflection makes me flinch, but I don't have time to put on makeup. I wipe the mascara from under my eyes and throw my hair into a messy bun.

I groan. I cannot go to school like this.

I grab my makeup bag—maybe I can put some on in the truck—and run back downstairs, where Mom is sitting in the living room.

"Hi, Mom. Bye, Mom," I say as I open the front door.

"Wait a second!" she says.

The moment I've been dreading. "Yeah?"

"I heard you slept at Cooper's last night."

"I accidentally fell asleep working on the scavenger-hunt stuff."

"Uh-huh . . ." She stands. "Well, we've never really talked about it because I've never needed to, since you were so hung up on school rather than boys, but . . . you know to use a condom, right? Do you need me to show you how—"

"Oh god, Mom!" I scream. "Please stop talking right now."

She worries her lip.

"It wasn't like that," I say. "You don't have to worry. And if anything ever comes even close to that, then yes, believe me, being friends with Fern has meant learning everything I need to know. Don't worry."

She nods. "Okay. Good. Please don't let it happen again."

"Okay. Bye." I make a run for it before things get any more awkward.

"You good?" Cooper asks when I get in the car.

"Uh, other than the fact that my mom wanted to demonstrate how to use a condom, yes."

Cooper's face turns a brighter shade of red than I've ever seen. "I'm going to pretend like I didn't hear that."

"Perfect. Let's go."

Cooper's sleeping in calculus.

I try to be inconspicuous when I snap a photo and send it to him with a message that simply says, **slacker.**

His phone must startle him because his eyes shoot open. He pulls it out of his pocket and holds it under his desk to check the message. His dimple makes an appearance as he reads it and types something.

My phone lights up on my desk.

Summer Cooper: **well if someone hadn't kept me up all night**

I glance back at him, his ears pink.

Summer Cooper: **shit I didn't mean it like that. obviously.**

Summer Cooper: **I'm too tired for this conversation. Please ignore me.**

I snort.

Half the class—and Ms. Hanby—turns to look at me.

"Would you like to share what's so funny about derivatives, Ms. Mitchell?" our teacher says.

A thin coat of sweat dampens my face instantaneously. I've never gotten in trouble in class. *Ever.*

"Nothing," I say. "I was just . . . sneezing and coughing at the same time. Body malfunction."

Someone laughs behind me. *Cooper.*

I press my lips together so I don't laugh again.

"Well, perhaps you should see the nurse if it happens again," Ms. Hanby says, glancing from Cooper back to me.

I nod. "Will do."

Ms. Hanby goes back to walking us through the problem on the board, and I scratch the side of my face with my middle finger.

I grin to myself as Cooper's muffled laughter fills my whole chest and nestles itself between my ribs.

Chapter Twenty-Two

Between my music and the sewing machine, I don't hear the doorbell ring the next morning. And I don't hear the footsteps climbing the attic stairs. I don't know anyone's there until someone taps my shoulder.

"Hang on," I shout over the music. "I have to finish edgestitching this seam real quick."

"Bitch, I didn't come all this way to watch you sew."

I turn around so fast, the chair almost topples over.

"Fernie!" I scream. She laughs as I jump up and tackle her in a hug. "What are you doing here?"

"You didn't make it to New York, so I figured I'd come to you," she says. She looks around my room—at Mom's art hanging on the wall, at my makeshift curtains, at my single dresser and clothing rack, at the old TV and DVD player—and turns back to me, her face stamped with apprehension. "We have to save you from this place."

I chuckle. "It's not as awful as I thought it'd be."

"They've brainwashed you," she says. "We need an extraction plan."

I laugh but she doesn't crack. I shake my head at her concern. "How'd you know where to find me?"

"I texted your mom last night. She gave me the address." She sits on the edge of the bed. "I'm on my way to Rhode Island, so I figured I'd stop by and spend the day with you."

"What's in Rhode Island?"

She finally grins. "I'm doing a collab with Spider Spices. They were going to send me some of their products to make videos at home, but then they emailed yesterday to see if I'd want to come try dishes featuring their spices at some restaurant they own in Rhode Island. Obviously I wasn't going to pass up this chance, but honestly, I'm pretty fucking stressed. It's a massive opportunity. I really need it to go well."

"Wow, that sounds huge," I say. Part of me is envious of my friend. Big things are happening for her, and collaborating with such a popular brand could open a lot of doors for her future. But . . . for the first time probably ever, a bigger part of me is *relieved* I'm not in that position. It's been nice knowing my biggest worry lately is whether I'm going to get riddles written in time or whether the Caffeinated Cat will be open when I'm in need of a harvest spice latte.

Things that don't involve me stressing about my whole future being on the line.

"It is. I'm really excited." She nods at my sewing table. "What are you working on over there? I didn't realize you were back to sewing again."

"A little." I point to a minidress I made the other night. "My mom didn't let me bring much, so I've been piecing together some cute outfits from donated clothes."

Fern's eyes bulge as she takes in the black-and-white plaid mini pinafore dress. "That is so freaking cute! I'm so glad you're making stuff again. We should promote your clothes in my videos!"

"You review food, Fern," I remind her.

"I could talk food and fashion."

I wave her off. "It's a nice thought, but there would be no point. It's just a hobby." I stand and link our arms. "Anyway, we should head out. We don't want to be late."

She looks at me, confused, as I tug her toward the stairs. "Late for what?"

"A scavenger hunt." I grin. "But first, we need provisions."

Less than fifteen minutes later, we walk into the Caffeinated Cat, and Fern nearly keels over the second Marty approaches.

"Holy shit. What do they feed their cats here?" she asks. "Why is that thing the size of a taxi?"

I laugh and bend down to pet my favorite oversized cat. "He's a Maine coon."

"I have no idea what that means," she says, brushing the cat fur off her black pants. "Can we please just order coffee and get out of here?"

"I had no idea you hated cats so much," I say, leading her to the counter.

"I only hate them in person. Love watching TikTok videos of them," she says. "Which is how I know they're unpredictable assholes with fast reflexes who seem to enjoy messing with people."

"Hmm. That's pretty accurate."

When we reach the counter, I'm surprised to see Cooper working.

"Hey. Thought we were people-watching today?" I say, trying to mask my disappointment.

"Don't worry, Mitchell, I'm off in thirty." He glances behind me, where Fern is standing, and his eyes widen. She's freaking stunning, so I'm not surprised. And I refuse to be jealous of my friend. "Cooper, this is my friend—"

"Fern Berry," he says, cutting me off. Then he looks at me, his jaw still nearly on the floor. "You're friends with Fern Berry?"

Fern smiles at him, flirtation painted all over her perfect face. "Nice to meet you, Cooper. Ellis is my bestie."

"Nice to meet you." He turns back to me. "Why wouldn't you tell me that?"

I draw my eyebrows together, puzzled. "Why *would* I tell you that? How was I supposed to know you'd care? Or that you'd even know who she is?"

"Fair. Okay, well, what can I get for you guys? It's on me," he says.

What is happening right now? "You're not paying for our stuff, Cooper."

"She's Fern Berry, Ellis. I'm paying. And I already know what you want, so, Fern, what can I get for you?"

Fern looks at me. "I like him."

I try not to roll my eyes while she gives Cooper her order; then we head to the other end of the counter to wait for our drinks.

"So, who is he? How do you know him?" she asks. "It seems I interrupted plans you two had today."

I hadn't thought of it before, but yeah, I guess she did. And now that I know Cooper recognizes her and is clearly impressed and maybe even a little smitten, it's going to be a long day of trying to act like I'm not bothered.

"He's just a family friend. And you didn't interrupt anything," I tell her. "We made the scavenger hunt, so we were just going to hang out and watch everyone try to figure out the riddles."

"Sounds . . . fun," she says. But her face says otherwise.

Cooper puts our drinks on the counter with a bonus lemon cookie. "Meet you at the gazebo?"

"Sounds good," I say, patting an old gray cat on the head. Fern and I grab our order and give Cooper one last wave.

"So," Fern says as soon as we're outside, "are you guys hooking up, or . . . ?"

"Who? Me and Cooper? No." I shake my head emphatically. "Absolutely not."

"Mm-hmm," Fern hums, unconvinced.

"What? We're not."

"Your chemistry would say otherwise," she says with a cheeky smile. "But okay."

I take a sip of my latte, trying to hide the blush undoubtedly coloring my face.

Fern surveys the town, taking in the people walking around with their hot drinks and warm smiles, scavenger-hunt papers in hand; the small businesses with their items set up outside on the leaf-covered sidewalks; the town square draped in signs for the Harvest Hunt.

"I'll give it to you that this place is, like, unreasonably charming," she says. "But it's *so* little. What do you even do here?"

I lead her across the street to the gazebo. "I've mostly been helping out with this festival my aunt runs. Otherwise, I've just been hanging out, I guess."

"*You?* Hanging out?" She shoulders me playfully, and I roll my eyes.

"School hasn't been that hard, so I haven't had to study as much. And I've made some good friends who have been dragging me out of my comfort zone." I smile at her. "They even convinced me to go to a football game."

Her head swivels to me, her wild red hair blowing in the chilly breeze. "*What?* How on earth did that happen?"

"Everyone was going." I shrug. "Plus, a friend of mine was playing, so I went to cheer him on."

She shakes her head, bemused. "Man, Ellis Mitchell casually hanging out and going to football games. There must be something in the water here."

We sit on the gazebo steps, and I break the lemon cookie in two, handing her half as I tell her about the Bramble Falls autumn events. She takes a bite and freezes, her eyes bulging as she grips my forearm.

"Are you okay?" I ask, worried she might be choking.

"No," she says. But she begins chewing, her face a picture of pure bliss. She swallows and looks at me, holding up what's left of her half of the cookie. "Holy shit, Ellis. This is unreal."

I grin. "I know, right?"

"I legit might have to come back and review this place," she says, shoving the rest of it into her mouth. When she finally swallows, she takes a sip of her drink and brushes the cookie crumbs off her shirt. Then she turns to me. "In all seriousness, I think I get it now. I thought I needed to mount a whole rescue operation, but you're here having a grand old time."

My instinct is to tell her she's wrong. That I'm desperate to come home. But I'm not so sure that's true anymore.

I pull my legs in closer and wrap my arms around them. "I'm not going to pretend I don't miss New York, and I'm definitely stressed about how this might affect things with Columbia and my internship. But, I don't know . . ." I shrug. "Being here isn't the worst thing in the world."

Something about saying these words aloud uncoils some of the tension that's been sitting in my shoulders ever since my parents sat me down to tell me they were separating.

Fern smiles softly at me. "Don't take this the wrong way, but Bramble Falls kind of looks good on you. Maybe you needed a little sabbatical." Her face turns stern. "But you obviously belong with me in Manhattan, so don't get too attached to this place. I don't want to have to find another roommate for next year." She faux shudders, and I laugh.

"There's no danger in that, don't worry. The plan is still Columbia. We'll be selling all your stuff to make room for mine in just a few short months," I joke.

Fern shrugs. "Your clothes are cuter than mine, anyway. Sounds like just the excuse I need to take them over."

A while later, Cooper exits the shop, and my eyes snap to him.

"God, he's hot," Fern mumbles as we watch him approach. He's in a rust-colored sweater, dark jeans, and brown boots.

"Yup."

"Wish I had more time here. The things I could do with your little family friend . . ."

"Fern!"

She laughs. "What? You're thinking it too."

"Thinking of the things you could do with him? I'm definitely not."

"You know that's not what I mean."

"Well?" Cooper says as he gets closer. "Anyone come to complain to you about the riddles?"

"Not yet, but it's still early," I say. Fern scoots over, making space between us on the bench.

Cooper ambles over and sits in the open spot.

"So, are you just visiting Ellis, or are you here on official business?" Cooper asks Fern.

"I'm just here for our gorgeous girl," she says, grinning at Cooper. He glances at me for a split second, then nods at Fern. I know what he thinks of me doesn't matter, but my traitorous brain wonders if he's agreeing that I'm gorgeous. If he's as enamored with me as I am with him.

But seeing as his eyes are glued to my best friend, probably not.

I clear my throat and push the thought away. "Fern is actually stopping by on her way to meet with Spider Spices."

Cooper's eyebrows lift. "No way. That's awesome."

I lean back and sigh. I'm only making her sound cooler.

"Ellis!" A tiny body suddenly jumps on my back, and sticky fingers poking out of black gauntlet-covered sleeves wrap around my neck.

There's only one little guy this could be.

I stand up, and he hangs on. "Oh my gosh, everyone!" I exclaim. "Is that *Batman* on my back?"

"Oh man. I think so," Cooper says, going with the shtick. "I didn't realize Batman lived around here."

The little body unravels himself from me and drops to the ground. He lifts his mask. "It's just me!"

"Harley," Dorothy says, coming up behind him. "I've told you a hundred times you have to stop jumping on people. Sorry about that, Ellis."

"No worries," I say, ruffling Harley's hair.

She shakes the sheet of paper in her hand at me. "By the way, this scavenger hunt isn't for the faint of heart. Some of these are much too hard."

"Well, why didn't you choose the easier version?" I ask with a laugh.

She lifts her chin. "Because my girls all took the challenging one, and I'll be damned if they're going to show me up. I'm determined to finish the hunt first."

"*That* I get." I laugh and lean in conspiratorially. "Do you want the answers?"

She grins but shakes her head. "No, no. I have to beat them fair and square."

"All right. Well, a little challenge never hurt anyone," I tell her.

"*But* I'll give you a hint—one of the answers is an animal."

She looks down at the list and frowns. "Hmph. Okay, well, we're off to look for an animal, I suppose. Have a good day, Ellis."

Dorothy saunters over to Harley, who pulls his mask back down, returning to his superhero state.

When I turn around, Cooper is talking earnestly to Fern about how much he enjoys her account. He's gushing over the latest bakery she covered and asking questions about New York neighborhoods, which Fern enthusiastically answers.

I join them as Cooper takes his phone from his pocket and looks at it.

He turns to me. "Well, I'll let you two catch up."

"Um, sure," I say, swallowing my disappointment. "Everything okay?"

"Yeah. Jake just texted. He's with Slug and Chloe, so I'm going to go meet up with them. That way you two can have some time to visit each other without me talking Fern's ear off."

I nod. "Oh. Yeah, okay." I want to spend the day with him, getting drunk off his laugh and stifling my sighs every time his dimple pops, but I can't say I'm not happy to see his mind-meld with Fern come to an end.

Although, him hanging out with Chloe all day is probably worse.

"Talk later?" he says.

I force a smile. "Sounds good."

With one last wave to Fern, he walks across the lawn toward Sparrow Drive, where Chloe lives. I shake off my jealousy because it's ugly, and instead focus on the fact that I have my best friend in Bramble Falls, a tiny piece of home that I want to grasp on to as hard as I can for as long as she's here. "So," I say, turning back to Fern, "tell me everything I've missed."

She grins and dives right into narrating recent life in NYC with gusto.

Fern and I eat at the diner for lunch, which she describes as "finger-licking good." I introduce her to Aunt Naomi when we run into her on our way to the bookstore. We visit the small shops and stop into the art store to see Mom. We run into Jake picking up pizza for everyone, and Fern can't stop ogling him. By mid-afternoon, I think she might genuinely be convinced that the town has something in the water that makes the boys hot, the cats big, the food delish, and the people weirdly friendly.

When five o'clock rolls around, it's time for her to leave. But it feels like she just got here. My heart sinks as I hug her, desperately wishing she could stay with me in Bramble Falls. But having her here has been an affirmation that even if things are moving forward without me in New York, at least Fern and I will always be the same. I wish her luck, and she shimmies out of my unrelenting grip.

"Go enjoy that 'family friend' of yours," she says with a devious smirk. Then she hops in her Uber, and I watch as she heads east out of Bramble Falls.

I'm on my way home when Sloane texts. **Come meet up at Jake's! We're going bowling. You can bring your friend.** I grin at my phone and turn left onto Pine Street, toward Jake's house.

When I arrive, everyone's waiting outside for me.

"Mitchell!" Coop yells when he sees me walking up the driveway.

"Cuz! You made it!" Sloane calls.

"There she is!" Jake says with a huge grin as he jogs toward me. I yelp as he scoops me up and carries me over to our group of friends. He sets me down next to his SUV and says, "Get in, losers."

"I'm picking the playlist!" Asher announces as he opens the car door.

"Dream on, Ash," Jake says. "It's driver's choice."

Asher sighs. "I guess we all already know what we're listening to, then. . . ."

Jake slaps him on the shoulder. "Only to the goddess herself."

As Chloe, Hannah, Sloane, Asher, Preeti, Slug, and Jake climb into the vehicle, Cooper turns to me.

"How'd the rest of the day go with Fern Berry?" he asks.

"She's just Fern," I laugh. "And we had a great time. It was really sweet of her to surprise me." I arch an eyebrow at him. "I didn't realize you were still such a foodie, though."

He opens his mouth to answer, but he's interrupted by the sharp honk of the car horn.

"Come on, Coop!" Chloe calls out the front window as she leans over Jake. "Get in. I have to sit on your lap. There aren't enough seats."

Cooper tears his gaze from me and climbs into the SUV. Chloe sits on his lap, and I get into the open passenger seat next to Jake. He blasts his favorite playlist as he pulls out, and everyone, including Asher, starts dancing in their seats and scream-singing along to "Getaway Car." I turn around, grinning hard at this group of friends I've somehow acquired. Chloe holds her phone to my mouth, urging me to sing. I laugh and join in, singing into my pretend microphone.

When my eyes snag on Cooper, he grins and winks at me, and I turn to absolute goo.

Ugh, I am down bad.

Chapter Twenty-Three

The following Saturday, I'm totally dragging as Sloane and I make our way back to the town square, where kids are screaming and laughing from inside the hay-bale maze we spent all night building. We were here until almost two o'clock in the morning setting up the children's activities and came back at seven o'clock to prepare for the Autumn Spice Sprint. Now, endless gray clouds smother the afternoon sun.

And I still haven't satisfied my harvest spice latte addiction.

A chilly autumn breeze nips at my skin and sends leaves swirling all around us, decorating the ground in shades of orange, yellow, and crimson. Their familiar earthy scent mixes with the scent of cider and doughnuts wafting from the vendor tents and food trucks on the lawn. I tuck my chin into my red scarf and pull my cardigan tighter around me.

After my conversation with Fern last weekend, it's hard to ignore the way autumn in Bramble Falls has somehow filled the New York–shaped hole in my heart.

"How are you so happy?" Sloane grumbles between yawns. "I'm too tired to be happy."

I narrow my eyes at her. "What makes you think I'm happy?"

"Uh, you're smiling like a weirdo?"

"Oh." *Huh.* "I don't know. Fall just feels different here for some reason. Don't get me wrong, I love autumn in New York—there are all kinds of great farmers' markets in the city, the fashion is top-notch, and Central Park is an absolute dream. But somehow out here it just feels, like, distilled or something. There's an incomparable coziness to it."

"Yes! That's what I've been trying to tell you!" she says, throwing her hands in the air. "Come for the apple picking and pumpkin carving, stay for the coziness."

I smile at her as we enter the town square. "Hey, I'm just here for the harvest spice lattes."

"And the boy who makes them . . ."

I stop breathing. "What? Who? Cooper?"

"Precisely," she says with a smirk.

The blood drains from my face. If Sloane can tell I like him, then everyone can tell. *He* can tell. And that's not a topic I want to broach right now. Not with him and not with my cousin.

"What are you talking about? Cooper and I are friends. A few weeks ago you were saying the same thing about Jake and me."

"It's rare, but I was wrong," she says. "I mean, Jake definitely likes you, but your heart beats for our little baker boy."

"Little baker boy?" I shake my head. "I literally have no idea what you're talking about."

"There's no point in denying it because I *know*." She grins at me. "If it helps, I think he might like you, too. He's always staring at you."

I sigh. "Just shut up. He is not."

I'd know because *I'm* always staring at *him*.

"Yeah, okay."

"Attention, Bramble Falls residents and visitors!" Aunt Naomi shouts into her megaphone from the gazebo. "Welcome to this weekend's events! The Autumn Spice Sprint will begin in five minutes! Participants should make their way to the gazebo now!"

"There's Asher," Sloane says, nodding at where he's waiting to race with her. "Come cheer for us."

I follow Sloane to the gazebo and stand off to the side, desperately wishing we'd left twenty minutes earlier so we had time to stop for a coffee before the race.

My phone buzzes in my pocket.

Pen Thief Jake: **Are you coming tonight?** 👻 🔦 😉

The Boots and Blankets Bonfire is tonight, and I've never been happier to not have to set up for something. I'd probably fall asleep lugging wood to the fire pit. The second this race is over, I'm napping to my heart's content—or at least until Sloane drags me out of bed to come back here.

Me: **Yeah, I'll be there**

I slip my phone back into my pocket.

I'm watching Sloane smile shyly at Asher as he tells her something when Aunt Naomi approaches me.

"Are you racing?" she asks. "We still have a spot left for one more team."

"Oh no." I shake my head. "Definitely not. I don't even have a partner. I—"

"Listen up!" Aunt Naomi shouts into her megaphone, nearly bursting my eardrums. "Do we have any single racers? Anyone who needs a partner?"

The crowd goes silent and glances around.

"Aunt Naomi, I really don't—"

"My niece needs a partner," she announces, ignoring me. "Do I have a volunteer?"

I lower my eyes and try to shield my face with my hand, avoiding the stares I'm undoubtedly receiving right now.

"Cooper Barnett! Get your butt over here!" Aunt Naomi shouts.

My head whips to the Caffeinated Cat tent. Cooper's gaze meets mine as the older woman he's working with says something to him. When he doesn't budge, she gives him a little shove. He shakes his head at her, takes off his apron, and makes his way out of the tent, garnering cheers from a few people in the crowd.

How mortifying.

"All right, Mitchell," he says with a smirk as he approaches me. "You ready to win this thing?"

"You really don't have to be my partner," I assure him.

He stretches each arm across his body like he's warming up for a triathlon instead of a silly town race. "Oh yeah? Well, you can be the one to tell your aunt that. And Betty Lynn, for that matter," he says, pointing his thumb back at the tent. "I'm pretty sure she was about to fire me if I didn't run this race with you."

"What's with these small-town people being in everyone else's business?" I mutter.

He furrows his brow. "These *small-town people* are just excited."

I flinch at the annoyance lacing his tone. "I didn't mean . . ." I sigh. "Sorry. You're right. I'm just tired." And Sloane's comment clearly got under my skin, putting me on edge.

"It's fine." He shakes out his muscles like he's shaking off my snide comment. "For the record, I don't mind racing. But I don't like to lose any more than you do."

He flashes me his lopsided grin, letting me know I'm forgiven—or at least that we're moving on from it. Hopefully the former.

"Well, perfect. I guess we just have to win this thing, then."

His dimple sinks into his cheek as I stand there with my hands on my hips, once again displaying a fake confidence.

Because, in reality, my athleticism rivals that of a newborn giraffe.

Aunt Naomi holds up her megaphone again and shouts at the crowd. "For this year's race, participants will run in teams of two and have to complete three tasks." She turns her attention to the teams. "Once you and your partner reach the bottom of the hay bale drop-off, you'll run to your first task, where you'll have to wrap each other in toilet paper from head to toe, with the exception of your face. When you're both mummified, you can sprint to my favorite task—apple bobbing. As a team, you must retrieve five apples. Each teammate must retrieve at least one. The final task is a three-legged race. You will stand next to your partner, tie your inside legs together with a rope, and run to the finish line. If your rope comes untied, you'll have to stop to retie it. The first team to smash their pumpkins at the end wins!"

The crowd whoops and applauds as we make our way to our starting markers—bales of hay stacked into climbable steps. I set my scarf in the leaves next to us, and the seven other teams step up to their bales. Sloane and Asher give each other a high five.

Cooper bumps my shoulder with his. "We've got this."

I nod, forcing myself to focus on the obstacle in front of me instead of his amber irises.

"On your marks, get set . . . ," Aunt Naomi shouts, "go!"

Cooper bolts forward, his long legs taking the wobbly, makeshift steps two at a time. When he reaches the top, he extends his hand toward me instead of jumping off the ledge. I take it, and he pulls me up the last two steps and onto the landing with him.

"Pick up the pace, Mitchell," he says, letting me go as he leaps off the edge and lands gracefully.

I follow him, tumbling into the leaves below with a thud.

"Are you okay?" he laughs.

"I'm fine."

On either side of me, teams sprint away with a chaotic sense of urgency, everyone screaming at their partner to move faster.

I definitely underestimated how seriously people take this race.

"Focus," Cooper says. "Eyes on the prize, not on the competition."

My eyes fall on him.

Which is, of course, not at all what he means.

I stand and brush the leaves off my butt. "Right. Let's go."

We sprint to the first task, my trusty Frye boots slipping on the grass.

"Do I need to carry you again?" Cooper shouts at me over his shoulder.

"Shush. I'm not that slow," I pant. He sprints ahead, leaving me trailing behind him. Because I actually *am* that slow.

By the time I get to the pile of toilet paper rolls, Cooper is already waiting on a knee for me.

"We're doomed," he says, unrolling the toilet paper around my feet.

"No, we're not. We're going to win."

"You're delusional." He makes his way up my leg with the toilet paper.

"No, I'm *optimistic*."

"Yeah, you keep telling yourself that, Mitchell," he says, pushing to his feet. "Now, put your hands up and spin. It'll be faster."

I twirl in circles while he holds the roll in place, unraveling the toilet paper around my waist and up my torso. A jolt of electricity zips through me when his hand skims my ribs, rousing every nerve ending and covering me in goose bumps. Then he grabs a new roll and starts on my arms, moving at an impressive speed. Standing this close, I take in his familiar scent—sugar, citrus, laundry detergent. It's the scent of horseback riding and of homecoming and of his bedspread. I want to bottle it up.

Once my arms are done, he continues to my head, bringing the toilet paper around my forehead and down the back of my head, tearing the end and tucking it into the wrapped portion on my neck while I secretly memorize him.

"You're up," he says. "Maybe you'll be better at this than you are at running."

"Ha-ha," I say, picking up a fresh roll of toilet paper. I bend down and start wrapping him up as quickly as I can—partly because I want to win this race but mostly to avoid looking at his very kissable face any longer.

The more I'm around him, the less I trust myself not to do something foolish.

Two teams to the right of us sprint to the next task. The rest are only trailing by seconds.

"Shit," I mutter.

"Just hurry," Cooper says.

I hold the end of the new roll to his waist, and he begins to spin. Within seconds, his torso is covered, and I'm wrapping his arms at lightning speed.

"Jeez, don't hurt yourself," Cooper says, laughing.

"We aren't losing this thing." I move to his second arm, then up his neck. Then, stepping closer, I push up on my tiptoes to reach around his head. Our eyes lock as I wrap the toilet paper over the thick hair I'm dying to run my fingers through. With our faces only inches apart, his gaze dips to my lips then back up, and my breath hitches.

It would be so easy to close the distance between us, to lean forward and press my lips to his.

"Are you done, or . . . ?" he rasps.

"Oh, um, yeah." I clear my throat and secure the end of the toilet paper before backing away from him.

With two teams ahead of us, we sprint to the large steel tubs full of floating red and green apples.

"I've never bobbed for apples before!" I shout to him.

"Are you serious?"

"Don't judge me!" I laugh.

We drop to our knees on opposite sides of our tub.

"Hands behind your back. You can only use your mouth," he says. "It's harder than it sounds."

"I think I can handle it," I tell him.

I lean forward, aiming for a green apple directly in front of me. I snap at it, sending it toward the bottom of the tub before it bobs back to the surface, away from me. I ignore Cooper's laughter across from me and go for another one, this time moving slower and more purposefully. Still, the apple dips beneath the water and escapes my bite.

Sitting upright with dripping hair, I fold my arms over my chest. "Are you going to help me, or do you think we can win by just sitting here looking pretty?"

"Aw, you think I'm pretty?"

"Oh my god," I mutter, splashing him. "Just help."

He chuckles before leaning into the tub. A couple seconds later, he pops up with water pouring from his hair and a bright green apple obscuring his giant grin.

I shake my head and go for another one. Only this time, determined to get the small red apple that seemed like an easy catch, my weight shifts, and I lean too far in, falling forward into the tub. My head is nearly fully submerged before I catch myself with one hand in the water.

I burst out of the tub, gasping from the shock of the cold, only to find Cooper laughing so hard he's practically wheezing.

I glare at him. "You think this is funny, huh?"

"I'm so sorry, but yeah, I really do."

"We're going to lose! Losing isn't funny!"

He dips his head and grabs another apple in his mouth like it's the easiest thing in the world.

"We're only going to lose if you can't get one," he says, placing the second apple with his other catch.

Then he leans down and gets another one. He sets it in the pile.

"I was born and raised in Bramble Falls. I can do this all day." He shrugs, a hint of amusement behind his arrogant smirk. "Let's go, city girl. Our team is depending on you."

I frown and pick out another floating apple. I bob for it, only to come up with nothing. Again.

The final team sprints away from the tubs and heads toward the ropes for the three-legged race. Most teams seem to be struggling with it, though, and I wonder if we might be able to catch up.

I nod at the teams ahead of us. "I think we still have a chance. What's the secret to getting an apple?"

"I wouldn't call it a secret, but you can't be all delicate and slow or else you just end up pushing it around. You have to dive right in."

I climb back onto my knees beside him, close enough that his body heat warms the side of me. Taking a deep breath, I dive quickly at the red apple I've homed in on.

And this time the apple crunches between my teeth.

"Hell yeah! You did it!" Cooper shouts.

It was pure luck, but whatever.

I can't stop smiling as I drop it into our pile. Cooper snags one last apple, gives me a high five, and we're off to the next task.

"Hurry!" I shout to Cooper once we get to our rope. He stands next to me and holds his hand out, but instead of giving him the rope, I attach our legs with a perfect bowline knot.

"Whoa," he says as I tug on it to test it out. "You've never bobbed for apples, but you can do *that*?"

"I was a Cub Scout."

His eyebrows shoot up. "Seriously? That's pretty badass."

"You can shower me with compliments later," I say, trying to ignore the flutter in my stomach. "Right now we have to go. Inside legs first." We step forward in unison. Inside legs. Outside legs. Inside legs.

Soon, with most teams falling or their knots coming untied, Sloane and Asher are the only people ahead of us.

"We're coming for you, cuz!" I shout to Sloane.

She glances back and screams through her giggles. "Faster, Asher!"

"Your legs are too short to go much faster!" I hear him say to her.

"Just shut up and run," she laughs.

They speed up, and Cooper glances at me. "Ready to sprint?"

I nod, and we pick up our pace.

Ahead of us, Sloane and Asher are stopped, retying their rope.

"We might actually be able to do this!" I say.

"Stay steady," Cooper says. "If you get too excited, you'll—"

Suddenly, I'm tripping over a fallen branch that was hidden beneath the leaves—and taking Cooper down with me. We land on the ground in a heap of tangled and twisted limbs, Cooper grunting as he falls on top of me.

His cheek is pressed to the side of my head when his whole body begins to shake with his contagious laughter. We lie there, chest to chest, cracking up until our stomachs hurt.

Teams pass us by, and finally Cooper leans to the side and hovers over me. His eyes are watery but bright, crinkling at the corners as he looks down at me with a smile that nearly knocks the wind out of me. My fingers itch to reach up and push his hair out of his eyes, to trace along his jaw, to touch the divot in his cheek.

A few yards away, Sloane and Asher throw their pumpkins on the finish line, pulling me from my trance. Sloane does cartwheels across the lawn while Asher celebrates with a goofy victory dance that seems to meld choreography from Beyoncé's "Single Ladies" video and Jenna Ortega's dance in *Wednesday*. Then the two best friends collide in a hug.

Cooper sighs. "Well, we lost."

"You don't say," I laugh. He maneuvers off me, and I immediately wish I could rewind time and press pause.

We sit, and I untie the knot, freeing our legs. When I look up, Cooper's eyes are traveling over my face, almost like he's studying me. When his gaze finally meets mine, my pulse feels like it's misfiring, and a flush creeps across my cheeks.

I dip my chin, suddenly shy, fighting the urge to hide from him. "What?"

He doesn't answer as he reaches his hand into my hair and pulls out a leaf. He tosses it on the ground. A rivulet of water trails down his cheek and drips from his chin as he swallows, his eyes never leaving mine. Then, slowly, he leans in. I hold my breath, wondering if I'm imagining it.

Wondering if I'm imagining what's about to happen.

"That was the closest race in years!" Sloane yells, running over to us holding a medal.

Cooper shoots upright and looks away, running his hand through his wet hair. "I should get back to the tent."

I open my mouth to say something, but I can't find words.

Sloane keeps talking, but my focus is on the boy walking away from me.

Because seriously, what the hell just happened?

Chapter Twenty-Four

Sloane and I spend the rest of the day catching up on sleep. When I wake up, I feel like a whole new person—with a fresh outlook on what transpired at the end of the race.

Obviously, I imagined Cooper leaning in.

I was simply sleep-deprived and physically exhausted, and I misread the situation.

Still, I spend extra time on my hair, curling it into loose waves that fall over my oversized Babaà sweater, and give myself a soft smoky eye. My lips shine with a pale pink gloss as I head downstairs.

"Damn. You realize it's going to be dark, right?" Sloane says. "No one's going to see how amazing you look."

"I spent the afternoon covered in dirt, leaves, and wet toilet paper. I needed to feel human again."

"Okay, heard. You ready, then?" Sloane grabs her jacket and we head out.

The night air has a bite. I stretch my sleeves down over my

hands, tucking my fingers into the soft fabric, and I gaze up at the sky. The clouds cleared while we were sleeping, and now every star in the universe feels visible from Saffron Lane tonight, sparkling and blinking like they're communicating in Morse code. The breathtaking black expanse is a canvas of shimmering lights.

This flawless sky is one thing I'll miss once I'm back in New York City.

"So, it seemed like you and Cooper had fun today," Sloane says, giving me a sidelong glance.

"What about it, Sloane?"

"I don't know. You say you're just friends, but . . ."

"But what? I'm moving back to New York soon," I remind her. "Not to mention, there's something clearly going on between him and Chloe."

Sloane scoffs. "Please. If he were into Chloe, I think he would have made a move by now. She's firmly in the friend zone."

"Well, so am I. And *barely*! I just made it out of the acquaintance zone. A few weeks ago, Cooper couldn't stand to be in the same room as me. I barely know him, or at least who he is *now*."

"You've spent more time with Cooper this past month than I have in the last two years combined! You know him." Sloane sighs. "But I will accept your crappy excuses and drop it for tonight."

"Thank you."

"But tomorrow is fair game," she says.

I roll my eyes, elbowing her gently in the side, and she laughs.

When we reach downtown, my mouth gapes. In just a few hours, the volunteers have transformed the square into a wonderland. The gazebo is wrapped in fairy lights, and a song from

Folklore pours from giant speakers inside. Strings of globe lights drape from tree to tree. A giant bonfire is already ablaze, with log benches and folding chairs placed around it. Lanterns hang from posts in the ground, illuminating a path to where tables of food and drinks are set up, and hollowed-out pumpkins filled with candles are scattered throughout the leaf-covered lawn, adding to the fall vibe.

The Boots and Blankets Bonfire is absolutely enchanting.

After meeting Asher by the tables of food and grabbing cups of hot mulled cider, the three of us make our way to the bonfire. We squish together on a log bench, and I sip my drink while Sloane talks about the upcoming school play.

I'm completely zoned out when, across the fire, Cooper walks over with Slug and some guys from our calculus class, his mussed hair, black hoodie, and gray sweatpants glowing orange in the firelight. He throws his head back, laughing at a joke his friend tells, and I can't tear my eyes away from him.

Cooper puts his hood up and stares into the fire, flames dancing in his eyes behind the black-framed glasses that drive me wild. He grins, and I study the curve of his upper lip and the way his one canine slightly overlaps the tooth next to it. I notice the scar on his left eyebrow, and I take in the way his dimple creates a crater when he bites his bottom lip.

Admiring Cooper Barnett might be my favorite Bramble Falls activity.

As if he can sense me watching him, Cooper's gaze meets mine. The fire crackles and pops between us, turning wood to ash, and all I can think is, *Maybe he did lean in. . . .*

"What do you think?" Sloane says to my right. I drag my eyes from Cooper and settle them on my cousin.

"Sorry. About what?"

"We're going to walk around and see who's here. You want to come?" she repeats.

"No, that's okay. It's freezing out here. I'm going to stay by the fire for a while."

Asher and Sloane slink off toward the gazebo, leaving me alone on the bench.

I sneak a glance across the fire, but Cooper is gone.

Friction warms my hands as I rub them together, and my breath creates a puff of white in the cold air. A song from *Fearless* comes on, and a bunch of girls cheer.

It seems a Swiftie was in charge of the playlist—another thing Bramble Falls got right tonight.

I'm humming along when someone plops down next to me.

"Hey, partner," Cooper says, setting a plate of treats on the bench to his left. He pulls my scarf from his front hoodie pocket. "You left this here earlier." He shifts his body so he's facing me and gingerly wraps it around my neck. My breath catches as his fingers graze my collarbone.

"Thanks," I breathe, meeting his amber eyes. I swallow and look away. *Pull yourself together, Ellis.* "You've just been carrying it around all day?"

He shrugs and faces the fire again. "Figured I'd see you at some point. We always seem to be in the same place." He grabs the plate next to him. "I also brought you treats."

"Oh, thanks." I take the plate, intensely aware of Cooper's

thigh and shoulder pressed to mine, despite him having plenty of space on the other end of the bench.

"So, what do you think of all this?" he asks, gesturing widely around us.

"It's beautiful. And *atmospheric* . . . but also freezing."

"I know, right?" He leans into me ever so slightly, warming my side with his radiating body heat. When his pinkie accidentally brushes mine, every one of my nerve endings buzzes. "I can't believe I forgot my blanket."

A soft breeze rustles the trees and feeds the fire. I try to tuck my head into my scarf.

"You want my hoodie?" Cooper asks.

"You'd freeze to death without it. I'll be okay but thank you."

"You gonna eat that?" He nods at the plate he handed to me. It's full of various desserts—macarons, cookies, brownies, scones, and cupcakes.

"Yeah, but I can share. This is a lot," I say, holding the plate in front of him.

"No, I'm good. Thanks."

I grab an orange cookie with chunks of Oreos sticking out of it.

"I haven't tried this kind yet," I say.

"I know. It's my favorite," Cooper says. "Oreo Creamsicle."

I'm not sure if knowing it's Cooper's favorite makes it taste even better, but I'm almost speechless when I take my first bite.

"Oh my god," I say through a mouthful of the dessert. "Cooper, this is the best thing I've ever eaten." I take another bite, the sweet, velvety dough practically melting on my tongue.

"The sexiest food ever?" He laughs.

"Yes, exactly!"

He nods, his dimple sinking into his cheek as he smiles shyly at me. "I baked it."

I stop chewing. "What?"

"All the cookies—well, all the pastries—at the Caffeinated Cat. I bake them."

I stare at him. Then at the cookie in my hand. Then back at him. "Are you serious?"

He laughs. "You shouldn't be so surprised. I'm pretty sure you knew me at my nerdiest stage when all I talked about was baking."

"Well, yeah, that's true," I say. He really was obsessed. "But baking as a hobby is different than baking for actual customers!"

I think back on this past month—all the times I ordered a cookie from him at the shop, or all the times he's brought me one, or the times I've gushed about them in front of him.

"Why haven't you mentioned it before now?" I ask.

"I guess I liked seeing your candid reactions. I liked that someone liked them so much without knowing I made them." He shrugs one shoulder. "And I liked knowing you weren't saying it just to be nice."

"Trust me, no one is giving you compliments on these cookies just to be nice."

Cooper blushes in the firelight. "Thanks."

"This explains so much." Like him being in awe of Fern. And Sloane calling him *little baker boy*. "I can't believe Sloane never told me. What a brat."

He laughs. "She probably assumed you knew. Everyone here knows. I can't believe you've gone this long without figuring it out."

"Apparently, I'm not that observant." I turn to him. "It's really cool you continued baking as you got older," I say, wondering what it'd be like to take a passion seriously enough to become as good as Cooper is at baking.

To have the time to dedicate to becoming that good.

"I love it," he says, simply. "My plan is to hopefully go to ICE after high school."

I stare at him. ". . . ICE?"

"Yeah, the Institute of Culinary Education. You know, in New York City. I'd love to open my own bakery one day."

"Oh. Wow." A thousand thoughts filter through my mind, the first being: *Cooper is planning on moving to New York City—my city.* And second: "So, you're planning on baking, like, as a career . . . ?"

"Yeah . . . ?" He tilts his head. "You say that like it's a bad thing."

"No. Baking just seems more like a hobby, you know? Not a realistic career path."

"Tell that to Baked by Melissa," he says, turning away from me and staring back at the fire.

"Well, sure, of course *some* people are going to get lucky. But there's no guarantee that you'll be one of the few to succeed. Did you know that most small businesses fail within their first five years?"

He shakes his head and fixes his eyes on me again. "Look, all I know is I'm not going to spend the rest of my life doing something I'm not passionate about. Not when doing something I love is an option. Nothing is guaranteed in any career, so I might as well be chasing my dreams."

I nod slowly, trying to wrap my head around how someone can be so laid-back about their future, how someone can just trust that everything will be fine—even when their dreams aren't the most practical.

How can Cooper have no fear of failure?

"Anyway," he says, standing, "have fun tonight. I'm sure I'll see you around."

"Wait!" Without thinking, I grab his hand. He looks at my fingers wrapped around his, then raises his eyes to mine. "I'm sorry. I didn't mean to upset you. What you do with your future is none of my business."

"I'm not upset." He squeezes my hand and lets go, offering me a small smile that doesn't meet his eyes.

He's clearly lying, and as I watch him walk back over to his friends, a cold, throbbing ache fills my chest.

Wow, way to be an asshole and ruin everything, Ellis.

I set my plate down next to me, my appetite now gone. Across the fire, Chloe joins Cooper. She says something to him, and he laughs. She rests her head on his shoulder.

Ugh. I cannot be here anymore.

I take out my phone and text Sloane to let her know I'm going home. As I stand, Cooper's eyes swing to me. I put my head down and throw my trash away.

After a cold walk home alone, I head up to the attic and change into my pajamas. I wipe off my makeup and climb into bed, where I scroll through my phone for the next thirty minutes, liking everyone's photos from the bonfire and my old friends' photos of their parties in New York.

But my mind is distracted.

I'm contemplating texting Cooper another apology when my phone buzzes in my hands, and his name appears on the screen.

Summer Cooper: **You awake?**

Me: **Yes.**

Summer Cooper: **Come outside.**

I bolt upright. Does that mean he's here?!

Me: **Now???**

Summer Cooper: **Yeah**

I groan, looking down at my outfit. My oversized sweatshirt and flannel pants are probably the least attractive clothes I own, but I don't have time to change if he's waiting outside.

Downstairs, I throw on a pair of boots and the men's Barbour jacket I thrifted a few years ago, and I head outside into the cold, ready for him to tell me what a massive jerk I am. Ready to hear that he doesn't want to talk to me ever again. Ready to apologize again for being, well, *my dad* earlier.

Ready to accept the end of a promising friendship.

Cooper's leaning against the lamppost with his arms crossed over his chest, the light from overhead accentuating the shadowed angles of his face. I close the door behind me, and he pushes off the post and meets me on the sidewalk.

"Hey," I say, my voice barely a whisper. I kick at a lone red maple leaf, staring at its long stem instead of the boy in front of me. "I didn't think you'd talk to me again. After what I said, I mean."

Silence lingers for a moment before he exhales and says, "You were right. I was upset."

I finally look up, my stomach plummeting with his admission. "I know. I'm so sorry. I—"

Cooper holds up his hand. "I'm not done." I press my lips together and nod. He chews the inside of his cheek before continuing. "I was upset, *but* I thought about it, and I don't think this is about me at all."

"What do you mean?"

"I . . . I think you've grown up in a world where the only important things are money and status, and now, you have this warped sense of what the future should look like—when, in reality, it can look however you *want* it to look. But I don't think you've figured that out yet." My brow furrows, and he quickly adds, "And I don't mean that as a dig. I think you're brilliant and driven, and you can do literally *anything* you want to do, Ellis. But *you* don't seem to believe it." He shrugs. "So, no, I'm not upset anymore. I'm not going to stop being friends with you. Instead," he says with a smirk, "I'm just going to have to prove to you that I can be one of the few who succeed and that the future is whatever you make it. That you just have to chase after the things you want."

I stare at him. A flurry of relief, disbelief, and *awe* swirls inside me.

I don't agree with him—I don't think the future can look however a person wants it to look just by having drive and passion, at least not when the future they envision involves unrealistic expectations and lofty, impractical dreams. He makes it sound as simple as plucking a career from a tree and declaring it yours.

But the world doesn't work that way.

Sure, it's about drive and perseverance, but it's also about luck and connections and setting yourself up for success by being realistic.

Still, he's not upset with me, and that's more than I could have asked for tonight. And moving forward, I can be supportive of his dream-chasing regardless of what I think about it.

"You can speak now," he says with a dimpled grin, sliding his hands into his hoodie pocket.

"Okay. Well, who knows, maybe you *will* prove me wrong. You do bake a killer cookie."

He laughs and shakes his head. "Thank you."

"I'm still really sorry," I tell him.

"I know. And I forgive you."

"Thank you. So, is that why you walked here? To tell me you're not upset with me?"

"No, actually," he says. "I've come to take you to the next event."

I draw my eyebrows together. "What do you mean? There's no other event on the fridge calendar."

His lips tilt upward into a mischievous smile. "This is an unsanctioned annual event. You won't find it on your aunt's Bramble Falls calendar."

"Oh."

"So, are you in?" he asks, his eager eyes lighting up and drawing me in.

Taylor Swift's voice rides the breeze from the direction of the bonfire two blocks away.

And I never saw you coming. . . .

I exhale. *Me neither, Taylor. Me neither.*

"Okay," I say. "But I have to go change my clothes."

"No, you don't."

"Unless we're going to hang out in a dumpster, yes I do."

His smile widens, turning my insides to mush. Then he grabs my hand in his, and I forget to breathe as my skin tingles against his. Suddenly, I don't care what I'm wearing.

"You look perfect. Now let's go." He pulls me down the sidewalk, back toward town.

And even though I'm following without a fight, he doesn't let go.

Chapter Twenty-Five

"Why are we here?" I ask Cooper as we climb out of his car at Bramble Falls High.

"You'll see." He leads me around the side of the school, where colorful lights move about in the distance and laughter floats along the cold breeze. As we step into the dark woods behind the school, I cling to Cooper's forearm, my grip on him tightening as the trees grow thicker and the woods grow darker. I'm not generally afraid of the dark, but it's creepy out here.

Then we enter a clearing, where a swarm of seniors wearing glow sticks around their necks and wrists are hanging out.

"Uh, what is this?" I ask.

"Just a friendly game of glow-stick Ghost in the Graveyard," Cooper says. "The senior class does it every year after the bonfire. It's tradition."

I shake my head. *This* is what Jake meant when he asked if I was coming tonight.

I find him in the crowd, talking with some redheaded girl I've seen around school. When he sees me, he grins and waves.

Cooper leads me over to a box full of glow sticks, and after cracking two pink bracelets and a green necklace, he puts them on me, keeping his eyes fixed on the light-up jewelry. He cracks a yellow necklace and puts it on himself, then hands me a neon-blue bracelet to put on him. I'm not even sure he notices when his finger sweeps over the inside of my wrist, but my heart stutters at the subtle contact. I stick the end of the glow stick into the plastic connector piece and hope he doesn't notice how being this close to him makes my hands tremble.

What is wrong with me?

"Okay, everyone!" our senior class president, Kayla McIntire, shouts over everyone. Cooper hands me a mini flash-light from another box, and the crowd grows silent as we all give Kayla our attention. "Welcome to the tenth annual senior-class Ghost in the Graveyard night! In just a minute I will draw a name from this hat," she says, pointing to a literal top hat being held by our class treasurer. "Every single senior's name is in it. If I draw someone who isn't here, we'll go to the next per-son. If your name is drawn, you're the ghost, which means your job is to hide from everyone else. The boundaries have been marked—if you come to yellow caution tape, do not cross it, or you'll be out of bounds. Those not chosen as the ghost will stay here at home base and count, one o'clock, two o'clock, and so on until midnight. At that point you'll all spread out and try to find the ghost.

"If you see the ghost, you shout, 'Ghost in the graveyard!' Then everyone has to run back here before getting tagged by the ghost.

As you can see," she says, pointing to the trees lining the clearing, "home base is clearly marked with glow sticks around the tree trunks so you can find it. If anyone is tagged, they become the new ghost. Anyone have any questions?"

Everyone looks around at one another, but no questions are asked.

"Okay, then. Let's do this," Kayla says.

Anticipation swells among the crowd as she sticks her hand into the hat and mixes the names around. She snatches one up and unfolds the small piece of paper.

"Cooper Barnett!" she reads. "You here, Coop?"

He turns to me. "You going to be okay on your own?"

"Yeah, of course." I nod at Jake across the circle of seniors. "I can always just hang with Jake."

He glances at his friend. "Right." Then he puts his hand up. "I'm here," he announces. Some people whoop and whisper excitedly.

"Come on up!" Kayla says, dropping the piece of paper back into the hat.

Before heading over to Kayla, he leans in close, his breath tickling my ear. "I know how much you hate to lose, so let's see if you can find me before anyone else."

Then he's off to take on his title as Ghost.

"Challenge accepted," I call after him.

He grins at me over his shoulder. "Good luck."

Leaving his glow sticks behind, Cooper makes his way deeper into the woods while I hang back with my classmates and count to midnight. I decide not to stay with Jake because I actually want to find Cooper, and I know Jake will be loud and make everything a joke.

Because he really is like an excitable puppy.

But as soon as we disperse, I'm having regrets. A twig snaps to my right. I swing my flashlight in the direction of the sound just as something makes a swooshing noise to my left. These woods are terrifying. How am I supposed to know if the sounds I'm hearing are seniors or animals?

As I wander aimlessly, wondering if I'll be able to find my way back to home base despite it being marked with glow sticks, I consider whether Cooper would have any sort of strategy right now. He definitely wouldn't have climbed a tree because of his fear of heights. But if he's on the ground, where would he think no one would look?

I scan the woods. Where would I go if I were him?

I turn left, trekking back to the tree line, where yellow caution tape runs along the perimeter. For the next ten minutes, I hike through the silence, searching for big piles of leaves that could be a camouflaged body or a hollowed-out tree he could hide in if he were brave enough. Completely alone in the dark, I fight the urge to be loud in order to scare off any creatures of the night.

Since the goal is to spot the ghost before he can tag me, hopefully I can get eyes on Cooper before he sees m—

I freeze as somebody dashes across the path in front of me. Somebody not wearing glow sticks. Beneath the moonlit sky, in the space between scraggly bare branches, I make out the angles of his face. An outline ingrained in my brain.

"Ghost in the graveyard!" I call as loudly as I can just before Cooper lunges at me. I scream and turn to run. I make it three steps before his strong arm wraps around my waist, pulling me close and lifting me off the ground as he spins.

I laugh, and he sets me down in front of a tree. "How'd you find me so fast, cheater?"

I lift my chin as I face him. "I didn't cheat. But I'm not revealing my secrets."

He steps closer. "There isn't a single other person around. I need to know how you thought to come over here," he says, gesturing at where we're standing—where the front and side perimeter tape meet. "Did you sneak away from the group and follow me when you were supposed to be counting?"

"That would be cheating."

"Oh, I know," he says.

"Then you know I didn't." I cross my arms. He stares at me, waiting, and I sigh. "With such a vast area for you to hide in, it seemed logical that most people would fan out in front of home base. I thought if *I* were hiding, I'd stay along the edge because it seems like the least likely place for people to look. With the boundary line being right here, it gives people less space to cover and therefore, a slimmer chance of finding someone."

"Smart," Cooper says, impressed.

"A little bit of logic. A lot of luck." I shrug. "Plus, most people had their flashlights pointed up into the trees, but I knew you wouldn't be in one because you're afraid of heights."

"I'm not—"

"Yes, you are," I say, cutting him off. "You refused to sit on

Aunt Naomi's roof to watch fireworks with me on the Fourth of July that summer."

He steps closer and smiles. "You couldn't have just forgotten that little detail, huh?"

"Never." I try to smile. I try to turn away and head back to home base. It's the smart thing to do. But he's *so* close, looking at me with those eyes that steal the air from my lungs, and suddenly I can't put one foot in front of the other. I can't fathom walking away even if I could.

And concealed in the darkness of the woods, with his tousled hair blowing softly in the breeze, I can't imagine not saying exactly what I'm thinking in this moment.

"I remember *all* your details, Cooper Barnett," I whisper. "They're my favorite thing to memorize."

Cooper's eyes widen. I step toward him, and his sharp intake of breath seems to echo through the silence.

The air between us is thick and heavy and charged.

"Earlier, at the end of the race," I say nervously, "were you . . . were you going to kiss me?"

In the distance, someone calls Cooper's name. Everyone's waiting on him—on us—but I started this, and I need to know how it ends.

His voice is raspy and quiet when he replies. "I shouldn't . . . It doesn't matter."

"Maybe it does," I say. "Tell me."

"But Jake . . ." He shakes his head. "I can't do this."

"What about him?" I ask, confused.

"He likes you."

"Okay, but I don't like *him*."

"You haven't made that particularly clear," he says.

"Actually, I have. I pretty explicitly told him we're just friends."

He frowns. "Well, he's still holding on to hope."

A beat of silence passes between us.

"Just tell me, Coop," I whisper.

He sighs and throws his hood up, as if he's trying to hide from me. "All right, fine. Maybe I was thinking about kissing you. But I shouldn't have been."

I open my mouth, then close it, unsure how to respond even though I asked for the answer. He looks as if he's organizing his thoughts before he looks at the ground and continues.

"When I told you I was hurt because you stopped talking to me after you went back to New York, that was the truth. But it wasn't that simple." He presses his lips together, like he's warring with himself over saying more, and my pulse quickens. "I know we were young, but I fell for you that summer." His eyes raise to mine. "You were the first and only girl who's ever broken my heart."

The woods suddenly seem darker, quieter. "What?" I breathe.

"I fell for this gorgeous, funny, laid-back girl who always wanted to try new things, and you made me feel like I could do anything. *Be* anything. But also like I didn't *need* to be anything other than who I was. I always felt like the best version of myself when I was around you. And then you were gone, and I was devastated."

"Cooper . . ."

"Do you remember the day you sat across from me in my

bedroom and suggested we be each other's first kiss?"

"Of course." I'd felt like I was the only girl in my school who hadn't been kissed. I'd wanted to be able to go home and not have to lie about it anymore.

"You said you just wanted to see what kissing was like before going to high school, what all the fuss was about. I knew it didn't mean anything to you. But I also already knew I'd never feel the same way about any other girl, so that kiss meant *everything* to me." He draws his eyebrows together. "Even after you stopped responding to my texts, I thought if I just waited until you came back the next summer, things would go back to how they were. We'd spend another summer together, and then I'd tell you how I felt and hope like hell you finally felt it too."

"But I never came back," I whisper.

He nods. "Until now. And you're different, but you're still the girl I knew in a lot of ways. Too many ways, if I'm being honest."

I step forward until we're toe to toe. Slowly, hesitantly, my hand reaches out to trace the details of his face, skimming along his jawline, my thumb sweeping over his cheek where his dimple is hiding. His eyes stay trained on mine as I press up on my toes, push his hood off, and let my fingers get lost in the hair they've been longing to touch.

"I got over you, Ellis," he says, his voice low.

"Good. I wouldn't have wanted you to be heartbroken forever," I tell him. I lean in until our noses touch, the air between us shared, my heart thrashing like waves in a storm. Cooper's breath hitches. "But are you *still* over me?" I maneuver my lips closer, sliding both hands around his neck as I press my body closer to his.

He lets out a groan and backs away, the sudden loss of his heat leaving me cold, stunned, and baffled. "I'm not going to kiss you."

"Oh."

"Not because I don't want to," he clarifies. A humorless laugh escapes him. "I've wanted to kiss you again ever since the first time."

"But . . . ?"

"But it's already going to be hard enough when you leave next month," he says. His muscles are rigid and resolute, and I'd drop the subject if he said he didn't like me back. If he weren't interested. If I were reading his signals all wrong.

But he's just scared and trying to protect his heart. And I have no plans to break it again.

"We can figure it out." I take a step toward him, closing the distance between us. "I'm not going to ghost you again."

In the pink glow of my necklace, Cooper's conflicted eyes dart between mine. Finally he cups my cheek in his soft hand. He leans in slowly, and I close my eyes as he presses his lips to mine. The kiss is tentative, full of nerves and hesitance. But when I part my lips in invitation, Cooper groans, turning hungry and insistent, like he's waited for this moment his whole life.

His fingers slide into my hair, and he walks us backward until I'm pinned between him and a tree. When my tongue meets his, Cooper's whole body sinks into mine, all of his solid muscles pressed against my soft curves, leaving both of us breathless—but who needs to breathe when a kiss is this magical? His fingers trail over the angles of my face, like he's trying to memorize me the way I've already memorized him. They travel under my coat, then under my sweatshirt, and his cold fingers settle on my waist. A small sound escapes me at the feel of his skin on mine, and I try to pull him closer, as if that's even possible.

Eventually the kiss turns measured, deliberate, and gentle again. I could die happy here in these woods with this perfect boy.

He pulls away and traces my bottom lip with his thumb.

"That was, um . . ." He trails off.

"We should do it again sometime," I say with a laugh.

But Cooper squeezes his eyes closed, looking almost *tormented.*

"What's wrong?" I take his hand.

"I shouldn't have told you all that," he says. "And I definitely shouldn't have kissed you."

"What?"

He shakes his head. "It's just so hard to be around you and pretend I'm still over you. I'm sorry."

I knit my brow. "What are you saying, Cooper?"

"I'm saying that this"—he gestures between us—"can't happen. *We* can't happen."

"No." My stomach knots. "Why?"

"Besides the fact that I don't want to hurt my friend?" he says. "I don't trust you."

"What?"

"You're leaving soon, Ellis." He focuses on the dark, leaf-littered ground. "I don't believe you won't move on once you're gone again. Out of sight, out of mind, just like last time."

"I would never do that again. I swear," I tell him, my chest tightening. He's slipping away. I'm losing him again, right after getting a taste of what things could be like.

Cooper takes a step backward, pulling his hand from mine.

"Can we just . . . forget this happened?"

There's no way I can forget this happened. Kissing Cooper will be forever ingrained in my mind. An unshakable core memory I will dream about. It's the kiss I'll measure every other one against.

But if he doesn't want to be with me, what am I supposed to do? I can't make him want me.

"Please, Ellis," he rasps.

I pinch my eyebrows together, fighting off the urge to cry and instead letting my hurt fuel my anger. "Fine. Then stop being so damn nice to me."

"You want me to be mean to you?" he asks, confused.

"I want you to stop bringing me cookies and lattes. I want you to stop saving me when I fall off ladders or taking horseback rides with me. I want you to stop pulling all-nighters just to help me. And I want you to stop making me bacon!"

He tries not to smile, but he can't suppress it. "No bacon. Noted."

"I'm serious, Cooper. If you're saying this isn't happening, then fine, I'll respect that. But I want you to stop making me fall for you."

His smile fades. "Okay. Fair."

"Okay." I nod. "Then consider it forgotten."

He huffs out a breath. My heart is crumbling, and he's *relieved*.

I blink back tears as a voice to our left calls for Cooper.

"Sounds like they've sent out a search party for us," he says.

"Yeah. I guess we better get back."

I brush past him, hoping the memory of his lips on mine somehow gets lost in these dark woods.

Chapter Twenty-Six

"Sloane, wake up." My cousin grumbles as I shake her.

Her eyelids flutter open. "What? What time is it?"

"Three a.m."

I tried to keep playing the game. I tried to pretend like nothing happened. But that proved to be impossible, and ultimately I trekked the two miles back home in the freezing cold after everyone was searching for the ghost after me.

"Three a.m.? Go away, you psycho," she says, throwing a pillow over her head.

"I need you," I tell her, trying to keep my voice from breaking the way my heart is.

She bolts upright, making me jump as she throws the pillow off her face and swings her legs over the bed, suddenly wide awake. "Let's go."

"Um, what? Where?"

"I googled how to get rid of a body years ago, specifically for this occasion. I've got you, girl. No questions asked."

Despite my shitstorm of a night, a deep laugh unexpectedly rumbles out of me. “Shut up.”

“I’m not kidding. I’ve got three pretty legit ways and two questionable ones. I’m willing to try any of them.” She worries her lip. “One way might require more Mountain Dew than we have on hand, though.”

I lay my head on her shoulder, unable to stop the embarrassing snort-laugh that escapes. “I don’t need to get rid of a body. Well, not yet, anyway.”

“Okay . . . Then why are you waking me up at this hour? What do you need?”

I lift my head and look at her. “Can I sleep in here?”

“Um, okay?” She draws her eyebrows together as she scoots back into bed and pulls the comforter over her.

I crawl in next to her. “Sorry. I just don’t really want to be alone right now.”

“You gonna to tell me what’s wrong?”

My eyes follow a crack in the ceiling until it dead-ends into the wall. “You were right.”

“Of course I was.” She pauses. “But about what?”

“About Cooper.” I swallow. “About me liking Cooper.”

“I knew it! But why’s that bad?” She gasps. “Wait. Did something happen?”

“You could say that.” I turn my head to face her. “We kissed.”

She screams, and I slap my hand over her mouth. “You’re going to wake up our moms.”

“Sorry,” she whispers. “But also, oh my god!” She throws her pillow over her face and squeals into it. “Okay,” she says, putting it back under her head, "I'm ready. How was it?"

I don't have to think about the answer. "Perfect."

"So what's the problem? Or did you just wake me up to tell me about it? Because I am here for it. Spill."

"He told me to forget it happened."

"*What?*" She sits up. "Why?"

I tell her about his Jake concerns. And, as she settles in next to me again, I explain his reluctance to let me break his heart a second time.

"He has a point," I say. "I *am* leaving soon—it's been part of why I was trying to talk myself out of liking him. But he's going to school in the city next year. In less than a year, we'll be living in the same place again. This doesn't have to be some month-long fling where everyone ends up hurt."

"Is that what you want? Something serious and long-term with him?"

"I . . . think so." The reality of that slams into me like a tsunami. He's the exception to the rule. I lay my head on Sloane's shoulder. "I really like him."

"It sounds like he really likes you, too."

"Maybe, but it doesn't matter." I sigh. "He doesn't want to be with me."

"I'm sorry." She leans her head against mine. "But there's still time—you don't leave for another month. Maybe he'll change his mind."

"Yeah," I say. "Maybe."

But I know he won't.

Sloane takes my hand beneath the blanket and holds it. "It's his loss, cuz."

I close my eyes and try to tell myself she's right.

But if that's the case, then why do I feel like I'm the one who lost tonight?

I don't know how to face him.

That's all I can think as I pull up my Khaite jeans, tug my beige Rowe turtleneck sweater over my head, and slip into my Stuart Weitzman boots.

Nothing feels worse than knowing I screwed up our friendship, too.

Things will *never* be what they were before last night.

I stand in front of the mirror. Immaculate makeup and flawless, wavy hair make me look like I'm fine. Great, even. Like I didn't lose a second of sleep over what happened—over what I'll never get back.

I straighten my shoulders and take a deep breath. "You *are* fine, Ellis," I say. "You've got this."

According to Sloane, every year Bramble Falls sells hollow mini plastic pumpkins in the town square. Those planning to ask someone to the Pumpkin Prom buy one and typically put a note inside with their proposal. The following two weeks are full of people finding mini pumpkins on their stoops, in their mailboxes, on their desks at work or school, or in their cars. The costumed dance is a way for everyone in Bramble Falls to have another prom night.

Yet another opportunity for me to go to a dance without Cooper. *Yay.*

Sloane and I walk toward town square, where our table is already set up. We volunteered weeks ago to sell the mini pumpkins, even though now it's the *last* thing I want to do today.

"You look good," she says, eyeing me.

"That's the idea."

"What? Look good so he has regrets?"

"No. Look good in hopes that I feel better," I say as we approach the Caffeinated Cat.

"Is it working?" she asks.

"Maybe a little." We stop in front of the cat-café window. "But not enough that I can walk in there. Can you get my drink for me?" Cooper is scheduled to work until noon.

Not that I've memorized his work schedule.

"I got you," she says.

"Thanks."

Sloane heads in, and just before I head over to the table, my eyes betray me and sneak a look through the window, where Cooper grins at Sloane before glancing behind her—like maybe he's looking for someone. Then his eyes bounce to the window, directly at me.

I book it out of there, crossing the street with our money box in hand, and take a seat at our table. Five minutes later, Sloane joins me, setting my harvest spice latte in front of me.

"He's also acting fine," she says with a sigh.

"He probably *is* fine," I tell her.

"I highly doubt it, based on what you told me." I slide the cash box over to her and she unlocks it as our first customer approaches the table. I take a sip of my drink, keeping my eyes trained on the black-haired man in front of me rather than on the building across the street.

"Do you think I can call out of school for the next few weeks until I leave?" I ask Sloane after the guy is gone. "I could say I have mono."

"Ellis, I love you, but you're not altering your life for a boy. You're going to go to school. You're going to get your straight As and continue being teacher's pet, and then you're going to go out with Jake."

I spit out my coffee. "I'm sorry, what?"

"Show Coop you're not hung up on him. Maybe you'll have a chance at being friends again."

"Like, I get your logic but also, no." I shake my head. "It'll seem like I'm trying to make him jealous."

She shrugs. "Making him jealous might be a perk, I guess."

"I'm not trying to play games. I just want to move on from this."

"Then do it with Jake."

I sigh. My cousin just doesn't get it. Cooper is the only exception. I don't want or need a guy to fawn over. If he doesn't want to be with me, then I just want to survive the next few weeks here and get home as unscathed as possible.

We spend the next three hours selling dozens of pumpkins. If I've learned one thing being in Bramble Falls, it's that the people here take their fall events seriously. And this one is no exception. Sloane says it's one of the most anticipated events of the year, and as the day goes on, there's no denying it. Everyone's excitement is palpable.

We're so busy taking money, passing out pumpkins, and chatting with people, that I don't notice when noon rolls around.

I don't notice when Cooper gets into the line.

Our eyes collide when he steps up to the table. Neither of us says anything. What is there to say?

Sloane clears her throat. "Do you need a pumpkin?"

He swings his eyes to her, and he holds out his money. "Yeah. Thanks."

My heart feels like it's being shredded as I hand him a pumpkin. He takes it, and nausea rolls through me when his fingers graze mine.

But I'm my dad's daughter. So I give him a convincingly genuine smile. "I hope you and Chloe have a fantastic time at the prom."

His eyebrows shoot up. "I—"

"Be on your way now, Coop," Sloane says, shooing him away with her hands. "Next!"

He glances at her, probably figuring out that she knows about last night, and nods.

I'm giving him what he asked for. Even if it's killing me, I'm pretending last night didn't happen. The least he can do is give me space.

He shoots me one last unreadable look and leaves, taking his future Pumpkin Prom proposal with him.

Chapter Twenty-Seven

Over the next week, I keep my head down at school. When Jake texts me at lunch, asking where I am, I tell him I'm meeting with my guidance counselor about college stuff or tutoring freshmen who have study hall during that time. Really, I skip eating and do homework in the library.

I do not once look in Cooper's direction.

When he asked me to forget the kiss happened, I'm sure he meant he still wanted to be friends. But I don't know *how*. I don't want to axe him from my life, but things are different now, no matter how much he wants to pretend like they're not.

It's easier to avoid him until I go back to the city.

But Jake is nothing if not persistent, and by Friday—after four days of incessant begging and complaining—I'm back at our lunch table.

"You're coming tonight, right?" he asks on Friday as he slides into the seat next to me with his food. Cooper eases onto the bench across from us, sitting next to Slug.

"To the drive-in movies?" I shrug. "Maybe. I haven't been to one since . . ." My eyes meet Cooper's, and I wonder if he's also remembering *Free Willy*. "Well, since middle school."

"We always put a mattress in the bed of Cooper's truck and load it up with blankets and pillows. It's a good time," Jake says, throwing his arm over my shoulder. "Think of it as more time to hang out with your favorite person."

I glance at Cooper. He looks at his tray and says, "You should come."

"Okay," I say because I don't have a good excuse not to. At least not without screaming from the rooftops that it'll be too hard to sit there with Cooper, knowing what it's like to kiss him and knowing it won't happen again.

Jake grins at me. "Perfect. We'll swing by and pick you up then."

At the end of the day, Sloane meets me at my locker instead of the flagpole out front, excited to tell me that she and Asher are going to the Pumpkin Prom together. "As friends, of course," she's sure to add.

I grin at her, genuinely thrilled to see her happy, even if I'm a miserable sack of potatoes. But then I spot Cooper walking down the hall behind her, and my smile quickly disappears as I duck my head behind my open locker door.

"Uh, what are you doing?" Sloane asks once I'm practically *inside* my locker.

"Is he gone?" I whisper, sinking farther in.

"Who—"

"No, he's not gone," Cooper's voice says. "He's hoping you two can talk."

"I'll, uh . . . leave you two to it," Sloane says. I close my eyes and sigh. Then I pull myself out of my locker and face Cooper. Behind him my cousin backs away with a grimace and mouths, *Sorry!*

I close my locker, swing my backpack over my shoulder, and turn my attention to Cooper. "What do you want to talk about?"

"I don't know." He shrugs. "About the fact that I hate how awkward things are between us now. About the fact you've been avoiding me."

"I don't know what to say to you."

"I mean, same, but can we maybe figure it out? Because not talking—not being friends—it kind of really sucks."

I look up at him, and the earnestness on his face tugs at my heart.

"It's not like I'm having fun avoiding you, Coop. And it's definitely not easy. But being around you is even harder." He drops his head, and guilt pulses through me, despite *him* being the one who said we can't be anything. I sigh. "*But* I suppose, like you said last month, avoiding each other isn't really possible, especially since we have mutual friends, and this town is Polly Pocket–sized." The slightest grin appears on Cooper's face. "So I'll stop dodging you and *try* to pretend like everything's fine, okay?"

He stuffs his hands into his jeans pockets and looks at the floor, his smile falling. "I really wish you didn't have to pretend."

"So do I." I shrug. "Maybe one day I won't—once I get over you the way you got over me."

Cooper stares at me like he wants to say something. But he doesn't. Instead the tick-tick-ticking of the clock hanging on the wall over our heads fills the empty space between us in the now otherwise-silent hall.

He finally nods. "I better let you get back to Sloane."

"Okay. I'll see you tonight."

My whole chest hurts when his eyes meet mine and he forces a smile. "Yeah." He turns to go. "See you, Mitchell."

I spend the next few hours at home dreading tonight.

"You need to chill out," Sloane says, lying on my bed. "It's going to be fine. You're going to ignore Cooper. If Chloe's there, you won't even look in their vicinity."

"Shoot. Do you think she'll be there?" Of course she'll be there. "How am I supposed to watch them cuddling during a movie?"

"You're not. Like I said, you'll ignore them," she says. "You'll focus on having fun with Jake. Even if you don't *like* like him, he's a fun guy. Worst-case scenario, you'll tell him the back of the truck is cramped and suggest you guys grab a blanket and sit together outside the truck—where you won't be able to see Cooper."

"Yeah. Okay. You're right," I say. "You have to come with us. I need you there."

"I already have plans with Asher, sorry."

I throw on my low-rise Agolde jeans and toss her a look. "Right. And when are you going to spill the tea about what's going on *there*?"

Sloane's face turns pink. "Nothing is going on. We've been best friends my whole life."

"Mm-hmm."

"Please shut up," she says.

I pretend to zip my lips. If she's not ready to tell me, I can wait. I have my own problems right now anyway.

Like the fact that Jake's voice is carrying up the stairs. "Let's go, Ellis!"

"If I text you nine-one-one, you better come save me," I tell my cousin.

"You got it," she says.

Jake and I hop in the back of the truck, and he informs me that due to space, it's just the four of us tonight—him and me, Chloe and Cooper.

Fantastic.

Five minutes later, we pull into the drive-in theater for double-feature horror-movie night, where *Scream* will play first, followed by *Hereditary*, neither of which I've seen. Cooper backs the truck into a parking spot so the bed is facing the movie screen. After he and Chloe hop out of the front seat, Jake scoots as far over as he can, so he's jammed against the side, and I sit next to him.

Cooper hooks the speaker to the truck, then avoids eye contact as he sits next to me. Chloe squeezes in next to him, forcing me to be mashed between him and Jake. "Sorry," he says.

Jake lifts his arm to make space, setting it over my shoulder and pulling me closer. The fact that Cooper doesn't do the same—put his arm around Chloe to make space—isn't lost on me. With my arm pressed to Cooper's, my whole body tingles, wanting *more*.

I hate this so much. Why on earth did I agree to this torture?

"Everyone comfy enough?" Jake asks, throwing blankets over all of us.

"Yeah," Cooper and I mutter in unison.

"No. I'm too squished," Chloe says. I can't decide if she's actually suffering over there, or if she just wants Cooper's arm around her. Either way, he only inches closer to me. By the time we're all situated and the movie starts, Chloe has more space than any of us.

I lean my head back on Jake's arm and replay Sloane's words in my head. *Ignore Cooper and Chloe.*

Which is harder than I thought it'd be, considering we're all smashed together.

A while later, the cold air cuts through my striped cashmere sweater, and I shiver. Cooper doesn't look at me and he says nothing, but he pulls the blanket up so it's covering more of our top halves, then he lowers his arm.

But beneath the blankets, in the nearly nonexistent space between our legs, his knuckles graze mine before he settles his hand there.

And he doesn't move it.

I close my eyes. The touch is subtle, the backs of our hands pressed to each other, but it's *something*.

I should pull my hand away. I should tell Jake I want to move a blanket to the ground, outside the truck where I can't see Cooper, but I can't.

Because it hurts to get mere crumbs, but it also feels *so right*.

So, we watch the rest of *Scream* like that.

When the movie ends, Jake announces he needs to stretch. Cooper's hand slips away as he pushes the blanket off us, and we all pile out of the bed.

I use the bathroom and wait in a mile-long line for popcorn

for the next movie, then head back to the truck, where Cooper, Chloe, and Jake are waiting—and a mini pumpkin is sitting on the opened tailgate.

I stop short of the truck and look at them. Cooper is staring at the blank movie screen, gnawing at his lip, Chloe's eyes are flitting between the three of us, and Jake is watching me as he nervously cracks his knuckles.

I slowly approach. "What, um, is happening?"

"Open it," Jake says, gesturing at the pumpkin.

"That's . . . for me?" I ask. I glance at Cooper, who seems to be avoiding looking at me.

"It is," Jake says, now grinning.

Oh no.

Now would be a great time for the ground to open up and swallow me.

I set my popcorn on the tailgate, and it topples over and spills. But I don't even care.

My hands are shaking as I pull the top off the mini pumpkin. I reach in, grab the note, and unfold it.

Dear New Girl,

Roses are red,
And you're really pretty.
Will you be my date for the Pumpkin Prom
If you're not back in New York City?

Jake

Written on a piece of purple-lined paper in purple ink.

My brow furrows. I know for a fact I only let him borrow paper once, and I definitely saw him writing on it that day.

Holy shit. "Did you write this on the first day of school? After you asked for a pen?" I ask him.

He shrugs. "I'm a mastermind. I knew the first time I saw you that nothing was going to stop me from asking."

I can't help but laugh. Taylor Swift would adore Jake Keller. "But I worked at the table all day. You never came to get a pumpkin."

He nods at Cooper. "I sent my boy to get it for me so you wouldn't suspect anything."

Oh. My. God. The day after we kissed, Cooper had to get a pumpkin so Jake could ask me to the Pumpkin Prom.

This whole thing is so messed up.

"Well?" Jake says. "I'm sort of dying over here."

Oh. "Um . . ." Cooper finally looks at me as he and Chloe wait for my response.

I want to go to the Pumpkin Prom with Cooper. I want to wear a cute couple costume and dance the night away with him. I want to kiss him and laugh with him and hold his hand while he walks me home.

But he made it clear that isn't going to happen. Ever.

I swallow and look at Jake. "Yeah, okay. Let's go to the Pumpkin Prom together."

"Hell yes!" he shouts, a huge smile spreading across his handsome face. "Now pick up your popcorn and get your ass up here."

Cooper slides over, making space for me, and the movie starts.

But this time there are no small, kind gestures or hidden touches beneath the blanket.

The only thing between us now is the knowledge of what might have been if I hadn't stopped talking to him three years ago.

Chapter Twenty-Eight

It's another overcast autumn day in Bramble Falls. With the end of October in sight, the breeze carries a chill as Aunt Naomi, Mom, Sloane, and I walk around the Lively Farm, where the annual A-maize-ing Corn Maze event is being held. A potato-sack slide, a Ferris wheel, and a haunted house have been set up alongside various other fair-type rides in the big open field next to endless acres of cornstalks.

The whole town seems to be here, and all of them come to say hi to Aunt Naomi. It's honestly amazing to see a woman be so confidently in charge. Street Media seems allergic to promoting women.

I'm going to change that, though—even if being here has set me back.

While Aunt Naomi and Sloane are in line for corn dogs, Mom grins at me.

"What?" I ask.

"I saw the clothes you've been working on."

I blush. "Oh."

"They're really good."

"Thanks."

"And I swear I wasn't snooping," she says. "But I was putting your clean clothes in your room, and your sketchbook was open on your bed. . . . Those designs are incredible, Ellis."

"They're okay," I say, looking at the ground.

"How are you the most self-assured person I know—until it comes to *this*?" she asks. "They're unique and beautiful and, whether it was intentional or not, they *so* perfectly capture fall in this town."

"Yeah?" My lips involuntarily curve up at the corners. It was entirely intentional.

She nods. "They're perfect."

"Thanks, Mommy." I lay my head on her shoulder and she laughs.

"You haven't called me Mommy in, like, ten years. I miss it."

"Maybe I should start again," I say.

"You're welcome to, but people might think you're a weirdo." I lift my head and she turns to me. "Are you still miserable here?"

I shake my head, truthfully. "No. I've had fun here, actually." But I'm ready to go back to the city—now more than ever, given the Cooper situation. I'm ready to get back to my internship and to my real, drama-free life and to my future.

Only a couple more weeks.

A few minutes later, Sloane bounces over to us with her mom trailing behind.

"Want to hop on some rides?" she asks me as she practically inhales her corn dog.

"Sure."

"Maybe something that doesn't spin, though. I'm not trying to puke all over this cute shirt you gave me," she says, looking down at the blue plaid button-down I cropped for her. She takes my hand and pulls me toward the rides.

"You two have fun," Mom calls from behind me.

Since Aunt Naomi and the Lively family found enough volunteers and don't need us today, Sloane and I spend the next few hours riding every ride and drinking lemonade and eating fried Oreos. At some point, we meet up with Asher and eventually run into Jake and Slug. We all attend the goat show and the community art show, and it takes everything in me not to ask where Cooper is. At four thirty, Jake and Slug saunter off to the pie-eating contest, and Sloane, Asher, and I grab a map and enter the thirty-acre corn maze.

"You guys are cheaters if you're going to use a map," I tell them.

"Believe me, we *want* a map. This thing gets intense. It's massive and easy to get lost. Not to mention people rarely have phone service out here," Sloane says.

She's right about the cell service—I haven't had it all day. This farm is like a dead zone. But: "It's a maze. It's supposed to be a challenge," I say.

Sloane looks at Asher. "Fold it up," he says with a shrug. "We'll have it in case. Let's see if we can do this without it."

She sighs as she folds it and shoves it into her pocket. And we're off.

We make our way through the towering cornstalks, slipping deeper into the twisty labyrinth with each step as the screams and laughter of the festivalgoers fade into the background.

After an hour of walking, Sloane lets out a groan. “My feet hurt.”

“Wimp,” I murmur.

She slaps my shoulder. “Shut up. Not all of us are fueled by a challenge.”

“Maybe not, but aren’t you fueled by the idea of getting out of here so you can lounge on the couch?”

“You have a point.” We come to a dead end, and she points to the right. “This way.”

“No. We’ve already been down there,” I tell her.

Asher glances to the right. “Really?”

I point to a lopsided cornstalk. “Yeah, that cornstalk is familiar.”

Sloane laughs. “You’re joking, right?”

“No?”

“Ellis, there are literally thousands of cornstalks out here.”

“Yeah, and I’ve been trying to memorize any weird ones so we know if we’re going in circles,” I explain.

Sloane throws her hands in the air. “But there’s probably more than one lopsided cornstalk!” She takes my hand and tries to pull me to the right. “Come on. We both already know you have no sense of direction.”

I tug my hand from her grip. “That’s true, but I’m sure of this. Let’s just go left.”

“That’s in the opposite direction that we need to go,

though. That'll just take us deeper into the maze."

"Maybe, but sometimes you need to go deeper to take the right path out," I argue.

She looks at Asher. "What do you think, Ash?"

His eyes flicker between the two of us as he rubs the back of his neck. "Uh . . . I'm not sure. . . . But sorry, Ellis, I think Sloane's right on this."

I scoff. "Okay, fine. You guys go that way, and I'll go this way. We'll make it a race to the end."

Sloane shakes her head. "I'm not letting you walk around in a corn maze by yourself at dusk."

"I have my phone flashlight if I need it," I tell her. "But I won't because you two will be the ones needing to use your map to get out of here once you realize you're walking in circles."

Sloane lifts her eyebrows and puts her hands on her hips. "Fine. We'll race you. But only because I need to take you down a few pegs, Ms. Know-it-all."

I smile. "Excellent. I'll see you at the end—if you ever make it."

She smirks. "See ya, cuz. Let's go, Asher."

They head right, and I turn left.

Then left again. Then right. Then left. And soon I'm pretty sure I'm the one walking in circles.

The sun is fading and above me, the sky is a mixture of deep oranges and dark clouds. I pass a few families wandering through, but for the most part, the maze is empty at this hour.

"Shoot," I whisper to myself. I take my phone out. No reception. Holding it as high as I can, I walk around, hoping for some bars. But I get nothing.

I'm slipping my phone back into my pocket and turning the corner when I slam right into someone.

Cooper.

"Oh—um—hey—" I stammer.

He looks around. "Are you alone in here?"

"Yeah, I'm racing Sloane to the end."

"How's it going?"

"Okay," I lie. "What are you doing?"

"My mom wouldn't let me stay home, so I figured if I had to come, at least I could be alone in here."

"Oh," I say, shifting my weight uncomfortably. "In that case, I'll leave you to it. Good luck . . ."

I step around him, but he calls out, "Wait." I turn to face him. "I'm so lost. Care if I follow you?"

I pause, not really sure how to say no. And then there's the annoying fact that I don't really *want* to say no, even if being around him makes me sad. "Sure."

I turn and resume walking aimlessly ahead, with the faux confidence of someone with a plan. *Fake it till you make it.*

After a few minutes of awkward silence, Cooper clears his throat. "So, I heard you made the shirt Sloane's wearing."

After this past week, it feels *impossible* to have a casual conversation with him, but I did say I'd try, so . . .

"I did. Did you run into her or something?"

"Yeah, I passed them about twenty minutes ago, and—"

"Oh?" I say, cutting him off. "Were they using their map?"

Cooper chuckles at my competitive side rearing its ugly face. "No, and they looked incredibly lost."

"Nice!" I say with a devilish grin.

He laughs and shakes his head. "*Anyway*, she was bragging about her shirt to Asher. I think it meant a lot to her."

"That's sweet, but it was as much for me as it was for her," I tell him as we veer right.

"What do you mean?"

I shrug. "It's just for fun, but I've been trying out different fabrics and designs here, so it was good practice. And it was sort of neat making something for someone other than myself. I've never done that before."

"Yeah? Well, it was still cool of you." Cooper kicks a corn husk lying on the dirt path and asks, "Have you ever considered doing it for more than fun?"

The question is so innocent, and yet I have to stop myself from laughing.

"No," I say. "I'm going to be a journalist."

"Because your dad is a journalist? I think that's what you said years ago."

I nod, both loving and hating how easy it is to fall back into being *us*.

"Used to be. Now he's the president of Street Media. And, yeah, I guess that's part of the reason. I grew up at the company, with my dad teaching me everything he knows. And I'm good at it."

"You're good at designing clothes, too."

I glance at him. "Thanks. But it's just a hobby. Do you know how many aspiring fashion designers there are in New York?"

"A lot, I imagine. But I think you could do it."

I offer him a smile. But he just doesn't get it. Even if I could get my dad on board—which would never happen—I have no connections in the saturated world of fashion. It'd be too risky to pin my whole future on *hopes* of succeeding when I have a guaranteed job in journalism.

"So, I was talking to Aunt Naomi about the parade this morning," I say, changing the subject. "And it got me thinking . . . you should make your own float."

He arches an eyebrow at me. "For what?"

"For your baked goods. You could turn your truck into a promotion for your own cookie business. Sexy Cookies, Inc." He laughs, and I grin at him. "Okay, maybe not that name, but I'm serious. I don't think Betty Lynn would mind handling the Caffeinated Cat float if you were doing your own. I could make a cookie costume this week."

He eyes me, smiling. "You'd have to wear the costume."

"Uh, no. I'm not signing up to dress in a ridiculous costume in front of the whole town," I laugh. "But I'll make it for you."

"Then who would drive the truck? You don't have your license."

"Jake will drive."

He nods slowly, thinking. "Yeah, okay. Let's do it." He's trying to be nonchalant about it, but I can read this boy like a book. *He's excited.*

A half hour later, we turn right again. The sky has grown dark, and I can no longer hear the rides or the crowds of people from the farm.

"You have no idea where we're going," Cooper finally says.

"Not a clue."

"Ellis," he groans.

I laugh. "I'm sorry. I was lost when you found me! It's not like I have a map."

He sighs. "I know you don't have a map, but you seemed like you had a plan."

"I did. Wander until I find my way out."

"Okay, but now what?"

"Keep wandering until we find our way out?" I suggest.

"We could cut through the corn and just walk straight until we find our way out," he says. "Even if we end up on the wrong side of the farm, we won't be stuck in here anymore."

I peer into the dark cornstalks. "Um, no."

"It's a better plan than yours."

"Except yours is terrifying," I argue.

"Why? There aren't any bloodthirsty children in there, I promise," he says with a laugh.

"There might be coyotes, though. Or bobcats." I sigh. "I don't have to worry about coyotes or bobcats in the city."

"No, you just have to worry about rats."

I shrug. "Meh, rats are just basically stray cats in New York. I'm used to those."

"Gross," he says with a shake of his head. "But okay, if you don't want to cut through the corn, I think maybe we should just sit tight."

"Like here? On the ground?"

"You can stand if you want. I'm just saying, Sloane knows you're in here. She probably already has people looking for you.

So we should stay in one place so we're not accidentally walking *away* from our rescue team," he says. "They're bound to find us eventually."

"Seems more likely we'll find the end before they find us."

He frowns at me. "We've both been in here for *hours*."

"Fine," I pout.

Cooper and I sit on the dirt path, cold and enveloped in silence, with our legs stretched out in front of us. I try not to think about how close his fingers are to mine as we lean back on our hands. And I try not to stare at the perfect slope of his nose or the curl of his eyelashes, or his full lips as he breathes puffs of warm air.

"Maybe we should keep walking," I say, desperate for a distraction. "It's freezing out here."

He taps my foot with his. "Nope. This is a good plan, even if it's not *your* plan."

I sigh and lie back. If I close my eyes, I can't stare at him.

The ground is hard and cold, but it doesn't even matter when he lies back next to me and lifts my arm. I open my eyes and draw my eyebrows together, confused, as he pushes my sleeve up.

"What are you doing?" I ask.

He touches a freckle on my arm, then runs his finger along my skin to the one next to it. Then to the next. "Do you remember when you were here that summer and we figured out we had a matching constellation of freckles?"

I grin at the memory. "I didn't," I say, reaching over and tracing the pattern of freckles on his arm. "But now I do, yeah. I remember thinking it was freaking weird."

He turns his head. "I probably should have, but I didn't. I

thought it meant we were, like, meant to be or something. Like I'd somehow met the love of my life in middle school."

"*Love*, huh?" I whisper.

He grins. "I was fourteen with a lot of feelings."

"And now?"

His smile falters. He stares at me a moment. "Now I'm almost eighteen with a lot of feelings."

I sincerely wish a coyote would jump out of the cornstalks and put me out of my misery.

I clear my throat and turn away from him. I can't do this.

"I hate that you're going to the Pumpkin Prom with Jake." His voice is quiet and yet it rattles everything in me awake.

"Well, it's not like you were going to ask me."

He pushes my sleeve back down. "I should have."

I turn away and close my eyes. "You can't say stuff like that, Cooper. You *can't*."

"I know. I'm sorry."

"Especially when you have Chloe," I say, looking at him again and growing frustrated.

"I told you Chloe and I aren't anything," he says. "I wouldn't have kissed you if we were."

"Then what's going on there? Because it's not nothing."

I say it as if I want to know.

I really, *really* don't. But I need to.

He sighs. "Chloe and I dated sophomore year for like two weeks. But then she dumped me for Slug."

I can't help it—I bark out a laugh. "Shut up. She did not." I shake my head. "That never happened."

Slug's nice and all, but no way.

"It did," he says with a smile. "But he told her he wouldn't date her because friends don't do that to friends. The following week, she wanted to get back together. She said breaking up with me was a lapse in judgment. But I told her no."

"Why? She obviously really likes you. Maybe it really was just a lapse in judgment."

The gravity of his gaze nearly paralyzes me. "Because she wasn't you," he says. "Because I felt nothing when she broke up with me. Because I figured if she couldn't destroy me the way you did, what was the point?"

My stomach flips and my heart squeezes and my insides melt. "Oh."

"It didn't matter, anyway. Turns out, she was just figuring out she wasn't into me *or* Slug—or any guy for that matter." He hesitates before continuing. "Because she likes girls."

My eyes widen. "Chloe's gay?"

Cooper nods. "She's not really out, though. Only her closest friends know. But she said if I trust you, I could tell you."

"I won't say anything," I promise.

"I know."

"I don't understand why she'd be okay with me knowing her secret, though," I say. "We're cool but not super close. . . ."

"Because she didn't want our friendship to scare you off. I haven't really dated anyone since her, and she said she could tell that you and I liked each other." He shrugs. "She was afraid you'd think there was more between us than there is."

I cringe thinking of how jealous I've been. She was so right.

Too bad this revelation doesn't make a difference for Cooper and me.

I turn away from him and stare at the sky, thinking about how unfair it all feels, as Cooper takes my hand in his and interlaces our fingers.

I don't look at him when I say, "You're confusing me."

"I'm sorry."

"I'm trying to give you what you asked for. I'm trying to pretend it never happened. I'm trying to make my feelings go away, and I'm trying to be friends with you again. But you're making it all really hard."

"I've regretted that night this entire past week," he says.

I roll my eyes. "Trust me, I know, Cooper. You don't need to remind me."

"No," he says. "I don't mean the kiss." I turn my head toward him. Our faces are only inches apart when he says, "I mean I've regretted saying we couldn't be anything. I've regretted telling you to forget it happened." His Adam's apple bobs. "I don't want to regret letting you walk away again, letting you leave, knowing this time could have been different."

"So, what are you saying?"

His eyes dart between mine before he closes them, the small space between us vanishing as he leans in and presses his lips to mine in a soft, reluctant kiss.

I reach up with my free hand and run my fingers along his neck until they're buried deep in his hair.

He stops kissing me, lets go of my hand, and shifts his body so his weight is resting on his elbow as he looks down at me.

I run my thumb over his ear and trace my fingertips along his jaw and over his eyebrow because I simply cannot stop touching him. I might be obsessed. "You said you don't trust me," I whisper.

He slowly nods. "Yeah, I know, but this week was torture. *Acting like I don't want you* is torture. You're a flight risk, and I don't want to end up hurt. But . . ." His gaze has me in a choke hold as I wait for whatever he'll say next. "I think you're a risk worth taking."

A million sparklers ignite inside me until I think I might combust. But then I remember one not-so-small problem. "What about Jake?"

Cooper's expression turns worried. "I honestly don't know. He'll be crushed. And probably pissed. I feel like shit about it."

"Same . . ." I tug on the collar of his hoodie. "But it also sounds like something we can figure out tomorrow."

He grins, letting me pull him closer, and kisses me again. His tongue slides along mine, and his weight collapses gently on top of me as he lowers himself. My hands find the small space where his shirt has ridden up, and they memorize the feel of his warm skin as goose bumps erupt across it. They travel the ridges of his back muscles, and heat pools in the pit of my belly as his fingertips skim down my ribs. My back arches of its own accord, pressing me even closer to him; our breaths become ragged as we drown in each other.

Then a bright light hits us.

"What the fuck?" someone says.

My heart stops beating.

Jake.

Chapter Twenty-Nine

Cooper jumps up *fast*. I'm climbing to my feet after him as Slug turns the corner. His eyes bounce between us as Jake's giant flashlight shines like a spotlight.

"Oh shit," he mutters.

Even in the dark, I can see Jake's jaw clenching, his nostrils flaring. He shakes his head, speechless, before grabbing a whistle from his pocket and blowing it, presumably to alert anyone else searching that we've been found.

"Let's go," he says, looking at his map. Probably just to avoid looking at us.

Cooper takes a step toward him. "Jake—"

"Not now," Jake says. He shoots me a glare and turns around. My whole chest collapses in on itself.

He shouldn't have found out this way.

Cooper glances at me before following a few strides behind Jake.

I walk beside Slug. No one says a word as the minutes drag on.

And then: "And to think I was *worried* when Sloane called and said no one could find Ellis," Jake says, eventually breaking the silence. "Turns out she was in *great* hands."

Cooper lets out an agonizing sigh. "I didn't—"

"No. You don't get to talk, Coop. Not tonight," Jake says.

Beside me, Slug shakes his head, but no one says anything else the rest of the way back.

By the time we all walk out of the corn maze, roughly fifteen people are waiting for us.

Mom flies over and throws her arms around me. "Oh, thank goodness. I was so worried."

"I'm fine. It's just a corn maze in Bramble Falls," I say. "There's not a whole lot that could have happened to me."

She lets go. "Um, it's freezing. Plus, there are coyotes and bobcats around here."

If Cooper didn't look so wrecked and Jake weren't so upset, I'd probably laugh at how similar Mom and I are.

But I can't think of anything besides my whole life imploding right now.

Sloane runs over. "Now that I know you're alive, I'm so excited to get to say, 'Told you so.'" She laughs, but when I don't (because I can't), her smile fades. "Oh no." She glances at the boys. "Sleeping in my room tonight?"

I nod, and Mom narrows her eyes at us. "Why? What's going on? What am I missing?"

"Nothing," Sloane says. "Let's get home."

My eyes connect with Cooper's as his mom finally releases him from a tight hug. Then I turn and follow Mom and Sloane over to Aunt Naomi, and we all walk to the car.

We pull out, and I rest my head against the cold window.

How can everything be so wonderful and so awful at the same time?

The next morning, I make my way to the town square, where I've asked Jake to meet me. I'd rather chew off my own hand than have this conversation, but it has to be done eventually. And I'm leaving for New York soon. I don't want to leave on a sour note.

I realize there's not much I can do about their friendship, but I don't want to leave with things messed up between him and Cooper, either.

Jake's sitting on the steps of the gazebo, scrolling on his phone, wearing jeans and a black jacket over a red-and-black flannel. He doesn't bother looking up when I sit next to him.

I bite my lip nervously. Because it doesn't matter how many times I cycled through the things I wanted to say. Now that I'm here, my brain is blank.

"Say what you have to say, Ellis," Jake says, finally hitting the button on the side of his phone and setting it on the ground beside him.

"I don't know what to say," I blurt. "Other than I'm sorry."

"What are you sorry for exactly?" He sighs.

"Cooper and I should have told you we liked each other."

"No. As one of my best friends, *Cooper* should have told me he was into you. You didn't owe me anything. You're just some girl passing through here," he says, shrugging.

Ouch.

"Maybe. But I still consider us friends," I say.

He scoffs. "Yeah, well, you did make it clear we were going to homecoming as *friends* when you agreed to go with me. I guess I was just an idiot for thinking we might become more eventually."

"I'm sorry. I never meant to lead you on."

He shakes his head. "That's the thing. You didn't. I thought a lot about it last night, and it's hard to be mad at you because you didn't do anything. You never said you liked me. You never did anything to give me the impression you ever would. It was just irrational hope, I guess." He finally turns to me. "But you didn't have to say yes to the Pumpkin Prom."

"I wanted to say yes," I tell him. It's half true. If I couldn't go with Cooper, I did want to go with Jake—as a friend I have a lot of fun with.

"Ellis, you like someone else. I'm not going to hold you to going with me."

"I'm not bailing on you again, Jake," I say. "You're not an obligation to me."

"Yeah, I know. But I *like* you. And it's okay that you don't like me back, but spending the night at prom with someone who'd rather be there with someone else doesn't sound all that fun, to be honest."

I nod. "Okay," I whisper.

Jake rests his elbows on his knees. "How long have you two . . ."

"We haven't," I say quickly. "I met Cooper when I visited one summer in middle school. We became really close friends and then had a falling out. Then I—"

Jake's posture stiffens. "Wait. *You're* the girl?"

"Huh?"

Jake digs his palms into his eyes. "No fucking way."

"What's happening right now?"

"Unbelievable." Jake shakes his head and looks at me. "I moved here freshman year. Cooper and I were nothing alike, but he was nice and befriended me, introduced me to everyone. But all he *ever* talked about was this girl he'd spent the summer with. It was so annoying," he laughs. "But then he got all quiet and sad because she stopped texting him. I was *so* glad when he started dating Chloe because I really thought it'd pull him out of his slump. But it didn't. Only time did."

I turn and look at my feet, ashamed that I was such an asshole.

"Why wouldn't he tell me you were the girl?" Jake asks.

"Because you liked me. He was afraid of upsetting you. Of ruining your friendship."

"But if he'd told me from the get-go . . ."

"Things between us were rocky and complicated. He wasn't trying to keep anything from you. He wanted you to be happy." I meet Jake's icy blue eyes. "We never intended to fall for each other."

"You say that, but there was never any other choice for Cooper." Jake's gaze travels to the Caffeinated Cat. "This is really messed up."

"Yeah." I pull my scarf tighter. "Do you hate me?"

Jake looks at me, his eyes softening. "No. I'm not even mad at you. I just . . . wish I'd known I didn't stand a chance."

"I'm sorry."

"You have nothing to be sorry for."

"Are we still friends?" I ask. "Or should I be keeping my

distance until I go back home? Because I really don't want to do that, but I will if it's what you want."

Jake hangs his head, and every second he doesn't answer feels like a new shard of glass is wedging its way into my heart. I *hate* this.

Finally, he sighs. "It's going to suck seeing you and Cooper together, but no, don't keep your distance. I'm not going to throw away a friendship because you don't like me." He gives me a slight smile. "Even though it makes no sense because I'm a catch."

I grin, a little weight lifting from my shoulders. "You know, you really are. If Cooper weren't in the picture—"

"Oh? 'Cause he's one of my best friends, but I'll murder him right now."

I laugh, and Jake smiles at me. "Please don't." After a beat of silence, I bump his shoulder with mine. "Thank you for understanding."

"Yeah," he says. Because what else is there to say?

"Are you going to talk to him?" I ask.

"Cooper? He's only called and texted about six hundred times today. I guess I could hit him up."

"Whenever you're ready."

He chews the inside of his cheek and looks out across the lawn.

I nudge him with my elbow. "Have I mentioned I'm sorry?"

"Yes, now please don't mention it again."

"Okay."

We part ways, and as Jake heads toward the Caffeinated Cat,

I walk home to wait to hear from Cooper for the first time since last night.

And I cross my fingers that when he calls, it won't be to say we made another mistake.

Chapter Thirty

I'm eating dinner with Sloane, Mom, and Aunt Naomi when Cooper texts.

Summer Cooper: **Can you come over?**

Me: **now?**

Summer Cooper: **Or whenever.**

Me: **Depends. Are you going to sit me down to give me bad news?**

Summer Cooper: **Just come over, Mitchell.**

I sigh, and all three women look at me.

"It's the moment of truth," I announce, setting my phone on the table. I told them everything on our way home from the corn maze. I hadn't been planning on it, but I was freaking out. So we stopped by the root beer stand, cranked the heat in the car, and drank floats while I rehashed the last two months. Afterward, Mom and Aunt Naomi brought every blanket they could find down to the living room and the four of us had an old-fashioned slumber party, rewatching *Practical Magic* while we waited for Cooper's text that never came.

Mom takes a deep breath. "Okay, go. Be back by ten. Text if you need me to come get you."

"Good luck, honey," Aunt Naomi says.

"If he tries to tell you Jake is more important, tell him to remember that I know how to get rid of a body," Sloane says.

I grab a jacket and head a few blocks over to Cooper's house. I'm about to knock on the front door when the garage door opens.

Cooper walks out and spots me. We stand there staring at each other for a moment.

"Did you talk to Jake?" I ask, like I'm tearing off a Band-Aid.

"Yeah." He gestures to the garage. "Come."

I huff out a breath. Not knowing where things stand between us is killing me. He grabs a bag that was sitting in the driveway, and I follow him into the garage, where his truck is parked.

He hits a button on the wall, and the garage door lowers. As soon as it's closed, Cooper strides over, lifts my chin between his thumb and forefinger, and kisses me.

"We've only kissed in the dark wilderness," he says. "I had to fix that."

I look at him through my lashes. "No complaints here."

He grins at me, but it's hard to reciprocate when I don't know what's going on.

"Does this mean things are okay with Jake?" I ask.

He sighs. "They're as good as can be expected, I think." I wilt. "*But* I think we'll be okay. Eventually."

"What'd he say?" I ask.

"Just that I should have told him I liked you, which . . . he's not wrong." He runs his hand through his hair, leaving it disheveled. "And that I should have told him when I was even considering acting on how I was feeling, which, again, he's not wrong. I messed up."

"It was a complicated situation."

"All I had to do was be honest. That part wasn't complicated." He turns and leans against his truck. "But since you apparently had a talk with him already, it helped that he knew who you were to me years ago."

"So . . . what about us?" I ask.

He draws his eyebrows together. "What about us?"

I look at the floor. "I don't know. I mean, Jake was a big concern of yours from the start. If he's upset . . ."

Cooper pushes off the truck and stands in front of me. He tucks my hair behind my ear, then gently lifts my chin so I'm looking at him. "I already told you I'm not letting you leave without trying to see what this could be."

"Okay, but—"

He puts his finger over my lips. "Stop. Jake will be fine. *Jake and I* will be fine."

I nod, and he moves his finger. "Now, I told you to come over for a reason."

"A reason other than ending my panic attack?"

"Yes." He points to plastic bags lining the wall. "I went to the store today and bought, well, everything."

"For . . . ?"

"For the parade. We're transforming the truck, right?"

"Oh. Yeah. Okay."

"But I have no idea what I'm doing," he says.

I walk over to the bags and start pulling stuff out, checking what he bought.

"All right, well, I've never made a float, but I do like designing fun stuff," I say.

"Exactly. I need that creative eye of yours."

"I think our best bet is going to be to wrap the whole truck in this green floral sheeting," I say, picking up a package from the floor. "So, let's do that—then we can wrap the foil fringe and vinyl twist around the bottom of the frame."

Cooper stares at me. "You lost me at 'floral sheeting.'"

I roll my eyes and grin at his befuddled expression. "Okay, you just stand there and hand me the tools."

"And look pretty?"

"Exactly."

I tear open the sheeting. "Typically, I'd say we should use a staple gun to secure this, but that won't work on metal. Do you have any heavy-duty double-sided tape maybe?"

"I didn't buy any, but we might have some in the house. Be right back."

Cooper runs in to get the tape, and I lay out the silver fringe around the truck. When he comes out with a new roll, we get the truck wrapped in the floral sheeting. Then we wrap the base of the truck in the silver foil fringe. Once we finish, the truck is well on its way to being transformed into a parade float.

"Now what?" Cooper asks.

"I'm not sure. I'd love to make it whimsical and fun, but . . ."

I gasp, my eyes widening with an idea. “Oh snap. I got it.” I start tearing the fringe off the truck.

“What are you doing?” he asks. “We literally just finished that.”

“Get the brown foil fringe from over there instead.”

“Yes, boss,” he says, but he looks skeptical.

We get the brown fringe on instead. Then we stand back.

“Okay,” I say, waving my hands at the truck, “The brown is the dirt path, the green is the grass, where—drumroll, please—” Cooper grins and shakes his head but indulges me, drumming his hands on his thighs—“the gingerbread house sits, covered in baked goods. Oversized, fake, giant ones, of course.”

“What?” Cooper chortles. “You want us to build a gingerbread house?”

“Yes! Well, something like one. We’ll use painted foam blocks to build it. We’ll get Sloane and Asher to help us make the giant desserts to stick on it. And then,” I say, grinning, “you’ll be standing in your cookie costume behind the house, passing out your cookies, and Jake will dress like a witch, driving you around. I mean, assuming things are okay by then.”

Cooper laughs. “Okay, I’m sold. But even if we’re good, you know Jake is going to say he’s too good-looking to dress like a witch. I can hear him now. . . .” He does his best Jake impression when he says, “It’ll scare off the ladies, man!”

He’s so right. “Fine. I’ll get Sloane to do it for us. It’ll be so fun,” I say. “But it *is* going to be a lot of work to finish in the next two weeks.”

Cooper shrugs. “I think we can do it. We’ll just meet here every day after school.”

"Except Wednesday because you work."

An amused smile spreads over his face. "Why do you know that?"

I shrug. "Details."

Cooper steps toward me. "I keep wondering if this is real life."

I take the final step toward him and wrap my arms around his neck. "Same, though."

He leans down and presses his lips to mine, but before we can get too swept away in each other, I back away.

"Can I ask you a question?" I ask.

"Anything."

My cheeks heat before the words are even out of my mouth. "Are you, um . . . are you my boyfriend?"

He raises his eyebrows, then a slow, crooked grin forms. "Do you want me to be?"

"Depends. Now that the thrill of the chase is over, are you going to stop showing up places with cookies for me?"

"Um, the chase was not thrilling. Like I said, it was torture not being with you. And you told me I wasn't allowed to bring you cookies anymore. Or make you bacon."

"That was before. I want all the cookies and bacon now," I tell him.

"Okay. Then consider all the cookies and bacon yours." He rests his forehead against mine and smiles. "And consider me your boyfriend."

My face feels like it might split in half, I'm smiling so hard. "Okay. Good."

He leans in to kiss me.

"Cooper?" his mom calls from inside.

He pauses and makes a sound somewhere between a groan and a whine. "Doesn't she know I'm just trying to kiss my girlfriend?"

I laugh. "I should probably go anyway."

The door behind Cooper swings open, and I take a step away from him. His mom grins knowingly at us.

"Sorry," she says. "I was just making sure you were alive out here."

"Alive and well, Mom," Cooper says. "I'm going to walk Ellis home, though."

"Good to see you again, Amanda," I say.

"You too, Ellis. Can't wait to see more of you around here," she says with a wink before retreating back inside.

"I take it you told your mom?" I ask.

He shrugs. "Yeah. My mom's my first best friend. I tell her pretty much everything."

Oh my god. And I thought I couldn't possibly like him more than I already did.

"What?" he asks, confused, making me realize I'm staring at him.

"Nothing. I just think you're the best thing to ever happen to me, Cooper Barnett."

"Likewise, Mitchell."

I press up on my toes and kiss him.

When we finally tear ourselves apart ten minutes later, drunk on gooey feelings and the newness of *us*, Cooper takes my hand in his and holds it the whole walk to Aunt Naomi's.

I know it's too early for the L-word, and yet it's there, bursting from the seams, begging to be spoken. And as Cooper kisses me good night at the door, I bury the word in the depths of my stomach with the kaleidoscope of butterflies he gives me.

And I leave it there for the exact right moment, maybe after he's been my boyfriend for longer than two hours.

Chapter Thirty-One

When I walk into lunch on Thursday, Slug is in my usual seat beside Jake. Until today, I've continued sitting there while Cooper's kept his distance, sitting next to Chloe a little ways down our table, just like he used to do when he was avoiding me. Because even though things are different, Cooper and I decided not to subject Jake to seeing us together.

The whispers around the school are probably misery enough for him.

"Get out of my seat," I say to Slug.

Slug glances at Jake before saying, "It's my seat now. You can go sit over there." He nods at *his* usual spot across from Jake.

"Wait . . ." I draw my eyebrows together and turn to Jake. "Do you not want me to sit by you anymore?"

He's been quiet this week, but we've been okay. At least I *thought* so.

"No. I want you to sit over there," he says, nodding across the table.

I press my lips together. I hate this. But Jake gets whatever he wants right now, and if that means space from me, then it is what it is. Still, my heart feels like it's being stabbed with a thumbtack.

I'm on my way around the table when I hear Cooper behind me. "What's going on?"

I look over my shoulder, where Cooper's standing across from Jake with his lunch. He glances at me, then back to Jake.

"Come on, dude, don't do that to her," Cooper says.

Jake rolls his eyes and sighs. "I'm not doing anything to her, Cooper. Sit down." He motions at the seat across from Slug.

"Uh, no, I'm sitting down there. I just—"

"Wanted to make sure I wasn't upsetting your girlfriend. Got it," Jake says. Cooper's cheeks turn pink. "But it looks like your seat is taken anyway. So sit."

Wouldn't you know it, one of Chloe's friends is sitting in Cooper's typical seat.

It's almost like it's all planned.

Cooper and I look at each other, uncomfortable. Then we sit.

"Perfect," Jake says. "Now, this is what's going to happen every day until Ellis leaves."

"What?" I ask.

"I'm tired of you guys walking on eggshells around me," Jake says. "I appreciate you trying not to throw it in my face, but I can't take the awkward lunches anymore. Just sit there. Talk. Eat. Be normal. Please." He grins. "Believe me, I'm not anywhere near how pathetic Cooper was after you left when you were kids."

I give him a weak smile because it's all I can muster, and

Cooper nods. Acting like everything is normal is hard, even if he's asking for it.

But again, it's what he wants, so we try.

After lunch, Cooper follows me to my locker. He glances around as I put in my lock combination, then gives me a quick peck on the lips.

"Hey, we agreed no PDA," I say.

"I couldn't help it, and it's a terrible rule," he says, his dimple sinking into his cheek. "You're leaving in a couple of weeks. We should be kissing as much as possible before then."

"Hmm. You have a point."

He leans in and kisses me again. "A good one."

"Okay, but I'm going to be late for class, so go away," I tell him, grinning. "I'll bring your cookie costume over after school."

"You finished it?"

"Well, no, not yet. But almost, and I'm dying to show you what I have so far," I tell him. "It's *fantastic*, and you are going to look fantastic in it."

He laughs. "I'm scared."

"Oh, you should be."

He smiles as he walks backward away from me. "See you in econ, Mitchell."

This whole week has felt like a dream. A busy dream, but a dream nonetheless. Cooper and I have worked on his truck until ten p.m. almost every night—although, admittedly, a good chunk of that time has been spent sneaking kisses and subtle touches. Sloane and Asher came over to his place Tuesday to help build and paint the gingerbread house while Cooper and I made baked goods out of sheets of colorful foam. We just have to attach the baked goods to the house and do any other final touches tonight. Then, other than finishing the costume, we won't have to worry about parade preparation at all next week.

My next two classes drag on forever, full of note-taking and lectures. Then, finally, I get to go to econ, where Cooper is waiting for me.

He grabs a pencil out of his bag. "I heard we have a pop quiz today."

My blood freezes. "In here?"

"Yeah."

I rack my brain for the last time I even looked at my notes for this class. Two weeks ago, maybe?

Mr. Davies knocks his knuckles on the desk as the bell rings. "Everything away except a pencil."

"Cooper," I whisper, "I haven't studied."

"You'll be fine. You're the smartest person I know."

"Because I study!" Panic grips me.

"Relax, Ellis. You've got this."

Mr. Davies passes out our quizzes, and I take a deep breath. Shoulders back. *I've got this.*

I stare at the ten-question quiz.

I definitely *don't* have this.

We have fifteen minutes to complete the quiz before Mr. Davies says we're moving on, so I do my best to fill in the answers, then turn it in. But I struggle to focus for the remainder of class.

"What can I do for you, Ellis?" Mr. Davies asks when I

approach him after the bell rings, after everyone—including Cooper—has gone.

"Um, I know it's not something you normally do, but I was wondering if you'd be willing to grade my quiz," I ask. "Now, I mean."

He must see the worry eating away at me because he walks around his desk and grabs the stack of completed quizzes.

"I've been working on stuff for the parade . . . ," I say, feeling the need to explain myself before he uncovers my failing grade.

"Ah, yes, a hazard of living with your aunt, I suppose," he chuckles. He pulls my quiz from the pile and examines my answers. "Well, good news. You only missed three."

I think I might be sick. "So, a seventy percent."

"Three wrong answers is still decent, Ms. Mitchell."

I stare at nothing as I nod. "Thank you."

With my backpack slung over my shoulder and my eyes stinging, I leave the classroom, grab all my books from my locker, and head to the flagpole to meet Sloane, Asher, and Cooper.

"What were you doing?" Cooper asks.

"I got a C," I mumble, still in disbelief.

"He graded it for you?" Cooper asks, surprised. "Okay, well, it could have been worse, especially if you thought you wouldn't do well."

"I don't get Cs. In fact, I've never even gotten a B. *Ever.*" I shake my head. "Do you guys think you can handle the float today? I need to study."

Cooper takes my hand. "Ellis, that ten-point quiz isn't going to drop your overall grade from an A. You'll probably have a ninety-nine instead of a hundred."

"That isn't the point. I've been distracted, Coop. College applications are due soon. I can't let my grades bomb at the finish line."

He sighs. "Okay."

"We'll send you pictures," Sloane offers.

"Sounds good," I tell her.

Cooper gives my hand a reassuring squeeze as we climb into the backseat of Sloane's car.

But nothing can make me feel better right now. I can't believe I let Columbia fall to the back burner.

I have to get it together.

Chapter Thirty-Two

I spend Friday evening with Mom, Aunt Naomi, and Sloane, passing out candy to trick-or-treaters and roasting marshmallows over a firepit in the driveway. Once we've turned off our porchlight and the town has grown quiet, I make my way to my room to study. I've just finished going through my physics notes when there's a tap at the attic window. I glance over and scream when I see someone's face.

I throw my hand over my chest and breathe. *Cooper.*

I jog over and throw the window open. "What are you doing?" I whisper.

He looks frozen in terror, crouched down in his pajamas and glasses. "I climbed the trellis."

I grin. "But why? You said you were going to bed. It's almost eleven."

"Because I've barely seen you since you got your average grade."

"You mean since yesterday," I laugh.

He frowns. "Well, you spent lunch in the library and actually focused in class. And I get it. I do. But you're also leaving soon, so let's watch a movie."

"Tonight?" I ask. "You have to work in the morning."

"Please let me in before I fall off the roof. I'll be fine tomorrow." I step back and let him crawl through the window. Once he's through, he stands and grins at me and whispers, "I just conquered my fear for you."

"I think you just conquered your fear for *you*."

"Fine. I conquered it for both of us," he says. "But I don't know how I'm getting back down, because I definitely broke that thing."

I pull him into me and kiss him. "Sounds like a problem for later."

He smiles against my lips. "If you keep kissing me, we will not get to a movie."

I shrug. "I was never one for cinema, anyway."

He laughs. "Ellis, go pick out a movie."

I pout. "You can't just show up here in your glasses and expect me to not want to kiss you."

He arches an eyebrow. ". . . this is a glasses problem?"

"Sure is," I tell him. "You in those glasses are hot, my guy."

"Huh. I had no idea. I'll keep that in mind for the future," he says with a smirk.

He kicks off his shoes and climbs into my bed while I put the old *Speed* DVD in.

"What is this?" he asks as it starts. He puts pillows behind him and lifts his arm, gesturing for me to join him. I crawl into the space between his arm and his body, snuggling against him with my cheek on his chest and his arm around me.

"You've never seen *Speed?* It's a classic. The perfect combination of romance and action."

"Okay." He pulls the blanket over us. "I'm intrigued."

For the next hour and a half, we cuddle in my bed, with me fighting the urge to kiss him while the tips of his fingers travel softly up and down my arm as we watch the movie.

When the credits start rolling, I look up at him. "I wish you could stay. I could fall asleep just like this."

"Me too." He kisses my forehead. "But we're already pushing our luck."

"I know," I sigh.

I sit up, and he pulls me in for a kiss.

"So, what's the plan?" he asks when he lets me go. "Do I have to jump off the roof? If that's the case, just kill me now."

"I'll walk you downstairs. Everyone's sleeping. You can use the front door."

We climb out of bed, and Cooper grabs his shoes before following me quietly down the steps. We sneak down the dark hallway, then down the next flight of steps.

We've just reached the front door when someone clears their throat. Cooper and I whip around to find Mom standing there with her arms crossed.

"Cooper," she says. "So nice to see you—in the middle of the night."

Cooper stands there frozen.

"He just stopped by to give me something for the parade," I blurt.

"Oh? Must have been something very important."

I sigh. "We just watched a movie. That's it."

"Mm-hmm." She turns to my boyfriend. "Good night, Cooper. Have a safe walk home."

Cooper nods and quickly escapes the house.

"You can't have boys sneaking into Naomi's house," Mom says once he's gone.

"I know."

"I'm putting condoms in your nightstand tomorrow."

"Mom . . . ," I groan. "We're not—"

She holds up her hand. "I don't care. Now go to sleep."

I nod and take the steps back up to the attic. If getting condoms put in my dresser drawer is the worst punishment I'm going to get for having a boy in my room this late, I'm not going to argue.

I climb back into my still-warm bed, where it now smells like Cooper, all citrus, sugar, and his laundry detergent, and my phone dings.

Summer Cooper: **I miss you already.**

Me: **Then come back.**

I click on his contact and hit the edit button.

Autumn Cooper: **I think your Mom would kill us. But at least we have the Pumpkin Prom tomorrow.**

Me: **Can't wait. ❤**

I bury my face in my Cooper-scented pillow and smile. What even is this life?

Chapter Thirty-Three

The sun is bright, but the air is cold the next day as Sloane and I walk to the Caffeinated Cat.

"We should have driven. It's freezing out here," Sloane whines.

"This is nothing. You should come visit me in New York. Try trekking a few blocks in the city." The temperatures might compare, but something about the city makes it feel colder.

"I'd love to come visit you," she says. "Maybe over winter break."

"Excellent. Then you can really experience a true New York City winter."

"Can we go ice skating at Rockefeller Center? And spend New Year's in Times Square?" she asks, growing excited. "Gah, please! That'd be so fun."

"Uh, that's quite touristy of you, but okay," I say.

"Well, I am a tourist. I've never *been* to the city. We should probably go see the Statue of Liberty and the Empire State Building, too."

I laugh. "We can if you want to."

"And Central Park."

"Okay, you make a list, and we'll visit as many as we can when you come," I tell her.

We've just passed the bookstore when Dorothy walks out of the florist. "Oh, Sloane, Ellis. I just heard the good news!" My cousin and I look at each other. Sloane shrugs. "About your mom putting an offer in on the house on Apple Blossom Lane," Dorothy adds.

"*My* mom?" I ask, my eyebrows drawn together. I shake my head and laugh. "Sorry, but that one's just a fake rumor. Probably shouldn't spread it."

"Well, I heard it directly from Joe Mercer," Dorothy says.

"I have no idea who that is, but he's mistaken," I tell her. I glance at Sloane, who's grown unusually quiet. Her eyes are wide with confusion.

"He owns Bramble Falls Realty . . . ," she mutters quietly.

"What?" I exhale.

Someone is wrong. Wires got crossed somewhere. Mom wouldn't buy a house in Bramble Falls. We're supposed to be home by Thanksgiving.

Still, my throat tightens.

"I have to go," I think I say.

I sprint home with Sloane on my tail. "Ellis, chill. We don't know what's true!"

Adrenaline carries me the two blocks home. I swing the door open and stomp into the kitchen, breathless. Mom looks up from her coffee and the art magazine she's reading.

"What's wrong?" she says, setting her mug on the table, concern carved into her face.

"Are you buying a house in Bramble Falls?" I ask.

Mom goes pale. She stands slowly, like she's approaching a skittish animal. "I was going to talk to you about it tomorrow. I just wanted you to enjoy your prom tonight."

"Talk to me about *what*, exactly, Mom?"

"I put in an offer. That doesn't mean we're getting the house."

"What the hell? Why would you put an offer in on a house *here*? We're going home soon." The whooshing blood in my ears crescendoes as panic suffocates me. "Are you . . . are you and Dad getting divorced?"

Mom looks at the floor. "I can't go back to him, Ellis."

My jaw falls open. "What are you talking about? This was supposed to be temporary."

"I know, honey. It was. But we're happy here, aren't we?" Her question is laced with hope. It infuriates me.

"No, Mom!" This is my fault—I made her think I could be happy here permanently. I blink back the tears threatening to flood this room. "I want to go home. Yes, Bramble Falls has been fine. It's not as awful as I expected it to be. I had fun. But I need to get back to my school and my internship. And to *Dad*! God, I've barely talked to him in two months. I miss him. Don't you get that?"

"I'd never stop you from visiting your dad, Ellis," she says.

"I don't want to *visit* him. I want to go home, where we *live*. Where I'm going to college next year!"

I can barely breathe.

"Moving here wouldn't mean you won't get into Columbia," she says.

I shake my head. She doesn't seem to understand what moving here means for me.

It means my parents will inevitably get a divorce. It means I won't have access to the same opportunities I'd have in New York—opportunities I *need* in order to have the best shot at getting into Columbia. It means I'll never see Dad because he's *always* working. It means his new intern will move up in the company while I'm forgotten—by both Dad and Mr. Street. It means the loss of my life as I knew it.

And I wouldn't be surprised if it means Mom asking me not to go to school in the city next.

This was probably her plan all along.

"I can't believe you're doing this to me," I say, my voice breaking.

"I'm not trying to do anything to you, sweetie," she says, stepping closer.

"You are so selfish."

"What?"

"You're moving me away from home—away from my goals—so that you can sit in your room and *paint*. You're punishing me because you hate Dad. And God forbid I want to be like him instead of you." I grit my teeth and take a step backward. "Do what you want, Mom. But I'm not moving here. I won't."

I turn around, where Sloane is staring at me, shocked. I brush past her.

As soon as the door closes behind me, I let my tears fall. And they don't let up the whole way to the Caffeinated Cat.

When I walk in, Cooper's face lights up. Until he realizes I'm crying.

Betty Lynn takes over at the register, and he follows me outside.

"What's wrong? What happened?" he asks, pulling me into a hug. But having his arms around me only makes me cry harder.

My dad would be so disappointed. *Stop being so emotional, Ellis.*

I wipe my face, clear my throat, and step back. "I'm leaving."

"To go where?"

"Home."

His face falls. "When?"

"Now," I tell him.

"Your mom didn't give you any warning? No notice? You're just . . . going?" he asks, like he can't wrap his head around it.

"My mom put in an offer on a house in Bramble Falls."

A whirlwind of questions passes over Cooper's face. "I'm so confused. She put in an offer here, but you guys are going back to the city?"

"She's staying. I'm going," I say.

"Are you coming back, then?"

"I don't know." I shrug. "I'll at least have to come back to get my stuff. But I'm going to try to talk some sense into my dad. I need him to fix whatever's happening between him and my mom. Worst case, I need him to talk my mom into letting me stay in the city with him, since she seems to suddenly think this is a permanent thing."

Cooper bites his lip. "Well, would that really be so bad? Finishing senior year here? With me?"

"Coop, I don't belong here."

"What are you talking about?" he asks. "People know and love you here. You *do* belong here. And we can figure out what comes next together." He takes my hand in his. "Don't go. Please."

"I have to. Everything is wrong. I mean, I got a C, and—"

He groans. "What are you talking about? Tell me this isn't about the C. It was one lousy C, Ellis!"

"It's not about the C. It's about what the C represents. I've gotten too comfortable here."

"So *what*? You've been happy. You've been letting yourself have fun for a change. How is that a bad thing?"

"Cooper, I feel like my whole future is slipping away."

"And what about us? What about *our* future?"

"We can still make this work. It was always the plan, right? I was always going back to the city."

"When you had to, sure. But you don't now. You have a choice," he says. "Your print is on this place. If you don't belong here, then I sure as hell don't belong in your life in New York."

"What do you mean? You'll be there for school next year."

"Yeah, and I'll be like an extra puzzle piece that doesn't have a place. How do I *fit* into your plans for your future?" He shakes his head. "I don't."

"You can't possibly be asking me to choose you over my future. To change all my plans for you."

"No. I'm asking you to change your plans for *you*, Ellis," he says, exasperated. "What we have is good. So fucking good. But maybe it's not good enough for you."

"Coop, come on."

"Don't go."

My eyes burn. "I have to. And if I'm going to catch the next bus, I have to go now."

He looks at the ground, but not before I see his eyes glassing over. He nods to himself, like he's weighing his words. "Then I guess this is goodbye." He holds my gaze as he drops my hand. "And it's the last one I'm going to say to you, Ellis."

"Cooper," I breathe.

"Have a nice life," he says as he turns and walks back into the café.

Forty-five minutes later, I'm on the back of the bus with nothing more than my phone and wallet, sobbing as Bramble Falls fades into the distance.

Chapter Thirty-Four

I use the key I keep in my wallet to let myself into the apartment. Sunlight floods the living room, revealing our spotless space. So spotless that it's almost lifeless. There's no evidence that Dad's been here since we left.

Mom always did the dishes, but there aren't any dirty ones on the counter or in the sink. She washed the laundry, but there are no dirty shirts thrown across the back of the couch or piled in the corner. She took out the trash, but the bin isn't overflowing.

I can't imagine Dad doing any of those things. Maybe he hired a housekeeper.

With the exception of a few condiments, the refrigerator is nearly empty. Not surprising since he's probably been getting takeout without Mom here to cook, but I am starving.

I try calling Dad for the hundredth time today as I make my way to my bedroom, but he doesn't answer. Mom has been calling and texting me since I left town, but I have nothing to say to her. Sloane texted to ask if I was okay, but I'm not and I don't feel like pretending to be. So I don't text her back. After grabbing a change of clothes, I hop in the shower because the bus was disgusting.

As I'm getting dressed fifteen minutes later, I'm still replaying my conversation with Cooper like a song on repeat. But when I get to the part where he says he doesn't belong in my life here, tears spill—just like they did every time I thought about it on the nearly three-hour bus ride here.

What would have happened when I came home in a few weeks? Would he have said the same thing? Was he always planning to break up with me when I left, or did he just not like being blindsided by my sudden departure? Does it even matter? He gave me an ultimatum—him or the future I've been working toward for years.

My thoughts continue to spiral, a heavy emptiness crushing my lungs, until the sound of the apartment door closing startles me. I trudge out to the hallway to let Dad know I'm here. Does he know Mom is buying a house in Bramble Falls? Was I the only one left in the dark?

I'm nearly to the living room when a woman's laugh floats through the apartment.

Who would be here on a Saturday afternoon? Maybe the new housekeeper?

When I turn the corner, Dad's there—standing behind a familiar blond woman, with his one arm around her waist, murmuring something in her ear. My feet stop moving, giving my brain time to figure out what's going on.

But I can't. The only explanation I can come up with is too devastating to consider.

Dad drops his arm and grins at her. "I'll just grab some clothes and we can go."

He turns and comes face-to-face with me. I've never seen him look so stricken.

"Ellis," he finally says. "What are you doing here?"

It takes all of me to unclench my teeth enough to answer. "What are *you* doing here?"

He glances at the woman. "You remember Catherine Howe, right? You met at the gala."

Yes, that's it—the executive producer with the gorgeous gold dress.

"And you're having a business meeting in our apartment on a Saturday?" I ask, not bothering to say hello to his *colleague*.

Dad tugs on his collar. "Does your mom know you're here?"

I shrug. "Don't know. Don't care. Does she know about *this*?" I point my finger between them.

"I'm going to go wait outside . . . ," Catherine mumbles.

Dad doesn't respond. He keeps his eyes glued on mine while she makes her way out. As soon as the door closes, he sighs. "Your mom knows, yes."

"So, you just thought since we were gone, it was okay to have an affair?" I ask. He stares at me but says nothing. I gasp as the realization occurs to me. "Oh my god. You were already having an affair. That's why we left in the first place."

No. No, no, no.

"Please tell me I'm wrong," I say, my voice cracking. I *need* to be wrong.

Dad runs his hand through his hair. “You’re not wrong.”

“But . . . why? I mean, how long?” I take a step back, shaking my head. “How *could* you?”

“Things between your mom and me have been rocky for a long time. You know that.”

“Well, yeah, because you’re sleeping with someone else!”

He sighs. “We were struggling long before that. We’ve been struggling since having you, if I’m being honest.”

My eyebrows shoot up. “Oh yes, please be honest, Dad. Please tell me about how my existence ruined your marriage. Dying to hear all about it.”

“That’s not what I mean, Ellis,” he says. “Can we sit?”

“Go right ahead. But I will not be sitting with you, no,” I say. “I can barely look at you right now.”

A flash of hurt passes over his face before he nods. He doesn’t sit as he continues. “I just meant that I didn’t realize your mom would change so much after we agreed she should quit her job and stay home with you.”

Images of Mom these past couple of months flicker through my mind. She’s been so happy working at the art store and painting again. I can’t imagine her *wanting* to give up her job doing something she loved. “Did you both agree? Or did you make her quit her job?”

He scoffs. “Of course I didn’t *make* her. I just told her I thought it would be best if *you* were her full-time job. Why should a nanny have raised you when your mom could contribute to our family in that way?”

“You can’t be serious right now.” I narrow my eyes at him.

"Then why didn't *you* do it? Why didn't you give up *your* career to raise me?"

Dad scoffs. "She worked at an art gallery, Ellis. She didn't make enough money to support us. She barely made more than she did when she was selling her own artwork."

"And let me guess, you made her give that up, too?"

"Again, I didn't *make* her do anything. We both agreed that painting was more of a hobby, and it was important for her to get a real job. So she started working at the gallery—until we had you."

I stare at him, suddenly feeling like a stranger to my own family. Like a spectator with a bird's-eye view of my own life, seeing it from a whole new perspective, discovering the truth behind my parents' dynamic.

I think I'm going to be sick.

"Okay, so to be clear," I say, "you made her give up everything that was important to her, everything that made her happy; then you decided you didn't like who she became while she dedicated her entire self to raising me and supporting our family because you told her to; *and then* you started having an affair with a younger woman *with* a career?"

The silence in our sterile apartment smothers me as the things I said to my mom swirl around in my head. I was *awful* to her.

"Ellie Belly . . ." Dad steps toward me.

"No. I've looked up to you my whole life, Dad. When you were too busy working when I was little, I became interested in what *you* were interested in so you'd acknowledge me. I've been *desperate* for your attention for as long as I can remember. Striving to make you proud of me. Trying to be just like you." I let my tears fall because I'm tired of trying to not be emotional for his sake. "I'm your *daughter*, and yet as soon as we were gone, you treated me like a client. Hell, if I *were* a client, I probably would have gotten a phone call that was longer than three minutes. And the worst part is that I became nothing but a nuisance to you because you were so wrapped up in your *girlfriend*. I mean, she's the reason you told me not to come the night I wanted to visit, right?"

Dad looks at the floor but says nothing.

"Yeah, that's what I thought." I walk over to the counter and grab my wallet and phone.

"Where are you going?"

"I don't know. Anywhere that isn't here."

"Stay. I'll cancel my plans with Catherine," he says.

"No, don't bother."

Dad follows me as I head to the door. "Your mom told me she's buying a house in Connecticut. I know you're mad at me right now, Ell, but please don't let that place derail you from the goals you've worked so hard toward."

I stop at the door. With my back to him, I close my eyes, trying not to scream. "You blew up our family, and the only thing you're worried about is whether I'm still going to get into Columbia?" I turn to face him, and for the first time, he doesn't look like the confident, invincible man I've always known. He looks . . . pathetic. I feel like, for the first time, I'm finally seeing my dad for who he really is.

He takes a step toward me. "Ellis—"

"No, Dad. I'm not interested in your advice, not if it gets me to where you are now." I shake my head as I turn the doorknob.

"I hope you miss Mom and me now that you've lost us. But, then again, I'm not sure you can miss someone you never really knew."

I walk out and slam the door closed, leaving behind the person I spent my life loving most in the whole world.

Chapter Thirty-Five

I wait outside Fern's apartment for forty-five minutes. When she finally pops out of the elevator, she's apologizing a mile a minute for taking so long to grab us food. As soon as I see the containers from the Nervous Donkey in her hands, I start crying.

"Oh, sweetie, what's wrong?" she asks, kneeling next to me.

"I'm so hungry," I say. "You brought me takeout."

She smiles softly. "I remembered you said you wanted to try this place. Judging by your panicked texts, I figured there was no time like the present."

"Thank you," I say through sniffles, climbing off the floor while Fern unlocks the door.

Inside, we collapse onto her black velvet couch, and she sets the food on the coffee table. A strangled sob escapes me as she lights a fall-scented candle and I'm reminded of Bramble Falls and everything I blew up there when I ran home to New York.

"Oh no," she says with wide eyes. She hurries to wrap me in a hug. "Whatever happened, it'll be okay," she murmurs into my hair. I nod, though I'm unconvinced, and she lets go and looks at me. "It will. I promise." She grabs a box of tissues from her end table and hands it to me. "We'll eat this delicious food and bake cookies. Then we can—"

Cookies. I bury my face in my hands as I turn into a blubbering mess thinking of Cooper.

"Ellis," Fern says, rubbing my back. "You're scaring me. Tell me what's going on."

I blow my nose and take a few deep breaths while my best friend waits patiently, her eyes filled with concern.

I choke out an overview of the disaster that happened between Cooper, Jake, and me. I cry as I tell her about my fight with Cooper, about him ending things. I tell her about Mom buying a house and all the horrible things I said to her. Then I tell her about Dad—about him banishing me and how I've become nonexistent to him these last two months, about his affair, about him asking Mom to give up a huge part of herself.

Fern leans back and shakes her head. "This is so much, Ellis. I'm so sorry you're going through all of this at once." I hiccup out another sob, and she reaches over and squeezes my hand. "If I'm going to be honest, your dad is kind of a dick, and that isn't some new revelation." I look at her, surprised. Fern and my dad have always gotten along great. "I never said anything because you worshipped him, but it always seemed like he was pushing an agenda. And now I think you're finally realizing the kind of hold he had on you."

I finish off the box of tissues and sigh. "Yeah, maybe, but it's a little too late. I ruined everything and everyone hates me."

Fern pulls her leg up onto the couch so she's facing me directly. "Things may seem bad right now, but you've never met a situation you couldn't plan your way out of. So—without considering anyone else's dreams for you—tell me: What do *you* want?"

"I . . ."

How do I even answer that question? I have no idea anymore.

"Think about it," Fern says, unpacking the food and handing me plastic utensils. "If you could be living the most ideal life right now, what would that look like? Would it be in the city? Or would it be in that little town?"

"I don't know," I say honestly. "Is there even anything here for me anymore?"

"Well, *I'm* here for you, babe. But let's think about it like this: Is Cooper part of this ideal life?"

I nod emphatically. "One hundred percent."

She hands me what appears to be a walking taco. "Then we'll figure out how to fix things with him," she says, grabbing a container holding a giant burrito. "I know it's raw right now, but do you want your dad to be a part of your life? Eventually?"

My eyes sting as I say, "I don't know how I'll feel 'eventually,' but right now, no."

"One less thing on your to-do list, then. But I have to remind you that without your dad, you will most likely not have a choice between the city and Bramble Falls—unless your mom lets you move in with me."

"Which she won't."

Fern shakes her head. "No, she won't. At least, not until next year. So you'll need to decide if patching things up with your dad is worth being here." I look at the floor. I can't even imagine trying to talk to him again. "You're probably going to need to fix things with your mom regardless, right?"

"For sure," I answer. I really messed up with her.

"Okay, so I think the plan is to go back to Connecticut and work things out with the people there. Then, with a little time and space, you can make a decision about your dad and New York."

She's right. That is the *only* thing I can really do right now.

I can't worry about Columbia or New York or Street Media and my future until I fix things in Bramble Falls.

"What are you doing the rest of the evening?" she asks.

I'd been planning on staying here. I thought we'd eat, and I'd cry until I had no tears left, and we'd put on a movie.

But now that I've gotten some clarity on what it is I need to do, the idea of wasting time wallowing makes me antsy.

"I'm going to head back to Bramble Falls," I tell her. "I have some work to do."

"Are you sure? You're welcome to stay." She takes a bite of her burrito.

My heart swells as I smile at my friend. God, I'm so grateful to have her. To know she'll always have my back the way I'll always have hers. Even if my dad isn't in the picture for a while, Fern is a big part of why the city feels like home to me. I'll still have my tether here, keeping me connected to New York, ready to help pull me back when it's time. But for now I need to head north.

"I know," I tell her. "But I'm going to go. Thank you for everything." I hold up my walking taco. "Especially the food. It's perfect for my trip to Port Authority."

"Of course. Call and let me know how it all goes," she says.

We hug goodbye, and with the city drenched in darkness, I hop on a bus back to Connecticut, leaving my old life behind and hoping like hell I can make it back before the Pumpkin Prom is over.

By the time I get back to Bramble Falls, the town is quiet. There are no lingering couples dressed in costumes, no leftover decorations, no music or snap-lock dance floor set up in the square.

It's too late to knock on Cooper's door, but there's no way I can do literally anything until I talk to him. I need to make things right. So I go to his house anyway.

His bedroom light is off, but the TV is on.

Me: **Are you awake?**

I wait for a response, but I'm left on read. Okay, then.

Me: **Come outside.**

A few seconds later, he appears in his window. At first he looks surprised to see me. Then his face sours, turning annoyed.

Autumn Cooper: **go away**

"I'm not going away, Cooper. Come out here," I shout, not caring if I wake up the whole neighborhood.

He rolls his eyes and disappears from the window. A few seconds later I meet him in front of his house.

"Hey," I say quietly.

"What do you want?"

"To talk."

"I don't want to talk," he says.

"Then listen."

He crosses his arms over his chest like armor. "I don't want to listen, either."

"Please, Coop. I'm sorry I bailed on you and missed the Pumpkin Prom. I'm sorry I didn't stay. It was a mistake."

"It was expected."

My heart aches. "Please don't say that."

"What do you want me to say? I've spent all day agonizing over what I could have done differently, Ellis, and all I came up with is that I never should have spoken to you again. I shouldn't have let you back into my life." His eyes look as hollow as I feel. "You know the old adage—when people show you who they are the first time, believe them."

"But I came back," I say weakly.

"That's not the point!" he yells. "I can't trust you to stay because leaving is what you do. You don't care about anyone or anything unless it gets you closer to your goals. And the worst part? You're so focused on what's at the end of this path that's been laid out for you, you hardly give a second thought to the people walking it with you. Instead you step on us and treat us like we're in your way. Like we're inconveniences or hurdles you have to get past on your way to reaching your dad's dreams. Because let's be clear, working at his company is not *your* dream, Ellis. Everyone who knows you knows it. But it doesn't matter, because even though deep down *you* know it too, you refuse to admit it. To forge your own path." He shakes his head and looks at the leaves scattered across the front yard. "And I'm not really interested in being another person in your life who's nothing more than a pit stop. Someone who doesn't matter."

I wilt as the weight of his words sinks into my bones because he's not wrong.

My chin quivers as I step toward him. "I'm so sorry. I want—"

"I actually don't care what you want. And I don't care about your empty apologies. I get that you'd rather not be here, so you were upset about your mom buying a house. But I can't be with someone who books it out of here without considering how it affects other people." He shrugs like he's given up, like he doesn't know what else to say to me. "You've only ever cared about yourself, and I'm over it. I'm not making the same mistake again. Now leave me alone."

He turns to go inside, and I don't bother stopping him.

Because what's the point? I always wanted to be my dad, and I've become him.

I don't deserve Cooper Barnett.

Chapter Thirty-Six

After having a long cry in the Bramble Falls gazebo, I sneak into Aunt Naomi's dark house. I close the door softly behind me, and there's a sudden movement on the couch as Mom jumps up.

"I've been so worried," she says. "Your dad said he didn't know where you were; Fern said you left there almost five hours ago; no one here had seen you. You can't do that to me, Ellis."

"Sorry." It's all I can say. I have nothing left in me.

Mom relaxes, her eyes softening. "Your dad said you found out—"

"Yeah. But I . . . I can't do this right now," I tell her. "Is it okay if we talk in the morning?"

"Of course. I'm here whenever you're ready."

I go to the attic, and after folding myself into a ball in my bed, I cry until I fall asleep with my face buried in my citrus-scented, salt-soaked pillow.

The next morning, I wake up to Sloane sitting on my bed with a plate of warm chocolate Pop-Tarts. She hands it to me as I pull myself up to sit.

"Heard you talked to Cooper last night," she said. "Figured you'd need chocolate. This was all we had."

I take a bite of the Pop-Tart. "It's perfect. Thank you."

"How are you?"

I set the plate next to me. "Not great." She offers an empathetic nod, and I pull at a string on my comforter. "Are you mad at me?"

"What? No," she says. "I was kind of upset because you made it sound like this is the last place in the world you want to be, but I don't know, it kind of seems like a you problem. I feel like everyone here has been really welcoming to you, and I don't think there's anything anyone can do to change how you feel."

"I don't hate it here. At all. Everyone has been great," I agree. "And you're right—this is totally a me problem. I freaked and then I bolted back to New York. It wasn't the right way to handle it, and I'm sorry . . . but that's not all." I swallow, picking at my nail polish. "I found out my dad's having an affair."

"What!" Sloane's expression is a mixture of shock and feral rage.

I won't be surprised if I find her disposing of Dad's body in a bathtub full of Mountain Dew later.

"And as soon as I found out," I continue, "I just wanted to be back here. I took this place for granted." I look at her. "And Cooper. I took him for granted too."

She bites her lip, her shoulders slumping. "He's not in a great place right now, as I'm sure you know."

"Yeah, I screwed up."

"Whatever happened between the two of you is your business, though. Don't forget that when people are prying and taking sides."

"Ugh, this week is going to suck, isn't it?"

"It's a small town, so yeah, it really is. I'm sorry. But it'll blow over." She stands. "I'm meeting Asher so we can go shopping for a witch costume for the parade. Do you want to come? It was your brilliant idea. . . ."

"No, I think I'll stay here and wallow. But thank you for still doing that."

"Of course. It's my dream role," she says with a grin.

As my cousin leaves to prepare for next weekend's parade, my eyes snag on a half-finished dress concept hanging alone on the curtain rod. I take one more bite of my Pop-Tart before I throw my blanket off, pull out the box of plaid shirts, and start sewing.

Because it's the only thing that can bring me an inkling of joy amid all the heartbreak.

I spend the rest of the week hidden in my room when I'm not at school. Word about me messing everything up got around to everyone in town quickly. I can't even get a coffee or walk down the sidewalk without people looking at me like I broke the thing dearest to them.

Because I did. Again.

Only this time, I had all the information—I knew how Cooper felt, and I knew he was scared I'd ditch him again. This time, he begged me not to go. He wanted to work through what was happening together. But I did it, anyway. I *broke him* anyway.

I don't blame anyone for hating me.

In a U-shaped hallway, it's nearly impossible to avoid Cooper, but I keep my eyes down. In class, I give him space. I don't look his way, but I know he's moved to the back of the room with Chloe, where he used to sit when he was avoiding me.

I haven't fixed my hair. I haven't put on makeup. I haven't slept, and I can't eat. I'm a walking breakup song, and I don't even care.

I'm at my locker on Friday, getting my books to take to the library for lunch period, when Jake stops and leans on the locker next to mine.

"Hey . . . ," I say. We haven't spoken at all this week, and I don't know what to say to anyone at this point. I moved seats so I'm not sitting by him in class anymore. If people feel like they have to choose sides, I know they're on Cooper's. I didn't want to make him feel weird or guilty about that.

"You look like shit," he says.

I lift my eyebrows in surprise. "That . . . is true. But it's still a really mean thing to say to me."

"Sorry. I'm just saying, you look like shit. Cooper looks like shit. Can't you two just look like shit together?"

"No." I close my locker. "He would very much like to look like shit as far away from me as possible."

"He's being an idiot."

"No, he's not. I shouldn't have left him like that."

"No, you shouldn't have, but you were upset," he says.

"I hurt him."

"Okay, but you're here now," he says, "and from what I hear, you're staying."

Am I? I still don't have a plan. At the moment, I'm just trying to survive my whole world crumbling.

"It doesn't matter. He hates me."

Jake sighs, exasperated. "He *loves* you, Ellis. He's loved you since he was fourteen."

Tears prick my eyes instantly. I should have told him I loved him the second I felt it. Instead I threw it all away.

I can't respond—not that I even know what to say—because if I try, I'll cry right here in the Bramble Falls High hallway. Jake must see it on my face because he pulls me into a hug.

"You two will get through this," he says quietly.

I nod even though I know that ship has sailed. "You better get to lunch before someone sees you fraternizing with the most hated person in town."

He lets go of me. "Fuck that. I'm going to the library with you."

"Um, why?"

He shrugs. "Because you're my friend."

A tear escapes the corner of my eye. I hurry and wipe it away. "Stop making me cry, asshole."

Jake laughs. "Sorry." He takes my books and carries them for me as we head toward the library. "On the bright side, if things *don't* work out with you and Cooper, you're in luck because no one else has scooped me up yet. I might consider giving you a second chance."

For the first time in a week, a laugh flies out of me.

I link arms with him. "Too soon, Jakey. Too soon."

Chapter Thirty-Seven

Aunt Naomi's house is chaos after school. Stressed voices stream from the kitchen, battling for attention as they all yell something about a budget. I peek my head in and recognize enough of them—including Cooper's mom—to know it's the tourism board. And if they're all here instead of at town hall, then it must be an emergency meeting.

Luckily, no one spots me, so I sneak upstairs. As I pass Mom's bedroom, classical music fills the hallway. I don't think I'll ever be ready for the conversation I need to have with her, but continuing to put it off isn't going to help me get back what I had last week. If I want to fix our relationship, I have to talk to her.

I rap my knuckles on the door, but she doesn't hear me. So I push inside and step into Mom's room, where she's seated in her spot in front of the window, humming. Her giant canvas conveys a crisp autumn night in Bramble Falls. A street is canopied by orange and yellow trees, illuminated by black lampposts lining the sidewalk. The light reflects off the wet street and highlights the back of a couple walking closely side by side, the girl's arm around the boy. They're tiny, only shapes, really, but the girl's hair is the color of mine, and the smallest stroke of brown reminds me of how Cooper's swoops over his ears. A sudden heaviness fills me.

"It's beautiful," I say, swallowing a strangled sob threatening to break free.

Mom startles. She whips around to face me. "I didn't know you were in here."

"I knocked, but you kind of go into your own world when you paint, so . . ."

She sets her paintbrush down and relaxes into her chair. "How are you?"

I shrug as I sit on her bed. "Okay, I guess. Everything is pretty sucky, but I think I'm coming to terms with it." I pause, trying to figure out how to begin this. Then: "I'm sorry for siding unfairly with Dad."

"I was never mad at you for it. We uprooted your whole life."

"But why didn't you just tell me about the affair?"

Mom sighs. "Your dad has always been your hero. I didn't want to break your heart."

"You didn't think I'd find out eventually?"

"Truthfully? I hoped you wouldn't," she says, her gaze dropping to the floor with the admission. I stare at her for a moment, considering how selfless it was of her to try to shield me from something that was causing her so much pain, especially while I was constantly casting all the blame on her. But after learning the whole truth from Dad, I owe her more than an apology for having his back when I should have had hers.

"Mom," I say quietly, and she looks at me. "I'm also so sorry for always acting like you never had any ambition. And for all the snarky comments I've made about you not having a job. I didn't mean any of it."

She leans forward and takes my hand in hers. "Listen, I need you to understand something. I know I gave up my career, but—"

"No, I never should have said what I said. You don't have to explain or justify anything."

"Let me finish, Ellis." I press my lips together and nod. "I know I gave up my career, but raising you meant *the world* to me. It gave me purpose after my art dreams were abandoned. And frankly, it was really hard work.

"Being a parent means making hundreds of decisions a day, constantly worrying about doing the right thing, blaming yourself for everything, being sad when your kid is sad, and being anxious about the future. It's an incredibly rewarding experience, don't get me wrong, but it's also exhausting. And your dad never dealt with any of it. He was never there to share any of it with, to celebrate or commiserate with, to discuss what we should do when Libby Prickett started spreading rumors about you or when you decided you wanted to dye your hair red. I didn't have anyone to turn and smile at when you won your first spelling bee or, later, your first debate. He was never there, and I came to accept it.

"But when I found out he was having an affair, I just . . . couldn't. I needed time and space to *process* it all, you know? I swear I was going to go back. *We* were going to go back. But being here"—she shakes her head—"made me realize how much he took from me. Piece by piece, he stole parts of me until I no longer recognized myself. Until I was living the life *he* wanted me to live instead of the life *I* wanted to live—one full of art and beauty and fun. And I saw the same thing happening to you, but I didn't know how to change it or stop it. You were *so* hell-bent on making him proud, on having the attention he never gave either of us when you were growing up, on living out his dreams for you so you could make him happy. . . .

"And then we were here, and I saw you becoming your own person instead of his reflection, his shadow. I spent the last two months trying to figure out what to do because, whether you see it or not, you've been the happiest I've ever seen you. And the designs you've created here, the confidence you've gained, the way you've embraced your passion . . . it's all been *inspiring*."

"You've inspired me with your art too," I tell her, tearing up. "I'm so sorry you lost yourself over the years. I wish I'd known this was such a big part of who you are."

"I lost myself, but I always had you, so it was worth it," she says, squeezing my hand. "Buying a house here was another one of those impossibly difficult parenting decisions I had to make on my own. But it was a decision I made for *both* of us. I understand if you're still mad. I've talked to your dad, and he's agreed that you can move back in with him if that's what you want to do. And whatever you decide to do with your future is obviously completely up to you—I'll support you in whatever you pursue. I just don't want you to have regrets."

I should be letting out a breath of relief—she's offering me everything I've wanted since the day they sat me down in the living room to tell me I was leaving the city. But things are different now. *I'm* different now. "Before we came here, I was so sure of what I wanted. There was never any question."

She nods. "I know. But that's life. It's unpredictable, and anything can happen at any time. Which is why you should live doing what makes you happy. What lights you up inside, what keeps that flame burning. And truthfully, I think journalism has always dulled all your blues to gray."

"What an artist thing to say."

She smiles. "You are the only person who has to live your life, Ellis. Your dad is the main character in his own story. Why not star in your own instead of being a side character in his?"

"Because what if I fail?"

"What if you don't? What if you take the world by storm?" she says. "Growing up is scary, but it's also full of possibilities. You can't only consider the worst things that could happen."

She's right. The idea of pursuing fashion *is* scary. But . . . maybe I shouldn't push myself away from the things that make me happy, the same way I shouldn't have tried to push her back toward a life that didn't make her happy.

"What are you thinking?" she asks. I must look how I feel—exhilarated yet absolutely petrified.

"I don't know. That going to school for fashion is risky but it excites me?"

"Some risks are worth taking," she says. My stomach knots. Cooper said something similar about me at the corn maze. *You're a risk worth taking.* "Whoa. What just happened? Your face just . . . crumpled."

"Nothing. I'm fine."

Mom frowns. "Please don't do that. It's okay to feel your feelings. You do not have to be fine, Ellis. I'm going to go out on a limb and guess it's about Cooper?"

I look at the floor as she sits back. "Yeah. He said he was afraid I'd leave, but he was taking the risk. I hurt him, and now he hates me."

"He doesn't hate you, honey. He just needs to know you care about him as much as he cares about you. That you'll take risks for him, too."

"But how do I show him that?"

"I can't answer that for you. I wish I could," she says. "But you'll come up with something. It might take some time, but luckily, I don't think he's going anywhere."

"Yeah, I guess."

Mom stands. "I'm going to rinse my paintbrushes and go help Naomi if we're good here."

"Yeah, we're good," I say. "What's going on down there?"

"They're having a budget meeting," she says. "They haven't raised quite as much money as they were hoping to."

"Oh. What does that mean for Aunt Naomi?" I ask.

"Well, I think she'll have to get a bit creative about how to fund next year's festival, but you know your aunt. She always figures it out." With a smile, she adds, "The same way you do."

I follow her out of her room. Before going downstairs, she turns to me. "You know I love you, right?"

"Yeah, I know. I love you, too."

She gives me a hug, then heads downstairs toward the yelling in the kitchen. I climb the attic steps, thinking about what she said.

Cooper needs to know I care about him. That I see him and I'm sorry.

As I get to the top step, my eyes land on my sewing machine, then on Cooper's whimsical cookie costume, which I finally finished a couple nights ago. I have an idea.

My brain quickly concocts a (potentially preposterous) plan, and I pull out my phone to text Fern: **What are the chances you can come to the Falling Leaves Festival in Bramble Falls tomorrow?**

I sit at my sewing machine. But before getting started, I text Sloane: **Hurry up and get home. I need you. (And no, there's no body.)**

If I can pull this off, maybe I can get back what I let slip away.

Chapter Thirty-Eight

After staying up all night, I meet Sloane at the high school with the dozens of other people participating in the parade.

"People are staring at you," she giggles as I waddle over to her. Her eyes trail down my getup—a giant, bright orange circle, covered in fabric that's folded and sewn together to look like Oreos, with orange spandex arms and legs attached.

Cooper's favorite Oreo Creamsicle cookie.

"I know," I say, a blush spreading across my cheeks. From somewhere in the crowd, Aunt Naomi shouts a ten-minute warning. "Where is he? This thing is starting soon."

"He said he'd meet me here early so he could change into his cookie costume," she says, searching the parking lot for his truck. "He's late, but he'll be here any second. He wouldn't miss it." Her green prosthetic witch nose peels up a bit when she smiles. "I still can't believe you're doing this."

I laugh. "I can't either, to be honest."

"It'll be worth it," she says.

"I hope so."

Sloane hugs me. "Worst-case scenario, we eat chocolate Pop-Tarts and watch *Practical Magic* for the fiftieth time tonight."

I hug her back. "Thank you. For everything."

She lets me go. "You'd do the same for me."

My whole chest expands. It means so much that she knows that. I don't know if it would have been true when I came here, but this place and these people have become important to me. I would do anything for them.

And I hope Cooper sees that today.

A few minutes later, he pulls in and parks in his assigned spot, immediately garnering attention. As people surround it, pointing and smiling at the quirky décor we worked so hard on, Cooper gets out with shower-dampened hair, gray sweatpants, and his blue Bramble Falls High hoodie.

God, he looks good.

"Okay, it's time," Sloane squeals. "You've got this."

My palms are suddenly sweaty, and my heart races as I head toward him, forcing one foot in front of the other.

He climbs onto the float and searches the crowd, presumably for Sloane, who was supposed to bring his costume. When he spots me, he freezes. If I weren't tottering over wearing his costume, I'm sure he'd jump out of the truck and make a break for it to avoid me. But instead he stares, his expression seeming torn between annoyed and amused.

When I finally reach him, he looks down at me and he sighs. "What are you doing, Ellis?"

"I was hoping you'd give me three minutes of your time. I just have to say something, and then I promise I will truly leave you alone if that's what you want."

"There's nothing left to say," he says, looking everywhere but my eyes. "Why don't you get that?"

"Please, Coop." I'm not above getting on my knees and begging at this point, but I really hope it doesn't come to that.

He hesitates, then says, "Fine. You have *two* minutes."

"Can you come down here?" I ask. He stares at me, jaw clenched, not budging.

Okay, then.

I take a deep breath, trying to fight the nerves curdling in the pit of my stomach. "You were right about me," I begin. "About everything. I've spent my whole life not really knowing who I am. Instead I've been the person I thought I *should* be, working toward dreams that weren't even mine to begin with. I've been awful to the people who've been there for me through all of it, and I've never allowed myself to get attached to anyone or anything that might hinder me from reaching my goals. Until I came here.

"You once said we have to chase after the things we want. It took me far too long to figure out that I wasn't doing that. Because what I *want* is to go to school for fashion, not journalism. I want to be in Bramble Falls until college. And I want *you*, the most thoughtful, the most fiercely loyal person I've ever met. You dream big and face your fears and take risks even when you might fail—and even when you're likely to end up heartbroken. You're my biggest inspiration to be better and bolder, and I would chase you forever if it meant you forgiving me for leaving, for ruining what we had.

"I messed up, and I know I deserve to deal with the consequences. But I'm really hoping those consequences don't involve losing you forever. If it's too late, I'll stop chasing you, if that's really what you want. But I don't think fourteen-year-old Cooper was wrong about us, and I hope you won't give up on me just yet."

He stands there, looking dumbstruck. When he opens his mouth, I suddenly remember what I'm holding.

"Wait, just . . . one more thing. Sorry. I promise I'm done after this. But I made you something." I take a step forward and pass the bundle up to him.

He takes it and shakes out the bunched-up fabric to reveal his present. "A new apron."

I nod. "A new apron with company branding." He looks at me, then back at the Cooper's Cookie Co. logo. "Obviously, I have no idea what you plan to call your bakery, but I thought—"

The sharp bark of a megaphone interrupts me. We both jump and turn toward the sound.

"All right, one minute until go time, everyone!" Aunt Naomi shouts.

"I said some really mean things to you," Cooper says, ignoring Aunt Naomi's warning.

"Nothing that was untrue."

"That's the thing. . . ." He bites his lip. "I don't think you're selfish, or that you only think of yourself. You showed up for your aunt at a ton of festival events this fall. You let Jake copy off your tests for the last two months so he wouldn't fail the class because he's lazy, you helped me with my float, and now *this*," he says, holding up the apron. "I was upset, and I didn't mean it. I'm sorry."

I shake my head. "You have nothing to be sorry for, Coop. And if you apologize again, I'm going to throw you off your float once we get moving."

He grins as Naomi chirps out a two-minute warning. Then his brow furrows. "Wait. Once *we* get moving?"

"Well, yeah. If you'll have me. I mean, I *am* dressed for it."

His eyes dip to my costume. "But you look ridiculous."

"I know," I laugh, glancing at Sloane as she slips into the front seat of the truck.

"You said you wouldn't wear it in the parade because it'd be embarrassing," Cooper says.

"It *is* embarrassing," I confirm. "But you're worth it."

A storm of unreadable thoughts and emotions thunders through his amber eyes. Then, finally, he says, "I don't want you to chase me anymore."

I stand there almost dazed, my heart shattering into a million pieces. But I came mentally prepared for this possible outcome. "Oh. Um, okay. I get it." I nod, blinking fast so I don't cry. Because even if Mom's right and it's okay to feel my feelings, I draw the line at crying in front of half the people in this town while wearing a ridiculous orange cookie costume. "I won't, then. Good luck with the parade."

The truck begins to pull away, and Sloane sticks her head out the window, calling behind her. "I'm sorry, Ellis. My mom will kill me if I hold up the parade."

I nod as I stumble backward. Then I turn to leave. Because Cooper was right—there's nothing left to say. There's nothing else to do.

But a few seconds later, a hand wraps around my wrist. I whip around. *Cooper.*

I glance at his float inching along Oak Avenue, and my eyes widen. "The parade is leaving without you. What are you doing?"

Cooper's lips slam into mine, and suddenly nothing else matters—not the parade, not the fact that I'm wearing this outlandish costume, not the whooping coming from the floats passing by. Time stands still. The ground beneath us shifts. My stomach swoops, and my heart melts.

When he pulls away, he rests his forehead on mine. "I meant I didn't want you to chase me anymore because I don't want to be running. I just want to be with you."

"You do?" A slow, hesitant smile nudges at my lips.

"Always."

I kiss him again, even though I can't stop grinning.

He pulls away, and I take the apron from his hand. I loop it over his head, and he arches an eyebrow at me.

"Go catch your float, and wear it," I tell him. "It's great for advertising. Plus, you'll look more professional handing out your cookies in it, considering you showed up in sweatpants."

"In my defense, I wasn't expecting someone to hijack my costume."

I shrug. "Sort of glad I did now. You look hot in sweatpants."

He flashes me a dimpled grin and pulls me in for one more kiss before turning around and kneeling in front of me.

"What are you doing?"

"We've got a float to catch and cookies to hand out," he says. "Hop on."

I laugh and climb onto his back. Doing his best not to ruin the costume, Cooper holds on to my legs and jogs us back to his truck.

An hour later, the parade is over and we're at the town square, now free of our costumes.

"Ready to check out this festival?" Cooper asks, coming up behind me and sliding his arm around my waist.

While I was working tirelessly to make Cooper's apron last night, dozens of volunteers turned this place into an autumn utopia. There are pumpkins everywhere, a petting zoo is now set up next to the leaf-garland-covered gazebo, and a DJ sits just on the edge of the lawn taking requests. There are vendors everywhere selling Falling Leaves Festival sweatshirts, scarves, and socks, apple cider, coffee, and pies. Games and activities, including apple bobbing and face painting, are set up on the lawn and lining the sidewalks.

It's beautiful. But the best part is the people. I don't know if I'll ever get over how much I've come to love this little community.

"Sure, but I need to find Fern first."

Cooper points to where Fern is sitting next to Jake at a picnic table in the shut-down street, and I pull him over to her.

"What's she doing here, anyway?" he asks.

"Making Falling Leaves Festival posts," I tell him.

"Why?"

"Because tourism is good for generating money, and Fern's videos go viral every time. She's declared Bramble Falls a must-visit destination." I turn to face him. "Which is also why I had her make a video about your cookies."

"Um, what?"

"It's not a charity offering," I quickly clarify. "I swear Fern literally could not stop talking about that lemon cookie you gave her when she visited. And now, whenever you're ready to sell them beyond the Caffeinated Cat, people will know your name. Just wait until you open your bakery."

He smiles and leans in to kiss me. "God, I love you." His smile falls as he rears back, like he surprised himself. "I mean—"

"I love you too," I tell him easily.

His eyes widen. "You . . . do . . . ?"

"Always."

He grins just before his lips crash into mine.

"Okay, you two, stop making me puke in my mouth," Fern teases as she approaches.

Cooper lets me go, and I turn my attention to Fern. "Thank you so much, Fernie," I say, pulling her into a tight hug. "I owe you."

She squeezes me before dropping her arms and looking at me with a familiar glint in her eye—my best friend is in her *element*. "Owe *me*?" she exclaims. "I should be thanking you! People are going absolutely berserk for this content. I've already had two reels go viral from this morning alone. I'm gonna milk this place for all it's worth, starting with Cooper's Cookies."

As she grabs Cooper by the arm and drags him back toward his float, he looks over his shoulder and shoots me a wink, once again awakening those pesky butterflies in my stomach. My lips turn upward in an unbridled grin, and I close my eyes, trying to savor this moment—the chilly breeze on my skin, the crunchy leaves beneath my boots, the smell of cinnamon and apple, the sound of laughter—because I truly can't remember the last time I was this happy.

And while Fern gets him posed for some photos, I open my eyes to savor the sight of the beautiful boy from Bramble Falls who captured my heart one autumn day at a time.

Epilogue

Thanksgiving on Apple Blossom Lane is unlike any holiday I've ever had, full of friends and laughter, and family. Downstairs, Aunt Naomi, Mom, Amanda, and Asher's mom are yelling over each other in the kitchen. Aunt Naomi suggested a friendly game of rummy, but it turns out I might have actually gotten my zeal for competition from my mom.

She's lost the last two games and refuses to serve dinner until she wins.

So Cooper, Sloane, Asher, and I are all hanging out in my room, awaiting our cold mashed potatoes and corn because Aunt Naomi won't just let her win *one*.

"I can't believe you two are working on college applications on a *holiday*," Sloane says as she throws a red shell at Asher in an actually friendly game of Mario Kart. "After the month we've had, you should be resting. Like normal people."

Aunt Naomi extended the Falling Leaves Festival another weekend to capitalize on all the attention Fern's viral posts were bringing to Bramble Falls. We had to help organize the continuation of the event, and then we volunteered to fill in for anyone who couldn't make it again. I spent two days painting pumpkins and ghosts on kids' faces while Sloane and Asher handed out mulled cider and Cooper worked his very own Cooper's Cookies Co. tent.

All the hard work paid off because during that additional weekend, Bramble Falls made more than double what they needed to fund next year's festival.

Cooper finishes typing something on his laptop, then says, "If we're going to starve to death, we might as well be productive while we wither away."

"Oh no. Now you sound like Ellis," Asher jokes. I throw a pillow at him, causing his Yoshi to fall off a cliff. "Aw, come on!"

"It's okay. You were going to lose, anyway," Sloane says to him as she crosses the finish line. Asher gives her a playful shove, and I exchange a knowing look with Cooper.

The last few weeks have flown by. Since the festival ended, I've worked relentlessly on creating a portfolio worthy of submitting to FIT, and even though there's still plenty of time before the application is due, I'm happy with what I've come up with. I realized there's a story to be told across the designs I made freshman and sophomore year through the new ones from this fall, the shift from oxford shirts to plaid ones a representation of the way my family and foundation shifted under me. I've been working on a few pieces that synthesize the two, including a maxi dress that starts as a crisp white oxford and then blends into draped flannel from the mid-torso down to the floor.

I think I might actually have a shot at getting in.

Dad's called a few times, but I'm not ready to talk to him. Last week he left a voicemail saying Mom told him about Cooper and that he'd like to meet him. He offered for us to stay with him over winter break, but even if Cooper comes with Sloane and me on our touristy trip through the city, I won't be staying with my dad.

I honestly have no idea if or when I'll be ready to forgive him—or to see the disappointment on his face when he learns I'm not applying to Columbia. Apparently, getting past wanting to make him happy is going to take some time.

"All right, I can't take it anymore. Time to snack on those cheese cubes in the fridge," Sloane says, standing. "And maybe harass your mom about dinner."

"Please do," I say, finishing up the portion of the application with my volunteer experiences. Listing the Falling Leaves Festival feels like cheating. I *did* help out, but I think I benefited more than Aunt Naomi.

"Yeah, I'm really not trying to die on Ellis's bedroom floor," Asher says.

He follows Sloane downstairs, and Cooper grins at me, his thick hair flopping over his forehead and his dimple lighting a spark in my belly.

"What?" I ask.

"I'm just really proud of you."

I smile at him. "Um, why?"

He nods at my computer. "This is a big deal."

I shrug, even though he's right. "I guess so."

He leans in and kisses me—something I don't think I'll ever get tired of.

"Okay, break it up, you two." I pull away from Cooper and turn to find Jake standing in the doorway with a covered dish.

"What's that?" I ask.

"Ham. My mom said if I was going to come here on Thanksgiving, I had to bring something."

"You can put it in the kitchen," I tell him.

"Wait!" Cooper says. "Bring it here."

"O-kay . . ." Jake carries it over and hands it to Cooper, who sets it on the bed.

I send Sloane a text: **Come fast.**

Cooper uncovers the dish, and we salivate over the hot sliced ham. Sloane and Asher come jogging into the room carrying a bag of cheese cubes.

"Friendsgiving," I announce.

We all pile onto my bed and eat straight from the dish while Jake tells us about his drama-filled Thanksgiving dinner, how he's been texting with Fern nonstop, and how he's pretty sure he's going to get his first-ever A—in physics, of course.

Just before we finish off the ham and cheese cubes, Sloane shouts, "Hold on!"

We all freeze, our final bites halfway to our mouths.

"We have to go around and say what we're thankful for, right?" she says. "It *is* Thanksgiving after all."

"Sure. I'll start," Asher says. "I'm thankful to be passing Spanish."

"Amen to that!" Jake says. They clink their cheese cubes together as if they're glasses. "I'm grateful for my parents—"

"Awww," I say, impressed by his genuinely sweet answer.

"You didn't let me finish," Jake says. "I'm grateful for my parents, whose awesome genes made me look this good."

I frown at him, and he laughs. Cooper rolls his eyes, and Sloane gives a look that says, *Well, he's not wrong.*

"Okay, I'll go next," Cooper says. "I'm grateful that I'm surrounded by supportive people . . . and that Ellis finally came to her senses and fell for me."

Everyone laughs.

"Sorry, bro. I think that means she actually *lost* her senses," Jake quips. I slap him on the arm, and he rubs it, pretending to be hurt.

"My turn," Sloane says, turning to look at me. "I'm thankful my cousin came to Bramble Falls, despite the shitty circumstances that brought her here." I smile at her. "I seriously don't know what I'm going to do without you next year."

"You'll still have Asher," I remind her.

She lays her head on his shoulder and sighs. "I suppose so. He just doesn't bring as much drama to the table."

"That's probably a good thing," I say.

"Definitely," Asher says, eyeing the other two boys, and I can't help but laugh.

I look around at my little group of friends, and my heart pinches.

I don't know what the future holds—whether I'll ever be close with Dad again, whether I'll get into FIT, or whether I'll have a successful fashion career—but I'm also not as worried about it as I used to be, because I know I have the best friends, who will be there regardless of what life throws my way.

"I guess I'm up," I say, my voice cracking with the building emotion. "First, I'm beyond grateful for all of you. . . ."

Jake hands me the tissue he used as a napkin. "Here, your eyes are leaking."

I take it and laugh. "Thanks, Jakey."

Cooper rubs circles on my back, and before we take our final bites of our Friendsgiving appetizers, I lay my head on his shoulder and add the truest statement I never thought I'd say:

"And I'm so grateful to be able to call both Bramble Falls *and* New York City *home*."

Acknowledgments

First and foremost, I want to thank my husband, David Wilson. I could get a million book deals and none of them would matter without him. From watching the kids to letting me vent and bounce ideas off him, to cooking dinners, dealing with my mood swings, and massaging my aching hands after twelve-hour drafting days, he's been there every step of the way, supporting me at every turn. He's my best friend, and there's no one I'd rather be on this twisty publishing ride with. David, thank you for dreaming big with me (can't wait to make our millions and buy that dream house). For the sacrifices you make to ensure I get writing time. For making me smile. For hugging me when I'm stressed and/or crying. For putting up with my anxiety. For being a husband worthy of a love-interest role in a romance novel haha. For being the best dad. For being understanding of my obsessive, workaholic behavior. And especially for making me dinner because I would die otherwise.

Thank you to my agent, Daniel Lazar, and his assistant, who

I really just consider a second agent, Torie Doherty-Munro, without whom this book would have never happened for me. I can't thank either of you enough for looking out for me in this wild world of publishing. I've thrown ideas and projects at you in every age category and various genres over the years, and you've taken it in stride, even when it's not your thing. I truly couldn't ask for better (or more communicative and responsive) advocates to have in my corner. Thank you, thank you, thank you.

Thank you to my editor, Kate Prosswimmer. Look what we created together! I'm beyond grateful for the opportunity to bring Ellis and Cooper to life in Bramble Falls. Thank you so much for the chance to write this book and for your ideas, insights, feedback, and fashion help (haha, seriously, though). It was such a pleasure to get to work with you! And thank you to Andrenae Jones for your input and all the stuff you do behind the scenes. I appreciate you.

Thank you so much to Amber Day for this absolutely gorgeous cover illustration. You captured Cooper and Ellis so unbelievably well (and did it so quickly, it truly made my forever-impatient heart so happy).

Thank you to Karen Sherman, Jen Strada, Tatyana Rosalia, and Elizabeth Blake-Linn for working hard to make this book what it is. Without you, it'd simply be sloppy sentences on a Word doc page. Thank you for helping turn it into something readable and pretty.

Thank you to Jess Burkhart—where would I be without you? (No, really.) Thank you for letting me complain to you literally all day about everything. For making me laugh. For being there when

I cry (which we know is a lot haha). For supporting me in all my endeavors. For making me work even when I don't want to. For gossiping with me. For reading anything I send to you in a panic and giving me honest feedback on it. For your advice. For answering all my horse-related and NYC-related questions for this book. I cannot wait to grow old together in our NYC penthouse (once David dies, since he won't move to NYC haha). Ily, bestie.

To Jessica James and Lynn Painter, thank you for letting me scream in your DMs about *all* the things, all the time. Thank you for all your support throughout the process of writing this book (and outside it). I'm so happy to be able to call you friends.

To my Do the Words writing group, including Erica Davis, Dea Poirier, Isabel Sterling, Vanessa Montalban, Amelinda Berube, and Shelly Page. Thank you all for your advice and your ears. You've all been amazing and supportive as I've talked nonstop about being on submission, working on three contracted books at once, and about my future projects. You provide a safe space to scream, and I truly appreciate it.

Thank you to Norah and Fiona, who are growing up way too fast. You make me laugh every day and are truly the best part of my life. Thank you for your patience, understanding, and unconditional love. You better never stop giving me hugs and snuggles.

Thank you to the rest of my family for all your support and enthusiasm. (I'm especially looking at you, Mom, Leah, and Marisa. And Papa D, for being the best salesperson, even when it embarrasses Debi haha.) And a big thank-you to my mom, Debi, and Dave, for babysitting whenever we need you, making this whole author thing possible. ❤

Thank you to my little "book club" (aka my friends who sometimes talk books when we meet up)—Joanna Cammel, Carolyn Tomello, Tammy Noska, and Laney Noska. Thank you for your support over the years, for your excitement whenever I have book news, and for buying my books and spreading the word about them. You guys are the best!

Thank you to librarians and teachers. You are absolute heroes. Thank you for making sure kids get books into their hands. Thank you for providing them with exactly what they need, exactly when they need it. Books open up whole new worlds, whole new experiences, whole new perspectives, and so often you're the reason they're discovering what's out there. Thank you for fostering a love for reading.

Thank you to bloggers/Instagrammers/Booktokers/influencers. Your support means *everything*. Nothing sells more books than word of mouth, and you're all out there putting in the work. You have no idea how much authors appreciate what you do. Thank you so much for screaming and flailing about all the books you love.

Thank you to the employees at Nervous Dog Coffee Bar for always being kind and providing me with the best lattes while I sat in the corner and drafted this book for hours on end every single day. And thank you for the inspiration behind the Caffeinated Cat's harvest spice latte.

Thank you to Ohio Cookie Co./Ohio Pie Co. for baking the best cookies ever, thereby providing the inspiration behind Cooper's sexy cookies. I highly recommend that anyone reading this go order some online immediately.

Thank you to *Gilmore Girls* and *Hart of Dixie* for providing me with small-town inspiration and endless comfort. To Taylor Swift, Ed Sheeran, Gracie Abrams, and Lewis Capaldi for putting out bangers with *all the vibes* for me to write to.

And to all the readers who don't fall into any category above, thank YOU. You are the reason I get to write books. Thank you for buying books and/or borrowing them from the library. Thank you for your love of reading, for your enthusiasm, for your support, for telling a friend about what you've been reading. You make publishing possible for authors, and we love you. Thank you, thank you.